She's Just a Friend

She's Just a Friend

Lisa Nicole Hankerson
& Siddeequah Perryman

URBAN BOOKS
www.urbanbooks.net

URBAN SOUL is published by

Urban Books
6 Vanderbilt Parkway
Dix Hills, NY 11746

ISBN 1-59983-008-6

First Printing: January 2007
10 9 8 7 6 5 4 3 2 1

Printed in the United States of America

Prelude

The rain was coming down harder than ever when Chris decided to stop at Frankie's for a drink before heading home. He had no desire to see Nikki right now. Not only did he feel guilty as hell for what had just happened, but he couldn't get Mina's words out of his head. *What did she mean?* Surely, Nikki would have told him. *And when did all of this happen? Recently? In the distant past?* It was killing him; he needed a drink badly.

Frankie reached under the bar, grabbed a shot glass, and slammed it down in front of Chris. "What'll you have, my friend?"

"Hey, Frankie, man, give me one of those lethal weapons you let me try a few weeks back, the one with five or six different kinds of liquor in it."

"Whoa! Is it like that?" Frankie asked, mixing up the shot. "Here you go; drink up."

Chris threw the colorful shot to the back of his throat and asked for vodka on the rocks next.

"What's going on, Chris? What's got you in this mood? I don't think I've ever seen you quite like this before. You look a mess . . . if you don't mind me saying so."

"You wouldn't believe me if I told you, man. You wouldn't believe me if I told you."

"Try me."

"Nah. I just want to drink." Chris didn't want to talk about any of the drama that was going on in his life. He wanted to pretend it wasn't happening. He could hear the rain beating on the pavement outside. It consoled him to imagine the water washing away every trace of Mina . . . and what he had done. He looked around Frankie's place and thought about the fact that it had all started right here—in the very spot he was sitting. And this is where it would end; he would never see her again. He couldn't now, even if he wanted to. She hated him for the things he said. He could still see the pain in those engaging eyes of hers.

Chris must have had five or more drinks when he heard his cell phone ring for the third time since he'd arrived. He didn't even check to see who it was. It didn't matter. He didn't want to talk to anyone in the condition he was in; it was going on midnight and he was drunk as hell. The room was starting to spin. He watched customers walk in and out as the hours went by. When he felt he'd had enough, he decided to get up from the bar and head to the empty black chaise longue across from the television. *Sports Center* was on, and he figured he would take a peek at the highlights and sober up a bit before attempting to drive home. It felt like hours had gone by when he looked up and saw Nikki walking right past him toward the bar. He was a bit confused because she was dressed quite provocatively, something he hadn't seen since their son, Corey, was born. She had on a black halter dress that fit her like a glove. Her breasts were protruding out of her plunging neckline, and she was wearing the highest pair of black heels he had ever seen her wear. She looked like she was waiting for someone. She kept checking her watch and looking around the room. He called out to her, but she didn't answer him. *What the hell is my wife doing here?* he thought. *Where is our son?*

Then the front door swung open. A tall, dark man walked in, accompanied by a sexy, white woman with short red hair. They were both dressed to kill. The dark stranger was decked out in what appeared to be an Armani suit and tie, and the redhead wore a red slip dress and heels. When Nikki saw them, she waved and motioned for them to come over to her, her cherry lips widening, spreading from ear to ear. Chris had never seen her with so much makeup on her face. He wasn't prepared for what came next. When the strangers approached Nikki, the man immediately slid his hand up Nikki's thigh underneath her dress. Nikki then uncrossed her legs and invited him to probe farther. And he did, causing her head to fall back in complete ecstasy, consumed by the pleasure she received. She appeared to be experiencing things she had never felt before. Chris was stunned. He couldn't move. He tried to get up, but his legs gave out on him. He called out to Nikki again, and this time she looked his way. She heard him, but instead of looking shocked to see him, she smiled deviously and then reached over, grabbing the redhead by the back of her neck and kissing her, all the while keeping her eyes on Chris. He watched as his wife slid her tongue down this stranger's mouth—a woman, no less. Nikki then reached around and untied her halter dress. Her breasts were now completely exposed as the dark man caressed them. He then started to suck on them, biting her nipples. Nikki continued to look at Chris, smiling at him. The redhead then knelt down and made her way between Nikki's legs as she straddled the bar stool. Nikki didn't appear to be wearing any panties, so the redhead slid her tongue inside her. The strange man then got on top of the bar in one swift jump and unbuckled his pants, completely exposing himself to the two women. He grabbed Nikki's head gently, forcing her to take all of him in her mouth. Chris couldn't believe what he was witnessing. His stomach was sick, he felt faint, and he couldn't breathe. He tried to call out to Nikki again, but now he couldn't. His voice was lost. He looked around the bar and noticed that it was completely empty. Where was everyone? he thought. Where was Frankie? Why wasn't he stopping this from happening?

"Nikki!" he cried out. "Nikki! Nikki!"

Chapter 1

The Reynoldses

Six months earlier

Nikki had exactly two hours to shop. It was amazing how tight her schedule was these days. Every minute truly counted and not usually in her favor. She had decided to swing by TJ Maxx to look for a pair of hiking boots to take on her trip to the cabin with the girls. She had been counting down the weeks and couldn't believe it was finally here. She couldn't wait to see Kay, Renee, and Lynda. Lynda especially. Nikki and Lynda had been the best of friends since high school and were inseparable. Nikki was pretty shy—until she met Lynda. Lynda was strong and exuded the kind of confidence every woman longed to have. They met the twins—Kay and Renee, the most dazzling and stunning set of identical twins they had ever come across—their freshman year at Clark Atlanta University. Kay and Renee were from South Carolina and had come to Clark University on full basketball scholarships. As a crew, they ruled the CAU campus.

Nikki promised herself she wouldn't get distracted on this

shopping spree, but she couldn't help but think of the good ol' days. She couldn't wait to see them again. It'd been a little under two years since they had all been in the same room together. As she walked toward the women's department she stopped quickly and grabbed a pack of wife-beaters for her husband, Chris. He was in desperate need of new ones. Her next stop was unexpected and unavoidable. Nikki found herself in the little boys' section, smiling and going through the racks of miniature men's clothing. As she stood there holding up and admiring a little denim jumper size 18 months, her life flashed before her eyes. She was a mother now. She stepped a few feet to the right and caught sight of herself in one of the full-length mirrors in the store. Nikki made a feeble attempt at using her hand as a comb, trying to catch stray hairs that were flying all over the place.

Ugh! she thought to herself. *Screw it!* She dug around in her bag, hoping and praying that she had a rubber band or some kind of scrunchie to pull her hair back. When she finally felt one deep at the bottom of her purse, she pulled it out and could feel all kinds of gook and lint under her fingernails. She was mortified that she had allowed herself to become so disheveled. Her mom used to tell her that "your purse mimics your life," and it definitely seemed to be a true statement for Nikki.

"I need to get my shit together," Nikki said to herself, letting out a long sigh. She and Chris had been married for almost thirteen years, and this was definitely the most she had ever let herself go. Her partying days long gone, she hadn't planned an event in over two years. It felt as if she and Chris had been holding their breath ever since their son, Corey, was born. They had decided to name him Corey Christopher Reynolds. They loved him so much, more than either of them could ever have thought possible. He was truly an angel as far as they were concerned. Her labor was nothing like the horror stories she had been told at her baby shower or by coworkers, who thought they were helping when they were really only scaring the shit out of her.

She had awakened around eight one Saturday morning experiencing some discomfort. Her stomach feeling tight, she was having slight difficulty breathing. Luckily, it was the weekend, so Chris was home in bed still asleep next to her. She shook him awake and told him how she was feeling and that they should probably call the doctor. He jumped up and paged their doctor immediately and then sat next to her, obviously very nervous about what was happening. He kept asking her if she thought this was "it." She kept telling him she thought so and tried to focus on breathing and remaining calm—for the both of them. By the time the doctor finally called back, Chris and Nikki were en route to the hospital. Her water had broken while Chris was helping her to get up off the bed. He lost it when he saw water trickling down her leg. All she remembered was him struggling to put a T-shirt on and hurriedly pulling jeans over his long legs. The hospital they chose was five miles away, so they arrived there in no time. Chris ran and got a nurse, who came to their car with a wheelchair. Nikki was admitted immediately, and less than an hour later Corey was born.

He had the brightest eyes she had ever seen. They looked like two big black marbles floating around on his tiny face. Nikki had never seen Chris look so proud of anything since she had known him. She looked in her husband's eyes that day and saw his loss for words. In the midst of all the drama surrounding her, Chris, and their newborn, he could only mouth the words "thank you" to her, and she would never forget it.

Of course, there was a price to pay for the beauty of childbirth, and God knows Nikki was paying it. No one told her she was going to bleed for a week or that she would have to wear oversized Maxi Pads that felt like diapers. Or that her nipples would be sore to the point that it brought tears to her eyes to have Corey latch on to eat. It had been miserable in the beginning. To top it all off, she and Chris hadn't been able to get back to a regular sex schedule since Corey's birth, and she was starting to wonder about the whole idea of getting married and having kids.

Her cell phone rang, snapping her out of her daydream—just in time to keep her from sinking into a mild and brief depression. She considered ignoring the call. (Shopping was the only time she had to actually slow down and relax a bit.) She looked at the number on the screen and felt her heart leap just a bit when she saw it was Chris calling from home. He was probably just calling to see how she was, but of course she was worried that there was something wrong with Corey. That was another thing that had changed: She was constantly walking around with her stomach in knots worried that something could happen, had happened, or would happen to her precious son. Poor Chris had taken a backseat to the baby since the day she found out she was pregnant.

"Hey, babe, everything okay?" she asked, hoping for the best. She didn't have the energy for any stress or drama today.

"Oh yeah. Just calling to see if you could pick me up some undershirts," Chris said. "I forgot to ask you before you ran out of here."

"I did not run out of the house; I was just walking fast and in a bit of a hurry, that's all. I'm looking at your shirts right now. I know you better than you know yourself." She smiled in amazement at her own ability to somehow remember all the details.

"Thanks, babe."

"You're welcome."

"Oh, and if you get home soon we may be able to get in a quickie while Corey is asleep."

"Good-bye!" Nikki said playfully, hanging up. Sex was

the last thing she wanted today, and she would stay out another two hours just to avoid it.

Nikki checked out at the front and walked out of TJ Maxx $175 poorer. In her shopping bag was a pair of Timberland hiking boots, two dresses, Chris's undershirts, and two outfits for Corey. Now she was starving, trying to fight the desire to hit the McDonald's next door to the shopping plaza. She had promised herself that fast food was just not an option, especially since she had been slack about working out lately, but the convenience factor won that argument once again—she found herself in the drive-through ordering a Quarter Pounder with cheese. *The fact that these places accept debit cards is just the devil himself,* she thought. The guy on the drive-through speaker gave her the total, which was somewhere around four bucks. Right before she started to drive around she decided to make a healthy choice and leaned over into the speaker. "Excuse me, sir. No mayo on that burger." She had to laugh out loud at what her diet had become. She really needed to make some changes before she found herself thirty pounds overweight and pregnant with her and Chris's second child.

Chapter 2

Let's Go

Lynda awoke to the sound of the captain's voice wishing her and the rest of the passengers of Flight 859 a safe and exciting visit in Atlanta. She was so happy when they landed she could barely contain herself. It had taken her forever to fall asleep with all of the turbulence they had experienced shortly after takeoff. *Ugh,* she thought, *flying is for the birds*. Besides, the guy seated next to her had talked her to damn death about his wife and their two fat kids. She couldn't believe he had straight-up called his own kids fat. When he said it, he saw her eyes widen and quickly assured her that it was okay and that he and his wife had accepted their kids' "condition." She was trying to quietly step over him and into the aisle to get her bags overhead without waking him and was almost home free when her shoulder bag accidentally flung behind her, slamming into the side of his head.

"Wha . . . wha . . ." he said, scrambling to get his wits about him.

"I am so sorry," Lynda said, totally embarrassed but laughing hard as hell inside.

"Oh no, I'm glad you woke me; I almost forgot to get your business card. It's almost impossible to find an affordable personal trainer in L.A.," he said, as Lynda dug around her bag, trying to find her business card holder.

"Not to mention, one as pretty as you," he said, trying to look charming. Which was impossible—he had dried-up drool on the left side of his mouth.

"Here you are," Lynda said, smiling, handing him her last two cards. They shook hands, and she could still hear him talking on her way up the aisle. She finally gave him a wave good-bye and ducked her head to exit the plane, having already forgotten his name, his wife's name, *and* his fat kids' names. It wasn't personal; she just hadn't planned on doing business during her visit to Atlanta. She wanted to devote this time to catching up with old friends and bringing closure to the events that led to her departure two years prior.

Before she could dial Nikki's number, her phone was already ringing. She looked at Nikki's name flashing on the screen of her cell phone and smiled. *That's my girl*. Lynda laughed to herself. *Impatient ass!*

"What's up, Nikki?"

"Heyyyy, Lynda," Nikki squealed, "I'm so happy you're here. You are here, aren't you?"

"Yes, I'm here. I'm on the train now, headed to get my rental. I can't wait to see you, Nikki. You know I'm gonna talk about you if you have a gut, right? Especially after I gave you all those exercises celebrities do to get rid of their stomachs. I know my godson weighed like ten pounds, but that's still no excuse," Lynda teased.

"Oh, please. Just because you've been out in L.A. training all those big-time people doesn't mean us girls in Atlanta need you coming here trying to talk shit about us. Chris doesn't have a problem with my body since the baby, and *you* don't have to see it, Ms. Lynda. So it's all good."

"Yeah, tell me anything . . . until those clothes come off," Lynda said, taking one final stab at Nikki.

"I bet you'll still want me," Nikki bragged.

"Whatever. I'm so over you," Lynda told Nikki. She knew they were both just playing, making fun of the old days. "I wouldn't have come here if I wasn't, believe me," Lynda said.

"Yeah, yeah, yeah. Well, hurry up and get your black ass to my house. Kay and Renee will be here soon, and I want us all to be here at about the same time."

"Wait, wait, wait. Did you say Kay and Renee?" Lynda asked, surprised.

"Well, yeah, Kay and Renee," Nikki repeated. "Why do you sound so shocked?"

"Nikki, you didn't tell me they were both coming; you just said that Kay was coming and bringing some friend of hers from work. Are you trying to have them kill each other right in front of us? Why do you want to open this weekend up for that kind of drama?"

"It won't be as dramatic as you think," Nikki reassured her. "Just calm down. Dang! They've actually talked a lot recently, so it won't be total mayhem if they end up in the same room together."

"Yeah, Nikki, but in a cabin all day and night?"

"It will be fine, trust me. I'll see you at my house shortly; I have to go get things ready for Chris and Corey before you get here. I can't just up and leave anymore, girl. It seems like I have to tell Chris the smallest things about taking care of this baby. He drives me nuts sometimes. Anyhow, I'll holler at you soon. Gotta go. See you when you get here," Nikki said, rushing to get off the phone.

"Bye," Lynda said, as the phone clicked on the other end. *This is about to be one crazy weekend,* she thought, as she looked around trying to find which way to go for Hertz.

Hopefully it would go okay, but something inside her told her she was in for a weekend she would not soon forget.

Nikki still had a ton of things to do before the girls arrived. She thought it would be best if the girls all rode together up to the cabin so they could talk on the way there, sort of the pre–catching up to all of the catching up they would do once they got there. Renee had been the only one to object to the cabin idea; instead, she tried to sell Nikki on staying at a local Atlanta hotel. But Nikki whined about wanting to do something different, and Renee finally gave in.

Nikki was in her bathroom upstairs hurriedly getting ready. As she saw herself in the mirror now, it suddenly struck her—she was, in fact, getting older. She leaned in to the mirror closely and noticed that her once youthful, taut skin was now just a little bit looser under her chin and around her eyes. It wasn't anything to worry about just yet, but she couldn't afford late nights, staying up eating Oreos and milk, like she used to be able to—at least not without doing some crunches to make up for it. Not getting too deeply involved with thoughts about aging, Nikki put the finishing touches on her hair with her flatiron. While primping and doing her hair she was examining herself from every angle in her black lace bra and panties. After her having Corey just ten months prior, the worst damage had been done to her lower stomach. She had some stretch marks here and there and was working hard as hell every day to get rid of the kangaroo-like pouch left behind. If she sucked her stomach in, it pretty much disappeared, but she couldn't go around sucking in forever.

Nikki turned around. Her ass was still tight and in-check. She laughed out loud at how ridiculously vain she could be.

"Baby, did you say that Corey needs a bottle now or before he goes to bed?" Chris yelled from downstairs.

Nikki wanted to run down the stairs and slap the shit out of him for yelling like he was crazy, as if he didn't know Corey was sleeping. Instead, she ran down the stairs silently, peeked over the banister, and said to him, "I'll be down in a minute, Chris."

Chris, clueless as to how infuriated his yelling had made her, looked at her like she was crazy. Nikki slipped on her clothes and boots and grabbed her suitcase as she looked around the room to make sure she had everything, running through a mental list of what she needed. She seemed to have packed it all up.

"Shit!" she exclaimed when she realized she had forgotten her birth control pills. She opened her nightstand and threw them in her purse, and headed downstairs. Chris was watching CNN with his long legs stretched out on the ottoman in their living room. He looked so handsome sitting there in his white T-shirt and boxers. Nikki laughed at the irony—as cute as he was, she could not wait to get out of that house. She needed a break from everything. Even though Chris meant well and was a great father, *there's just nothing like Mom*, she thought to herself. (She hadn't been away from him and the baby since going away on a job assignment to North Carolina to fill in for another anchor at the last minute. In spite of her objections, she was told she had to go. It was only for one night, so she lived—as did the baby.)

"Okay, babe, here's the deal," Nikki said, preparing to give Chris the rundown on what he needed to know so he could survive until she returned Sunday. "Chris! Are you listening?" Nikki was writing down the name of the cabin and emergency phone numbers.

Chris reluctantly got up and walked over to where Nikki was standing in the kitchen. "Okay, I'm all ears; tell me what I need to know, babe," he said.

"Okay, Corey is probably going to wake up in about an hour and a half. When he does, go ahead and give him some juice and maybe some fruit or crackers. After that, all he'll need is lunch. Just give him like a turkey or ham sandwich but make sure to cut it up in tiny pieces. Then for dinner, just give him some mashed potatoes and some chicken. Again, make sure you cut the chicken up real small, and then just give him some milk before bed. Oh, and, Chris, please don't forget to give him a bath," Nikki said, looking Chris directly in his eye. "And do not—I repeat, do not—let him go to sleep in the clothes he has on now; those are not pajamas."

"I got it, babe. You act like I'm retarded, like I don't know anything about how to take care of our son."

Nikki didn't acknowledge his comment.

"Me and little man will be fine," he added, walking behind Nikki and massaging her neck to loosen her up a bit.

"I know, Chris; I just want to make sure you have everything you need."

"Just go and have a good time." He kissed her on the cheek.

The doorbell rang seconds later, and Nikki ran to open it. She looked outside and realized that Lynda and Renee had arrived at the same time. She knew that Kay, always rushing in at the last minute, was going to be the late one—and she was. Renee and Lynda were having their own minireunion outside in the driveway when Nikki ran outside and jumped in the middle of both of them, hugging and kissing each of them. "I am so happy to see you girls," she squealed. "Come inside while I grab all of my junk so we can start loading up."

Chris, his arms held up in the air, stood in the doorway, blocking the ladies from entering the foyer. "Ladies, do not come in here all loud waking up this baby," he said.

"*Now* you don't want to wake him up, right?" Nikki rolled her eyes at Chris, even though she knew he was joking. It drove her nuts how totally oblivious he was of the baby's schedule and sleeping patterns—until it had a direct impact on him.

Lynda gave Chris a big hug and moved him out of the way so Renee could walk past him into the house. "Good to see you, Lynda," he said, smiling, holding her arm outstretched so he could take a good look at her. "Looks like you've been eating good out in L.A.—I mean healthy good; you must be fifteen pounds lighter, girl." Chris licked his lips playfully.

Nikki looked up at Lynda and Chris while she dug in her bag to look for the map she'd bought from Racetrac and packed by accident. She had to admit that Lynda did look damn good. Her personal training career had really taken off in L.A., and she had the looks to prove it. Nikki would have paid for Lynda's tight ass and hamstrings right about now. They weren't like bodybuilder tight, but tight enough to show through the leggings she had on. Just perfect.

"A map, Nikki?" Renee teased. "The cabin is only like an hour up 400; it's a straight shot!" Renee was making fun of Nikki's bad sense of direction.

"Don't worry about me and my map, and don't ask me to see it when our asses end up lost somewhere either. Maybe your little two-way or Palm Pilot or whatever other gadgets you have in your purse can tell us where we're going then?" Nikki said, laughing at Renee.

"Hey," Lynda said, "once Kay gets here, we're out, right?"

The room grew silent. Completely silent. Nikki looked over at Lynda, and at that very moment Lynda realized that Kay's arrival was going to be a total surprise to Renee. Nikki just stood there shaking her head in disgust.

"The baby's up," Chris said. No one actually heard the baby cry or make any other noise to let them know he was awake, but Chris headed up the stairs, taking them two at a time, trying to get out of the line of fire.

"Kay who?" Renee asked, looking dead at Nikki.

"Stop playing," Nikki said. "You know if I had told you that Kay was going to chill with us this weekend, you would have made up some lame excuse not to come. I didn't think it was fair to Lynda to fly all the way from California and not get to see all of us," Nikki said, defending her decision.

"I'm sorry," Lynda said, feeling like shit for letting the cat out of the bag.

"So does she know that I'm going to be here?" Renee asked Nikki.

"Umm . . . no," Nikki said.

"Nikki, you kill me . . . always setting something up!" Renee blew up.

The next thing they heard was trotting down the stairs, and all they could see was Chris's tall ass standing there, his eyes all bugged. "Shh, girls. Chill! The baby is 'sleep."

They all walked toward the living room area, away from the stairs, to talk more. "Listen, Renee," Nikki said, "I am sorry; I wasn't trying to play God here. But it's not like you and Kay haven't spoken since your fallout two years ago. I guess I just wanted us all together again—one last time at least."

The doorbell rang before Renee or anyone else could respond. Lynda was closest to the front door, so she ran and grabbed it.

"Lynda!" Kay said, reaching toward her to give her a hug.

"Kay! Kevin?" Lynda said, surprised to see them together. The tension got even tighter in the room.

"Kevin, what a surprise! Kay, you didn't tell me you were bringing your husband to the cabin with us." Nikki laughed, giving Kevin a hug in a lame attempt to be funny.

"That's cute, Nikki. Real cute. He's here to watch the game with Chris; didn't Chris tell you?" Everyone's eyes moved to Chris as he stood on the bottom of the stairs with a sheepish grin on his face—except Kevin's and Renee's. Their eyes were locked on each other.

"My bad. I forgot to tell you, babe. No big deal, though,

right? Come on, man. Let's go," Chris said, motioning Kevin to the den.

Kevin got his hugs in quickly, squeezing Lynda tight and then giving Renee a small hug that he wanted to appear as insignificant and innocent as possible. He was saved by the bell when he heard Chris calling his name from the den.

"Okay, here I come. Here I come. You ladies have a great time," he said, leaving Renee to deal with Kay.

When Kay looked up and saw her mirror image staring back at her from across the foyer, she kept her composure and continued to smile and chat as she walked into the house. "So I see we're all here." She shrugged, obviously commenting on Renee's presence. She walked over to Renee and gave her one of the weakest hugs imaginable.

"Hello, Kay," Renee said to her twin sister.

"Hi, Renee," Kay said.

"Can we go now?" Lynda asked, motioning toward the door.

"Yes, good idea. Let's ride," Nikki said.

The girls headed out toward Nikki's truck while Nikki and Kay went into the den to say their good-byes to Chris, the baby, and Kevin. In a matter of minutes, they were all set to go, everyone's bags packed horrifically in the back—any man would have shuddered at the sight. But they didn't care; it was just the girls and none of that mattered.

"Y'all ready?" Nikki asked, putting on her shades. She took the silence and the halfhearted "yups" as an acknowledgment that the girls were ready to head toward their destination, Cavendar Creek Cabins, for a weekend that would hopefully be full of surprises.

"You have my cell number, but I'll call to check on you guys," Nikki said to Chris.

"Keep an eye on that tire," Chris yelled, barely audible as Nikki drove away.

Chapter 3

The Key Party

"Touchdown! Yeah, baby! Yeah, yeah!" Kevin and Chris chanted, giving each other high fives. Mike Vick had run eighty yards for a touchdown. The Falcons were playing the Colts, and Vick was on fire.

"That was off the chain. Can you believe he made that run in overtime?" Kevin was excited to see the Falcons come from behind and win the game.

"Yeah, that was awesome. There's never been a quarterback in the league like Vick." Chris passed Kevin another beer.

"Yeah, he just needs to take us to the Super Bowl now!" Kevin said confidently.

"So how's the job treating you, Kev? You keepin' those guys in check over there?"

Kevin had landed a job as head coach at Morehouse College a little over a year ago. His previous job was as an assistant coach at Georgia Tech, where two of his best players were caught cheating. Kevin couldn't deal with the big fat complaint Dean Carter stuck on his record when he cursed him out for dogging the kids out so bad. Dean Carter, along with the help of the head coach, made it pretty difficult for Kevin after that day. He literally packed up his office one Monday morning and quit on the spot—he'd had enough. A former coworker at Tech transferred over to Morehouse and was able to put in a good word for Kevin, who was grateful for the break.

Chris and Kevin had been friends for several years now and didn't hang out much since he had a new job and Chris and Nikki had the baby. "So what's up, boy?" Chris said, shoving Kevin and damn near knocking him off the couch. "I know you were trippin' when you saw your girl Renee up in here. Ha, ha!"

"Man, that was a trip. I can't believe you didn't warn me or something, so I could have been a little prepared."

"Hey, Nikki put this thing together in a hurry, bruh. I didn't even know Renee was coming. I knew Kay was—because of you—and she told me that Lynda was coming to town, but she definitely left out the part about Renee."

"Man, your wife is a trip. She's always up to something. I know she brought them together so Kay and Renee can talk and shit. But—trust me—it's a bad idea. A real bad idea . . . hooking those two up again." Kevin shook his head.

"Why? I mean, I thought they squashed all that drama ever since you and Kay got married. I mean, I know Kay used to be a little jealous of you and Renee. But she's straight on where you stand, right? She doesn't still trip about that, does she?" Chris asked, trying to get to the real reason for Kevin's nervousness.

"Yeah, it's cool, man. So what's up with you and Nikki?"

"Aw, don't even try that, Kev. What's up? For real? You think I didn't check you and Renee out when you first walked in? More importantly, do you think Kay didn't notice?"

"Man, please," Kevin said, looking guilty as hell.

"I'm talking about the way your eyes were all locked up with hers. Y'all were tripping. Damn! When's the last time you saw Renee, anyway? Not since you and Kay got married, right?"

"Umm. Yeah, yeah. It's been a while. Been a long while. Yup."

Silence filled the room. "Kevin. What's up? Have you been seeing Renee on the side? Tell me you haven't!"

"Naw, man. Naw, that's crazy. Hell no!"

"Kevin?"

"What, man?"

"What's up?"

"I haven't been seeing her on the side. I haven't."

"So . . . when's the last time you saw her?"

"All right, all right. I did see her one other time before Kay and I got married," Kevin confessed. He still couldn't hide his feelings for Renee—after all this time.

The night Kevin and Renee met was a night he would never forget. It was love at first sight when Kevin saw her for the first time, sipping on a glass of wine at a nightclub. He couldn't believe his bad luck when he found out she was engaged but had a twin sister, Kay, whom he met later that night and mistook for Renee. Kay was unattached and a big flirt. She was beautiful and fun. He ended up dating Kay instead of the one he really wanted—Renee. Over time, he and Renee developed a friendship that didn't help the pent-up feelings he already had for her. Jason, Renee's fiancé, ended up being part of the "crew." Kevin and Jason didn't like each other too much. Jason knew Kevin had feelings for Renee and, even worse, suspected that Renee had feelings for Kevin as well. That caused a lot of tension whenever the whole gang got together. Things between Kevin and Renee took a serious turn when Nikki invited him and Kay to a "key party" a few years back. The key party changed many lives that night, especially Kevin's.

The key party had been unchartered territory for everyone. At this party, everybody knew everybody, and not just as acquaintances; they were all the best of friends. They each were allowed to switch partners and spend the night with each other. Whatever happened was supposed to remain a secret between each couple. Kevin ended up with Renee that night. That night confirmed what he had already known for months—he was in love with Renee, his wife's twin sister. That night also, pretty much, ended the friendship between Kevin and Jason. Jason went to Renee's house on that fateful night and found Kevin there. It had gotten pretty ugly, and neither Kevin nor Renee had been able to calm him down before he left hastily, yelling obscenities and making threats to the both of them.

Their friendship ended with Kevin beating Jason pretty bad in a straight-up brawl. He had found out that Jason put his hands on Renee a few times. Kevin went over to Jason's house in a rage and lost it. He and Jason hadn't spoken since.

"So what the hell, Kevin? What happened when you saw her?"

"Man, seriously, let's just leave that one alone. I saw her; she looked great. We just caught up. That's all."

"You're tripping, Kevin. How long ago was this? You know you need to tell me what happened. I mean, what can't you discuss? Man, stop playing and tell me what happened." Chris knew Kevin was hiding something, that there was more to the story than he was letting on.

"Chris, look. If I tell you this, you have got to keep it to yourself. For real, man, I can't even go any further if you can't promise that."

"Come on, Kevin, you know you can trust me. Now what the hell happened?"

Chapter 4

Truth or Dare

"Okay, okay, this is the deal: After the key party, I pretty much knew that I was all in with Renee. I mean I knew I had it bad for her, but that night removed all doubt. Then I went to her place a few days later to let her know how I felt. She wasn't feeling me, though; she tried to tell me that we couldn't be together because I was with her sister and that was wrong. She wouldn't budge. So I asked her for one last kiss to seal our fate and then promised her I would let it go. Well, when I left there I had every intention of ending it with Kay—I knew I was in love with her sister. What the hell kind of relationship could I possibly have with Kay knowing that . . . especially since they were twins?

"Renee begged me not to break up with Kay, but I didn't listen. I was prepared to tell Kay it was over. Kay was waiting for me at my place when I got home. She was pissed, of course, 'cause I hadn't spoken to her in days after the key party. Then I was looking all crazy because I had just left Jason's house after giving him that ass-whuppin' he so rightly deserved. She questioned me, asking me what was up and why I had been avoiding her. Then she noticed the scratches and blood on my hands. I explained to her that I beat Jason down because he put his hands on Renee. I think that's when she really realized that I loved Renee. She didn't say it, though; I could see it in her eyes. At that moment I knew I couldn't break up with her. I just couldn't do it. I mean I loved Kay, too; I never wanted to hurt her. I just happened to love her sister. I was confused."

Chris looked down, shaking his head.

"You think it's all ridiculous, don't you?" Kevin asked, hurt by Chris's reaction.

"No, man, it's just bad timing, I guess."

"Exactly," Kevin continued. "But then when I went to bed that night and I was holding Kay in my arms, it suddenly hit me—Renee was just not an option; I had to make a choice. Was I going to break Kay's heart and be alone because Renee had made it clear to me she wasn't going to be with me? Or should I try and make it work? I decided that night to try and make it work. But after the trip the girls made to Cali the following week, Kay and Renee were suddenly not speaking. I kept asking Kay, 'What happened?' but she just told me that they had fallen out and that she couldn't really discuss it with me. She kept saying she didn't want to bring it up ever again, that she and Renee were done, and that was that. She hated talking about it, so I stopped pushing. I tried to call Renee a few times to get it out of her, but she never returned my calls. This was like four months after the key party.

"Meanwhile, Kay and I were better than ever. Renee was almost a distant memory. I put all my energy into making it work with Kay, and it was working. It really was. We were happy—in spite of everything we had been through. One of those 'love conquers all' type of things, you know. Anyhow, Renee kept haunting me, man. For some reason I just couldn't let her go. All it would take was for me to hear a song that we danced to that night or to eat Chinese food and I would think about her all over again. I was losing it. So I tried calling her one last time. I really just wanted to see how she was doing. Had she gone back to Jason, or met someone else? As usual I left a message just asking her to call me to let me know how she was doing. In the past she hadn't returned my calls, but this time she did. By the time I heard from Renee it had been about six months since the key party. She apologized for blowing me off and wanted to see me. She 'missed me,' she said, and wondered how I was doing too. I suggested that we meet at the Houston's down the street from her place. I knew that was her favorite restaurant and figured it was as good a spot as any—oh, and their spinach dip is bangin'. Kay was working late so it was the perfect night to do it. When I arrived at the restaurant I saw Renee in a corner booth way in the back. She motioned me over to her. She looked fine as hell, as usual. Her hair was pinned up just like I liked it. All the feelings I had tucked away came crashing through instantly. I asked myself, what am I doing here? But I headed over to her, anyway. She got up and gave me the tightest squeeze. She was wearing some low-rider jeans that gripped her ass just right. All I know is she looked doooood. Damn! She felt good, too. It was so fucking crazy how different she felt in my arms, compared to Kay. You'll never understand how freakish it is, but she fit just right. We held each other for a while, and I didn't want to let her go."

"So, Renee, what's been up?" Kevin asked, escorting her to her side of the table before returning to his side to sit down.

"Not much has changed with me, Kevin. I'm still working hard at A-Plus Advertising. I got a promotion, though." She smiled. "I'm actually an account manager now, so I oversee all the account executives. It's a lot better for me; I was getting really bored. Now my days mainly consist in taking

clients out to lunch and chillin' at my desk, monitoring presentations. And I also do a lot of training, which I really enjoy."

"Oh, oh! You're not playing, huh? You're big time now! That's cool, Renee. I'm happy for you. Really, I am."

"Thanks. You're silly. I'm not big time, just trying to do my thing a little. You haven't changed a bit," she said, feeling slightly embarrassed. "It feels good, though—being in charge—but, trust me, I still have a boss that keeps me in check. So I haven't truly gotten there yet, but it's wonderful doing something a little different."

"I see you're still wearing Ralph Lauren perfume," Kevin said, smiling, trying to break through the small talk.

"I love it; I'll never wear anything else. I can't believe you remembered."

"I could tell she was impressed with me, dog."

"I remember everything!"

"I started tripping at this point, Chris. I was gazing into her eyes, mesmerized. I know it sounds like something out of a movie or something you'd read in a book, but I'm serious. On everything I love, she had me, man. Every time I'm with her, my body gets all warm and shit, like I'm a damn teenager. That's always how I knew it was different with her in comparison to Kay. I mean—don't get me wrong—I love the hell out of Kay. Really, I do, but at the time I just didn't feel the passion I felt for Renee when I was with her."

"Maybe it was the fact that you knew it was forbidden. Maybe it was the idea of it all that turned you on more than Renee herself."

"Nah, it's her, man. It's her. You just don't understand. I feel crazy as hell when I'm with her, like I can't control myself."

"Damn! That's messed up! Kay is such a great girl, Kev. You were trippin'."

"Trust me, I haven't finished yet. You think I was trippin'? Wait till you hear the rest. Okay, where was I?"

"You were telling Renee how good she smelled and were gazing into her eyes," Chris reminded him. "Go ahead. Finish the story. Get to the good shit . . . please!"

"Okay, we kept talking. We were talking about work. At the time I was still in hell working for Tech, complaining and wanting to quit bad. She was supportive as usual and told me I should quit, saying I could do anything I set my mind to. Then we got our drinks. She was drinking a Long Island iced tea, and I was sipping on a Corona. The conversation stayed pretty steady—until I brought up Jason."

"Kevin, I really don't want to talk about Jason with you."

"Why? Are you still pissed at me for going to his place that night and kicking his ass? I hope not, 'cause I'd do it again, Renee—in an instant. That was fucked up, what he did to you. No real man should ever put his hands on a woman. I mean, what was his problem? That muthafucka is crazy. I can't believe I ever called him my friend."

"I was on a roll, Chris. I was sounding crazier than Jason. Damn! He heated me up."

"Kevin, this is what I'm talking about! You get way too riled up when we talk about him. I mean, listen to you. It's over; it's in the past. That was so long ago. Let it go."

"I'll never let go of the fact that he hurt you. Will you?"

"I've actually found a way to get past it."

"Have you spoken to him since?"

"No. He keeps leaving messages on my machine telling me how sorry he is, wanting to explain, but I never return his calls."

"Yeah, I know what that feels like," Kevin said, taking a dig at Renee for giving him the same treatment.

"I'm not gonna lie. I was pissed that she never returned my calls, man; I had to throw that in there."

"I know, Kevin. I'm sorry about that. You just don't understand. I was really messed up after the whole key party incident. I was so confused and twisted up inside; I didn't know what was right or wrong for me. I was just lost."

"I feel you, Renee. I was a bit messed up, too, but I wasn't confused. I knew exactly what I wanted."

"Then I started looking deep into her eyes again. I reached across the table and took her hand in mine. She was looking at me, too; she knew what I was talking about. I think she felt it, too."

"*Kevin—about Jason—I know I said I didn't want to talk about it, but you have to know this. I haven't spoken to him since that night. I couldn't. I couldn't speak to anyone . . . especially after what happened on the trip to California with Kay, Nikki, and Lynda."*

"What the hell happened between you and Kay on that trip?"

"You mean she hasn't told you?"

"Nope! I tried and tried to get it out of her, but it was like this big secret. She just wouldn't tell me. She just told me that you guys were done—over—and that you may as well be dead as far as she was concerned."

"Isn't that something? Is that what she said? She's such a trip. I'll tell you what happened: Your girl tried to kill me in the car; we threw down and it was not pretty."

"What!"

"I was tripping at this point, Chris. Did you know about this, man?"

"Well, yeah, I did, Kev, but I couldn't say anything, dog. Nikki made me promise. She said that Kay didn't want you to know, that she had her reasons that didn't have anything to do with us, so she begged me not to tell you."

"Awwwwww! That's fucked up, Chris. That's real fucked up."

"Come on, man, you know how me and Nikki roll. I respect her shit, and she respects mine. I wouldn't expect her to tell a secret I asked her to keep either—not even to one of her girls."

"So what are you saying? You think Nikki doesn't have any secrets from you? Is that what you think?" Kevin started to get edgy. He felt betrayed that everyone but him knew what had happened on the trip to Cali.

"No, I'm sure she does have some secrets, but if she does, there's really nothing I can do about it—unless I find out about them. Then that's a different story."

"Whatever, Chris. All right, man. You and Nikki kill me. I guess that's why y'all are still happily married and all that good stuff."

"Come on, Kevin. Seriously, I figured Kay would tell you . . . eventually."

"Well, she didn't. I had to hear it from Renee. Anyways, let me finish my story."

"Okay, okay, okay. Cool. Go ahead. I'm listening."

"So she told me that Kay slapped the shit out of her and that they were going for broke in the backseat trying to hurt each other bad. It was an old-school fight, Chris—hair pulling, scratching. Just ridiculous. I couldn't believe that either of them was even capable," Kevin said, "but you never know with women."

"So what made Kay lose it in the car? What triggered her, Renee?"

"Well . . . brace yourself. Apparently she found out that you picked my key on the night of the key party, and Jason told her that you and I had sex that night."

"What! Awwwww, he's about to get another ass-whuppin', for real. That's bullshit! Who the hell does he think he is? Damn! That shit makes so much sense now. That night after I went home from leaving Jason's, Kay was looking at

me like the devil. I thought she was just mad that I had actually fought Jason over you, but now I understand it was much deeper than that."

"I know, Kevin. That's why she didn't tell you, I guess. She didn't want you to know that she knew."

"But we didn't even have sex!"

"I know, Kev, but she didn't know that. All she had to go on was what Jason told her—just his lies."

"I can't believe that she's known all this time that I picked your key. Damn! That's so fucked up. She must have been devastated."

"She was, Kevin. She was. That's how we ended up fighting. In the car we were the only ones not talking. Lynda and Nikki were chatting about some stuff up front when out of the blue she looked me dead in my face and said, 'You fucked him, didn't you?' She was so irrational; I couldn't get her to believe that nothing happened. It was the look in her eyes that frightened me. I mean I can hold my own, but when I looked my sister in the eye, I knew it was about to be on. She reared back and slapped me dead across my face and then started pounding me. It was unbelievable. I couldn't get her off me, so I was defending myself the best I could. Once I finally got some leverage I threw her back off me and her head hit the side window. She wasn't my sister at that moment. Nikki and Lynda were screaming and yelling, begging us to please stop, but we were too far gone on adrenaline. The last thing I remember was throwing a handful of hair in her face. Nikki stopped the car, and we all got out. My face was swollen from the fight, and Kay's head was pretty banged up, not to mention the small bald spot on the right side of her head. After Nikki pleaded with us to get back in since we were only seventy miles or so outside L.A., Lynda sat in the back with Kay, and I sat up front with Nikki. We rode in silence. Once we arrived at the hotel, Kay got on the phone

and called a cab immediately. She ended up taking a plane back to Georgia that day. It was all a big mess."

"Damn! No wonder you were all messed up. No wonder you didn't want to talk to anyone."

"I was truly sorry, man. She started to cry right there in the restaurant. I walked over to her and told her it was going to be okay. I promised her that it would. I grabbed her purse, paid the tab, and we got out of there. We'd had a few drinks between us, so I offered to drive her home. I told her I would take her to get her car in the morning somehow. She accepted. When we got back to her place, I walked her to the door. That was the first time I'd been to her place since that night. It brought back a lot of memories—good and bad. When we got to the door I looked at her, and she looked at me. We were standing there outside her door reading each other's minds. She was saying, 'Come in. Please come in.' And I was saying, 'Invite me in. Invite me in.' It was a trip, man."

"Renee, I'm sorry all of this happened. I feel like this is all my fault, like if you and Kay never met me that you would still be tight like sisters should be."

"It's not your fault, Kevin. It's not."

"Then we hugged. She buried her face in my shoulder. I squeezed her, not wanting to ever let her go."

"Well, did she invite you in?" Chris asked, excited.

"Hold on, man. I'm getting to that part. Just ease up, ease up. So we were still holding each other, and then I slowly pulled away. I wanted to kiss her. She stopped me—but not for the reasons I thought. She surprised me. She took me by the hand and invited me inside. My heart was pounding, man, I'm telling you. When we got inside she led me over to the couch and we sat down and got comfortable in each other's arms. I was stroking her hair and holding her, comforting her. It felt so right, man. We must have sat there on her couch like that for a solid hour—in silence. Shit! I had almost fallen asleep when she got up and headed for the kitchen. She returned with a huge piece of strawberry cheesecake and two forks. We were reenergized. We started chatting and I told her a few funny stories about some of my players. Then we started on the last movie we saw, debating on why it ended the way it did. There was some subtle flirting going on. She had a small crumb of cheesecake on the corner of her mouth that I had no problem removing and then licking it off my fingers. She thanked me with a light kiss on the lips. We were laughing and getting really comfortable with each other. We had both made a silent agreement not to let our talk at Houston's ruin our night."

"Hey, truth or dare?"

"What?"

"Truth or dare?"

"Truth," Kevin said.

"At this point we had already finished the cheesecake and were on to drinking some Reisling, feeling pretty good again."

"What's your favorite part on a woman's body?"

"Ha, ha! Okay, that's easy; I love a woman with nice legs."

"Really? I didn't know that. Are you a breast man or an ass man?"

"Hold up. Isn't that two questions? It's my turn, right?"

"Okay, okay. Sorry. Dang! Go ahead."

"All right, cool. Truth or dare?"

"Truth," she said excitedly, anticipating his question.

"What's your favorite sexual position?"

"She had the nerve to look a little embarrassed . . . like she didn't know she was headed for trouble suggesting this game."

"See? You just had to get freaky on me. Okay, this is probably gonna sound lame, but I like the good old-fashioned

missionary position the best. I like to be able to look at my partner when I'm making love to him."

"I gulped and looked at her like, 'Can I be your partner tonight?' Ha, ha! She kills me, man, kills me."

"*Okay, my turn, Kevin. Truth or dare?"*

"Truth."

"*So are you a breast man or an ass man?" she asked, looking pleased that she was still able to get her question out.*

"That's tough; I like both."

"*Don't be lame, Kevin. Come on. You* must *like one better than the other. If you absolutely had to choose—"*

"She was looking at me like, 'Please say *ass* . . . since I got these itty-bitty size-B titties.' "

"Ha, ha!" Chris started laughing hysterically. "Y'all are crazy. Hey, size B ain't bad at all. As long as I can fit one of those bad girls in my mouth—that's all I care about, for real. I can't believe you're playing 'truth or dare.' Now, that sounds like some shit my wife would do. Well, what did you tell her, man? Did you say breast or ass?" Chris asked, enjoying the story.

"Okay, chill, man, chill. I said, 'I like both, but if I had to choose, I would have to say the ass because it's attached to those legs I love oh so much.'

"She started smiling at me. Then she confidently crossed her tight legs one over the other. She knew I loved those legs of hers—it was all over her face."

"*Okay, my turn. Truth or dare?"*

"Truth," she said.

"Hmmm . . . have you ever been intimate with another woman?"

"Ewwwww. No!"

"Have you ever wanted to?"

"No, no, no. I mean, when I went to that strip club with Nikki and the girls I had more of an appreciation for women.

They definitely have beautiful bodies, but I have no desire to be with one. Hey! You're cheating; that's two questions. It's my turn now. Truth or dare?"

"Dare," he said, gleaming at her with this "now what the hell are you gonna do" look on his face. She looked at him the same.

"Okay. Umm, hmm. I dare you to get butt naked and run to the car and get my cell phone. I left it in your car."

"Now, I know you didn't just dare me to do that. Me? Butt-ass naked?"

"Okay, you can keep your underwear on, but everything else must go."

"You must not know who you're messing with, girl."

"Then I started unbuttoning my shirt. I had a 'wife-beater' underneath it. The game was starting to get real interesting. She was checking me out as I started taking off my clothes, so I started doing a little striptease for her, grinding like I was 'Sexual Chocolate' or something. She was cracking up. She took out a dollar from her purse and started motioning me to her with it. I started unbuttoning my pants and then pulled my underwear out for her to slide the dollar in it—and she did. Then I took my pants all the way off."

"Take it off. Take it off," she chanted.

"It was cool. I took my wife-beater off, all slow. She was loving it. We were having a good time. Then I did my dare. I ran outside damn near naked and got her cell phone like she requested. She was trippin' as I ran out the door; she couldn't believe I did it. I never did find the phone after searching for a while.

"When I got back inside the lights were off all over her town house. She was nowhere to be found. I started walking through the dark in my boxers, wondering like hell what she was up to. Then I yelled, 'Renee' and got no answer. I started toward her bedroom. I could see a flicker of light there."

"Hey, Renee?"

"When I got to the bedroom, there were a few candles lit all around the room, some on her dresser, her nightstand, and even a few in her bathroom. The room smelled good—just like her. I could smell Ralph Lauren all over the room. She had taken her clothes off, too. She just had her panties on and was kneeling on the bed. I thought I was going to die from sheer happiness. She had let her hair down and she looked amazing. Man, she took my breath away—literally. I was so taken by her beauty, Chris, man; I couldn't even speak. I just started walking toward her. She was drawing me like a magnet. It was obvious the game was over. She started moving toward me, sliding on her knees. Then she started touching me with her hands. They glided all over me slowly, all soft and warm. I was really nervous. It was so unexpected. I had always been the one in control before. And she had always resisted me. This time we both knew what we wanted. I never imagined her seducing me. I wasn't prepared. She got so close to me our bodies were touching. She could tell I didn't know what to do. She could tell that I was trippin', and so she kept on making the moves as I stood there, trying to get it together. I was breathing all heavy and shit . . . like I was about to explode or something. She slid her hands in my Calvins and started stroking me. I thought I was gonna come right there on the spot. I had to do something. I had to take back the control."

"*I wanna taste you," Kevin said.*

"She looked at me and smiled. It was a crooked smile. She was gonna let me do it; I couldn't believe it. I didn't know who I was in the room with for a minute. She was making moves I never dreamed she would. Then she lay back down on the bed, reached over to her nightstand, and turned her stereo on with the remote control. It was Sade. She knew how much I loved Sade. I started to wonder if it had all been planned, but I followed her lead. When she slid back on the bed, I slid, too. My hands started gliding up and down both of her thighs, so smooth and tight. They felt damn good. I had it all under control. Then I started going down on her, man. She was moaning and squirming, making these glorious sounds that pumped my manhood back up a bit. I was down there for a good fifteen minutes before she came—hard, all over my face. She tasted good and could tell . . . from the way I was licking my lips. I wanted all of her. She was gripping the sheets. I was putting in work for real. When she regained her composure she took my face in her hands and put her mouth up to my ear and whispered, 'You're making me crazy.' We were both breathing uncontrollably now from the excitement. This was madness. We were so damn caught up in the moment; there was no turning back now. We were both kneeling on the bed facing each other and started to kiss like we never had before. I could still taste her, and I knew she could taste her own juices, too. But she didn't seem to mind. My tongue was vibing with hers. Her eyes were closed, her hands caressing my head and mine squeezing her ass. We were both moaning passionately. My body was tingling all over. I could feel her heart pounding on my chest. Our bodies were wet with sweat. Then she started making her way down while still looking up at me. She was so damn sexy, man. She took me in her mouth; I took hold of her hair, twisting it slightly, tugging at it as her head went up and down. She was sucking me like she couldn't get enough. That turned me on even more—to see how much she was loving it. I tried to stop her after a while, not wanting to come yet, but she wouldn't let me. She kept telling me to come. She wanted it all, and so I let myself go and I came. She surprised me and took it all in—and then some. There was not one drop left by the time she was through. I was in awe. I felt like I had to be dreaming and was going to wake up any second now, but it wasn't a dream. It was real. It wasn't long before I was ready for a second round. I had to have her.

I wasn't gonna let her go without getting inside. She wanted it, too. She told me she wanted to feel me deep inside her. So I laid her down on the bed to be on top of her; I wanted to look in her eyes when I finally made love to her just like she wanted to look in mine. I wanted to see her sweet face, to kiss her and stroke her hair. I wanted to feel her underneath me.

"It was by far the best sex I'd ever had. She was making my body feel things it had never felt before, I'm telling you, man. I couldn't believe I could still go after she made me come, but— for some reason—I was still going strong. I had stamina I'd never had before. I was making love to her like we had just started. We made love until we both came again. I couldn't think straight; it was just so intense. When we were finished, I slid from on top of her and intertwined her hand in mind. I kissed her hand gently, then her lips. We were just staring at each other, lying there naked side by side, but unfortunately, the regret was already there in her eyes."

"Kevin," she whispered.

"Shhhhhh! Don't say it, Renee, please."

"Then she just smiled at me and closed her eyes. I watched her drift off to sleep. She looked so peaceful and content. I could have lain there next to her forever if she would have let me, but I knew this was all she could handle. I just knew. I watched her sleep for what seemed like hours before I fell out, too.

"When morning came, I could see the steam floating in the air from the bathroom. She had already gotten up, showered, and put on her clothes. I did the same before joining her in the kitchen. She made me pancakes and eggs. She was sitting at the table drinking a glass of orange juice when I walked into the room. She had a fluffy, white terry cloth robe on. Her hair was wet from washing it. She looked more beautiful sitting there than she ever had before. If I didn't know I was in trouble before, I knew I was headed for some now. How would I ever go back? I asked myself. But I could see it in her eyes that she was going to make me do just that.

"It was bad, man, so fucking bad. I went to kiss her good morning, and she kissed me back. But it wasn't the same; it was short and quick, the kiss of death. It was done. Over. Finished. I knew it. I didn't even want to talk to her about it, so I walked off and went back in the bedroom, gathered up the rest of my things, and started to walk out the door."

"Kevin, don't leave like this . . . please."

"What do you want from me, Renee? I sure as hell don't want to hear about how sorry you were that this happened, and I damn sure don't want to hear about Kay and how you can't do this to her."

"I know, Kevin. I know you don't. That's not what I was going to say. I think you know me well enough to know how I feel about all of that by now. I just wanted to say—"

"Then she got up from the table and walked over to me. She was tearing; I was trying to hold mine back. I felt like if I blinked just one more time, tears would start flowing, but I held it together. She tiptoed and kissed me gently. Then she took my face in her hands."

"I love you, Kevin. I always will. I don't regret one single moment we shared last night. Not one. I will cherish that moment for a lifetime. Nothing will change that—ever."

"Renee—"

"Don't, Kevin. Please don't. Just tell me you feel the same way . . . please."

"You know I do. You've always known that I loved you from the first day I met you."

"Then we hugged each other tightly; I didn't want to let her go, man, but I knew I had to. I knew that was the very last time I would ever hold her like that again."

"How the hell did you go back to Kay after that, man?"

Chris asked, concerned. "How could you marry her knowing how strongly you felt for her sister? That's crazy, Kev. Crazy."

"I don't know, man. It took me a few days to compose myself after I left Renee that morning. I didn't even go home for a while. I got a hotel over by Perimeter and did a lot of soul-searching. I thought about going back to Renee's and fighting for her, telling her that I wasn't gonna let her go, but I knew, deep down, that night that she and I could never happen. It wasn't reality; Kay was my reality. Kay and the choices I made back in the day to commit to her and make her mine: I had to stay true to that. And I loved Kay. She made me happy, for the most part. I just didn't want to start over. I couldn't even imagine falling in love with someone else. Me and Kay were comfortable with each other; we were compatible. I knew I could make a life with her if I gave it my all, so that's what I did.

"I saw Kay a few days later. She gave me the riot act on where the hell I'd been the last couple of days. I told her, 'I had to get away to think.' It wasn't the first time that I had needed to be alone to work through things. When I went back to Kay, I made a promise to myself to leave Renee in my past. I had to put her behind me. She was never going to be mine, and I didn't want her if she was going to always look at me with resentment and regret. I think she had some hope that she and Kay would be all right one day—but not if she was with me. And I had to respect her for that. I proposed to Kay about six months later, and I've never looked back since."

"So weren't you pissed at Renee, though? Didn't you feel used?"

"Not used—no—disappointed. Definitely disappointed; we both wanted that night to happen. We had for a long time. It was on both of us. She never gave me the impression before that night that this would be a new beginning for us; I knew that going in. I was just hopeful. That's all. But, deep down, I felt like that was going to be the last time I saw her. I think that's why we got so much into each other. We made the most of that night, since we didn't get a chance the night of the key party."

"Damn! Man, that's deep as hell. I wasn't expecting all this when I asked you what was up with the two of you. So how are you and Kay doing? You two all right?"

"Oh yeah, we're great. Better than ever. I mean this all happened a long, long time ago. I'm completely committed now; I wouldn't have married her otherwise. I love her but I just had to get Renee out of my system. That night changed things so that we could move on, both of us."

"So you never spoke to Renee after that morning?"

"Nope. Never—until today. I've thought of her from time to time, naturally, but I've never picked up the phone to call her. I had heard that she'd moved back to South Carolina to be with her dad. That's what Kay told me, anyway."

"Yeah. Nikki talks to Renee every so often, but not much. That's why I was surprised to see Renee going with them to the cabin today."

"Is she dating anyone?" Kevin asked.

"A banker, I think. I think that's what Nikki told me. So Kay doesn't ever talk to you about her?"

"Hell no! Not one single word. Renee's name doesn't come up—ever! That's cool. I'm happy for her that she's dating again—as long as it's not Jason. Ha!"

"No shit!" Chris said, changing Corey's diaper.

"Damn! Man, I still can't believe that you're a father sometimes."

"Yeah, it's a trip, man. It's no joke having a kid, man. Corey is a handful. I know Nikki's happy to be outta here, even if it is just for one night."

"Yeah, I hear you. How old is Corey now? Nine months?"

"Ten. I love it, though; I was made for fatherhood. It's

hard at times. We haven't slept in almost a year—especially Nikki. She loves being a mother, but I don't think she'll ever lose the part of her that likes to get into shit, you know—to be wild every now and then. It's only a matter of time before she's trying to round us all up. She denies it when I talk to her about it. I think she denies it for my sake, though . . . because she knows I'm happier with the life we have now."

"Damn! Yeah, she's definitely a good one, man. I hope you guys are together forever; don't ever let her go."

"Oh, not to worry, man. Me and Nikki are in it for the long haul, no doubt."

"All right, bet. Hey, Chris, of course I don't have to tell you again that what I just told you about me and Renee is between us, right?"

"Come on, man. Of course."

"I mean it, Chris, man. I know you tell Nikki everything, but you can't tell her this; she and Kay are still really good friends. She would lose it if she knew. I'm not trying to start trouble or lose my wife."

"I got it, man. I got it. Give me some credit," Chris said, putting his fist out for a pound from Kevin. "We're partners—for life."

"So when are you two planning on having some kids?"

"Shit! Not any time soon, man; I'm not ready for all that."

Kevin's and Chris' conversation tapered off as they finished watching the last minutes of the game and Kevin told Chris he was going to go ahead and bounce.

"All right, man. I'll holler at you later," Kevin said, heading toward the door.

On the way home Kevin reflected on the talk he'd had with Chris. He felt good about it. It was nice having someone he could talk to from the "old crew." He put Sade in the CD player and cruised all the way home reminiscing about how much he and Kay had been through.

Chapter 5

Catching Up

The ride to Cavendar Creek Cabins started out tense, to say the least. Nikki, grateful that Lynda had offered to drive, sat in the front passenger seat acting as DJ. Kay decided to spend the forty-five-minute drive staring quietly out the window, counting trees as they passed by. Renee spent her time on the phone talking to what seemed to be the new man in her life—from what Nikki could tell as she eavesdropped.

"Okay. You too. Bye," Renee said. It was the first time Nikki had seen Renee smile since she arrived.

"Well?" Nikki asked, turning around in her seat looking at Renee for an explanation.

"Well what?"

"Come on, Renee. Don't you dare try to act all secretive. I hope you don't think that you're gonna get away with playing the silent game while you're here. Just to reiterate, this trip is all about communication, talking to each other. Closing doors, opening new ones." Nikki had everyone's attention.

"Whatever, Nikki," Renee snapped. "Can we get in the damn cabin before we start baring our souls, please?"

"Yeah, I second that," Kay agreed.

"Okay, okay," Nikki conceded. "We don't have to bare our souls or anything. But can't we have a simple conversation? So, Renee, who were you talking to? Is it a secret?"

"No, it's not. I just met him, so I don't really want to jinx it by talking about him."

"Well, does he have a name?" Lynda chimed in.

"Derrick. Derrick Washington. He's a professor over at Morehouse."

"Wow! A professor? How old is he?" Nikki turned her body around completely to face Renee, while Kay, pretending not to be interested, was looking out the window.

Renee hesitated. "He's forty-seven," she said, bracing herself.

"Forty-seven?" Lynda and Nikki screamed in unison.

"That's a borderline old-ass man," Lynda said.

"Forty-seven isn't old, not really," Renee said defensively. "He doesn't look it; he's so handsome, debonair—Denzel-like."

"What? Oh, shit! Okay, I'm feeling you on the Denzel kick because Denzel is pushing fifty, and I'ma tell y'all right now, Denzel could easily—do you hear me? Easily—get the panties!" Nikki said, laughing out loud.

Kay finally chuckled. Nikki, knowing she would join in eventually, just smiled at her.

"Yeah, I feel you on Denzel, too," Kay said to Renee. "I would tear him apart."

Renee smiled at her sister. She couldn't believe she was talking to her—and with a smile on her face, at that. The only conversations they'd had since the long ride to Cali was to check in with each other about their father every so often. They always tried to hold it together for his sake. It was rough—phony at times, even—but they did it. They did not want him to know what had transpired between them. He would have been so disappointed.

"So have you slept with him yet?" Nikki asked Renee, cheesing.

"Damn! Get right to the point, why don't you?" Lynda said.

"Well, no, not yet; I only met him a few weeks ago. He's quite the gentleman. We kissed, though, if you must know." Renee beamed.

"Very interesting. So you've got yourself a real man, huh? And how was the kiss?" Nikki asked.

"It was awesome. It was one of those kisses that makes your entire body tingle. I felt it in my toes, I felt it everywhere."

"Awwww!" Nikki was impressed and a little envious. It had been a little while since she had been kissed to the point where she felt it in her toes. "That's wonderful, Renee. Hold on to him and appreciate it while you can; that shit doesn't last."

"Uh, Nikki, what are you talking about—with your perfect-ass husband?" Kay asked, perturbed.

"Whatever, Kay. Don't act like we're not in the same boat. I'm not saying that Chris can't kiss; he is a great kisser. But after years of kissing the same person, I'm just saying that you stop feeling it in your toes. You may feel it in your panties from time to time—but not in your toes. That's that 'love at first sight' kind of kiss. Once you're married, those kisses get so familiar, you can damn near do without them."

"Nikki, that's ridiculous." Lynda shook her head. "You are so dramatic."

"Well, I'm not really a kisser, personally," Kay joined in. "That's too much drama; I like to just get right down to it."

"I didn't know you didn't like to kiss, Kay," Renee told her sister.

"I don't hate it, but I don't love it. I've moved on in my

old age; that's elementary school stuff," bragged Kay, like she had a story to tell.

Everyone was hoping she didn't bring Kevin's name up. *Please, please don't bring his name up,* Nikki was chanting in her head.

"Yeah, Kevin and I don't even kiss anymore; we have graduated to much bigger and better things," said Kay, firing at Renee, who turned away and smiled, shaking her head.

"What? What's that look for?" Kay asked.

Oh, shit! Here we go, Lynda thought to herself.

"What are you looking like that for, Renee?" Kay asked, raising her voice.

"Kay, I'm not about to start in with you," Renee said, remaining calm.

"Oh, that's cool. I was just wondering why the hell you had that fucking grin on your face, but I'll just chalk it up to good old-fashioned jealousy."

"All right, all right, all right. That's enough, Kay. Damn! Can we please not get into this today? Please?" Lynda begged.

"Yeah. I second that motion," Nikki said as she turned up the radio. "I bet y'all can't shake your ass like Beyoncé did on that *Uh-Oh* video." Nikki put her hands up in the air, trying to shake hers in her seat.

Kay and Renee were both looking out the window again—away from each other; it seemed there would always be a divide between them.

Chapter 6

Cavendar Creek

The girls made it to the cabin in one piece; everything had gone smoothly with the check-in process. The cabin owners, an old white couple named John and Mary who'd been running the lot for ten years, were very nice. On their way out the door John and Mary informed the girls that a friend of theirs was already at the cabin waiting for them outside. They thanked them and made their journey through the woods to find their lot.

"You guys are going to love Angel," Kay told the girls once they were back in the truck. "She's so cool, she'll get along with all of us just fine. I'm going to warn you, though, she's kind of hot. Well actually, she's beautiful."

"Just great," Nikki said, sighing heavily.

"Oh, stop it with the jealous stuff, Nikki," Kay said. "She's not going to steal me from you." Kay hugged Nikki playfully.

Nikki had almost forgotten that Kay had invited Angel. Apparently she was a pretty new friend of Kay's. Nikki had always been somewhat skeptical about bringing outsiders around the crew. She knew it was silly, but she was kind of protective of her group of friends and just didn't want anyone coming between them.

"I'm glad we didn't come up here in the dark," Lynda said.

"I know I would have been scared as hell," Kay added.

When they pulled up they saw Angel waiting outside her car talking on her cell phone. Angel was just downright adorable. She stood about five four, had a pretty face with chiseled, model-like features. Her hair was cut really short, and stuck up and out haphazardly . . . but fly as hell and her skin looked great, almost airbrushed but you could tell it wasn't a bunch of makeup or foundation. She was quite striking. Nikki was the last one to get out of the truck. Angel gave Kay a hug first and then immediately turned to Renee and the rest of the girls, giving them small "brand-new" kind of hugs, introducing herself briefly. They all walked into the cabin, filing in one after another. It had a rustic feel to it, with a spiral staircase carved out of an actual tree trunk that led up to a loft area that all the girls had seen on the Web site.

"I want the loft!" they all screamed in unison like schoolgirls.

Something inside Kay told her to run for the staircase. It caused a chain reaction as they all dove toward the first step as if whoever got upstairs first determined who got dibs on it.

"Okay, calm down!" Nikki urged. "We agreed to pull straws, remember?"

Everyone slowed down and came back down the stairs adjusting their clothes, getting back into woman mode. Renee was the only one who kept her composure, as always. Lynda was under the kitchen sink looking at the selection of pots and pans, while Nikki and Kay went onto the balcony out of the back door.

"Check out this Jacuzzi!" Nikki and Kay yelled from outside. The girls ran toward the side door that led to the balcony.

"Nice," Angel said. "I love it!"

"This place is cleaner than my house," Nikki observed.

"Tell me about it. Mine too," Lynda agreed.

"Mine too!" Kay and Renee chimed in simultaneously before looking at each other, then turning away.

The girls leaned over the railing overlooking the creek that ran behind their cabin. They were all really enjoying being away from home in such a clean cool spot.

"I think a friend of mine came to this same set of cabins, like two years ago," Renee said.

"They said they signed some kind of book or journal that you can write in before you leave so people will know you've been here."

"We'll have to find it before we leave," Nikki promised.

"So what's for dinner?" Kay asked.

It had been hours since any of them had eaten. They all realized they were hungry.

"It's already two o'clock," Lynda said.

"I say we go to that Super Wal-Mart we passed on the way in and buy some stuff to cook for dinner and for a big breakfast tomorrow," Kay suggested. They all agreed that it was the best way to save some money; plus, they just liked the idea of having food to munch on.

"Let's go ahead and get this grocery shopping out of the way so we can get back and just chill," Nikki said. No one had taken off their shoes yet, so all they had to do was head back toward the truck. Nikki and Lynda got to the front door first, and Kay, Renee, and Angel were close behind.

The girls made it to Wal-Mart and back in record time. It was now three o'clock. They pulled straws and decided to take time to get settled into the cabin nicely and put their bags in their rooms. Nikki and Lynda ended up in the master bedroom, which included a bathroom. They both unpacked their bags as if they planned on staying a week instead of just one night. Nikki had her clothes folded neatly in the top dresser drawer with a bar of her favorite soap—Caress. Her mom had taught her to put soap in her drawers to make her clothes smell nice.

Lynda, beat from the plane ride and the drive to the cabin, passed out on the bed, attempting to take a little nap. Kay and Angel shared the loft, which had two twin beds separated by a huge cream bearskin rug. They spent their unpacking time with some much-needed Cuervo Gold and a flattened bag of Nacho chips Angel had stashed in her overnight bag.

Renee listened to all the cackling going on upstairs and found herself relieved that she had gotten stuck with the pullout queen-size bed in the living room alone. She was grateful for the twenty-seven-inch TV placed in front of the sofa. She had to have the TV on while she was sleeping since she hated the sound of crickets chirping and frogs croaking. The thought of being in the woods was enough to make her skin crawl; she hated bugs, and it also brought back unwanted memories of her ex-fiancé, Jason.

The last time she was in a cabin was a night that was supposed to be filled with romance; instead, it marked the end of a love that should never have been—Jason had a lot of demons that needed to be exorcised. He should not have been anyone's boyfriend, much less fiancé. Renee couldn't understand why, at times, he hated her so badly. There were so many good moments in the six months they were together when he was a perfect gentleman. Jason was a lawyer and paid as hell. He was biracial, about six feet tall with dreamy green eyes, and a killer smile. He was the type of brotha who wined and dined a woman, the type who seemed to know what women wanted and then delivered it each and every time . . . when she least expected it. Renee felt like she had hit the jackpot when she found Jason and they fell in love, but then after just a few months, things started to gradually change. Every once in a while, he had trouble getting it up, which in turn made him withdraw when they were making love. She started to feel like it was her. He insisted it wasn't but would never have any explanation. Then his temper started to show. He would go off on her for no reason, disrespecting her and calling her a tramp if she dressed too provocatively. But she loved him so much she would always accept his apologies. He would come across so remorseful, childlike even, when he did something to hurt her. His erratic behavior was infrequent at first, which led her to blindly let his good qualities outweigh his bad; she let herself believe that she somehow did something to provoke it and tried not to do anything to upset him. The memories brought Renee to tears but were thankfully interrupted by outrageous laughter from upstairs. Kay and Angel were having a ball, it seemed, and she felt a bit jealous.

"Kay, you're a trip, girl. I can't believe that you literally called Kevin a bore. That doesn't make any sense, because if you don't mind me saying so, your husband is fine as hell! That hunk of dark chocolate needs to be on a poster right on this wall in here next to my bed."

"Angel, chill, man! I didn't say he wasn't fine. I know he's fine, but that's just so overrated now after two years of marriage to the man. He's just so lame in the bedroom sometimes. I mean I can't even get him to use handcuffs."

"Now, Kay, just because you've turned into some crazed freak doesn't mean that everyone has to like it. Personally, I'm all for the traditional lovemaking. I can make love to my man with just me, him, and Luther!"

"Really?" asked Kay.

"Yes, really! What? I can't be traditional?"

"No, I didn't say all that," Kay said, rolling her eyes.

"So, seriously, girl, what are you going to do about Kevin? I mean you can't go on like this; you know you're going to have to tell him sooner or later."

"Well, I prefer later; besides, I still love him. I'll always love him. I just have to start putting myself first, that's all."

"So what was that little performance in the ride over here about?"

"What performance?"

"I overheard Nikki and Lynda talking about you and Renee fighting on the way here. Why were you guys arguing?"

"That's such a long story, and I'm so not in the mood to tell it."

"Give me a break, Kay. You better tell me what's up. I mean, aren't twins supposed to be close?"

"Well, the worst of it happened at this party Nikki threw a few years back—a key party."

Angel was caught off guard. "Wait. What are you talking about?"

"My sister and I . . . the reason we don't really get along anymore," Kay said. "It's because of this crazy party we had two years ago."

"Whoa! I think I've heard of that before," Angel said. "That's where you switch partners or something like that, right?"

"Exactly."

"How many people were there? Was it fun?"

"Trust me, it ended up being way more than I could handle," Kay said, trying to figure out how much she should really tell Angel. After all, she'd only known her a few months. But the tequila might as well have been a truth serum as it all started to come out shamelessly. "Okay, this is what happened:

"I can't blame Nikki at all, but she was the one in our

group always bringing everyone together to hang out and have a good time. None of us had kids, but our lives were busy and demanding. So her role in the group was important. She's one of the reasons the friendship between all the couples stayed alive. Anyway, there was Nikki and Chris, me and Kevin, Renee and Jason, and Lynda and Rick. Me and Renee met Nikki and Lynda in college at Clark. The guys all met through us, basically.

"One day Kevin and I both got invitations in the mail. I'll never forget them; they had a gold key on the front. I remember Kevin coming over to my place with his, and we both read them together, clueless as to what it all meant. Later in the week we all came together to find out. At the dinner party at Nikki's she explained the deal with the party and asked us all if we were in."

"Wait—you have to explain it to me, too," Angel interrupted. "I mean, exactly what did she say?"

"Nikki told us that the prelude to the key party would be held at a hotel—in this suite at the Residence Inn. We were all supposed to bring drinks and music and just hang out and party for most of the night. The women all had to bring their keys with a tag attached with their name on it. At the end of the party, each guy was supposed to pick a key out of the bowl by the door where all the ladies had dropped them. The ladies would all leave about thirty minutes before the guys and go to their own houses. The guys would then go to the house of the woman whose name was attached to their key."

"Wow! That sounds live as hell!" Angel was sitting up straight on the bed, her eyes bright and hungry for more.

"Oh, I forgot to tell you that back in the day we played 'spin the bottle' at one of Nikki's parties. Sounds harmless enough, I'm sure, but at that party my husband ended up in the closet with my sister, Renee. He came out of the closet with a hard-on and embarrassed us both."

Angel spat out her drink, she was laughing so hard.

"That's not funny," Kay fired back. The memories had started to get to her.

"I'm sorry . . . for real," Angel said. "Okay, go ahead, go ahead. Who ended up with who?"

"We weren't supposed to ever talk about it, but all of that came out later in the car."

"What car?" Angel asked.

"I'll get to that part."

"So was the party itself fun?"

"Oh yes. Definitely," Kay said. "If there's one thing we all did well together, it was party. At the hotel we listened to good music, ate a little bit, and drank a lot. We played a couple of games that I can't remember now. One of them was played with these scarves; it was something to get the sexual tension flowing. It worked, too. The other game was more like a game to see how well you knew your mate; it was fun. I think that at the end of the night we were all nervous, but we were curious as well. So the ladies left, and it all began. I went home and just waited for the door to open."

Angel was completely enthralled by the story. She hadn't taken her eyes off Kay the entire time.

"So who did you end up with?" Angel asked eagerly.

"Ummm . . . well, that's not really important to the story. The key is—no pun intended—who did my sister Renee end up with?"

"Please tell me it wasn't Kevin."

"Yup. I think they planned it. I always have, ever since I found out."

"How could they have planned it?"

"I don't know, Angel, but one day I'm going to find out."

"Damn! You sound a little bitter."

"Wouldn't you be, if your sister—your twin sister—had sex with your man?"

"Whoa! They had sex?"

"No, Angel, they just played Monopoly all night," Kay said sarcastically.

"My bad. Damn!"

"You know what? Let's pick this up later. Let's go see what the rest of the girls are doing."

"Are you kidding me? You're joking, right?"

"Seriously, I can't talk about this right now. It's bringing me down. I don't know what I was thinking bringing it up."

"You are killing me, Kay!"

"I know. I'm sorry, I'm out. I'm going to go see what Nikki and Lynda are doing."

"Okay, wait for me. Let me just change my clothes really quick. It's hot in here and I'm sweating like crazy."

Lynda woke up from her brief nap to the sound of the shower going. She shook her head, remembering how anal Nikki was about being clean. She would take three showers in one day sometimes, depending on what she was into. It brought back memories of their college days when they were roommates. That's the first time she started fantasizing about Nikki. Nikki was not shy about her body at all. She would take a shower, come out of the bathroom butt-ass naked, and have a straight-up conversation with you while she dried off and lotioned her body. That was one of the things that attracted Lynda to her. She didn't know what to do with those feelings she had when she was all but nineteen, but she knew something wasn't right.

"Hey, sleepyhead. You up?" Nikki said, surrounded by a cloud of steam coming from the bathroom.

"Yeah, I was so tired I figured I wouldn't be of any use to you guys tonight if I didn't get at least a half hour in."

"I know. Sometimes all you need is a catnap," Nikki said, lotioning herself, making sure her towel was secure.

"Umm . . . Nikki, you okay over there?" Lynda asked, noticing Nikki's newfound shyness.

"Sure. What do you mean?"

"Are you uncomfortable around me now?" Lynda asked.

"Why would I be uncomfortable, Lynda? Don't be ridiculous."

"Well, you just seem a little tense, that's all. And that's really strange coming from you. I mean it's not like I haven't seen you naked before. Do you think I'm gonna jump you or something?"

"Lynda, stop tripping. It sounds like you're the one with the problem. I'm cool. I'll be right back. I'm gonna get dressed, okay?" Nikki traipsed to the bathroom with her clothes tucked neatly under her arm.

"Okay," Lynda said, confused.

Chapter 7

Angel

Everyone except Kay ended up lounging around in the living room area. Angel broke the ice with a seemingly innocent, but loaded, question. "So what are we going to talk about for two whole days? By the way, whoever put this whole thing together picked a really nice place; I love it!"

"That would be me." Nikki, not having a humble bone in her body, pretended to give a gracious bow.

"Oh, okay, so you're the planner in this group, huh?" Angel asked.

"That's an understatement," Kay and Renee both said.

"Don't act like you guys didn't have fun with most of the things I've put together," Nikki argued. "No—you know what? Screw that! Y'all have loved everything we've done to some degree. Maybe it didn't all end up perfect, but we had some good times."

"She's right," Kay said.

"Thank you!" Nikki said with attitude in her voice but a smile on her face.

Kay brought over a tray with a bunch of cheese and meat

she had sliced up along with some crackers. The girls were finally in "chill" mode. Renee put the radio on for some background noise.

"Oh, I know—let me go and get all the board games I brought." Kay went upstairs and came back down with six different games.

"Ooooh," Renee said, "you brought Jenga; that's my favorite!"

"Okay, we've got Jenga, Taboo, Trivial Pursuit, Monopoly, Pictionary," Kay announced, "and some cards, just in case we have any 'spades' players in the house!"

"Let's play some of these later," Lynda suggested. "I kinda wanted to talk some, to catch up. I miss you guys."

"Yeah, I love to talk," Angel said.

"If we're about to catch up, I think I'm gonna need a drink. Anybody else want something while I'm up?" Nikki asked.

"Meeeeee," they all said, hopping up and scrambling toward the kitchen.

The girls had bought all kinds of liquor, and before long they were all set to chat: Nikki was drinking a martini with olives; Lynda had a rum and Coke; Kay had a vodka gimlet; Renee was drinking Absolut with cranberry; and Angel was sipping on an ice-cold Corona stuffed with a slice of lime.

"So give us some info for us to kind of get to know you, Angel," said Renee, making sure there was no jealousy in her tone.

"I guess I should start with how I know Kay," said Angel. "She actually sold me my studio several months ago. I was having a really hard time finding a place here. I had convinced myself that it just wasn't something I could do. Anyway, I was at this hair salon on Peachtree when I overheard two other customers talking about their real estate agent. I kind of butted in and asked if they had a card for her. They went on and on about how great she was and really urged me to give her a call. I called Kay the next day and I knew right over the phone that we were going to get along great."

"So how old are you?" Nikki asked.

"I'm twenty-seven. So, anyway, where was I? Okay, okay . . . after Kay sold me my place we kept in touch and met up a few times to have drinks and that's kind of how it went."

"Did you grow up in Atlanta?" Lynda took a long sip on her cocktail.

"No. New York. My mom lives here too. She is a nurse at Grady Hospital, and my dad has been a cop for twenty-three years. He's still in New York. Believe it or not, I always wanted to follow in his footsteps and go into law enforcement, but I always felt, because of my size, people wouldn't take me seriously."

Lynda had been admiring Angel's small frame since she'd met her. She was a really pretty girl and appeared to have the brains to go along with her looks.

"No way," said Kay. "You wanted to be a cop?"

"Still do. Well, I did until I—"

Everyone slowed down on their drinks, waiting for Angel to finish her sentence. But their waiting was in vain. Angel stood up and went to pour herself another drink. When she got up, the low-waist, hip-hugging, velour jogging pants she wore couldn't cover up the tattoo—an eight ball on the small of her back. Nikki and Renee must have seen it at the same time. When Angel came back and took a seat, they both started in with the same question for her.

"What is your tattoo all about? What does it mean?" Nikki asked.

"I didn't know you had a tattoo," Kay said, intrigued and bewildered. She spun Angel around to get a good look.

"Oh, it's a silly tattoo I got in college," Angel told them, trying to brush the whole thing off.

"What does it mean?" asked Lynda. "Did you play a lot of pool back then or what?"

Angel, recognizing that the spotlight was on her, knew there was no way out, so she decided to go with the truth. She looked up after taking a sip of her drink and began to tell her story. "Everyone has their secrets, right, ladies?" she asked. "As a matter of fact I will tell you all about my tattoo as long as everyone here is willing to come off a secret . . . even if it's just a small one to start with. But it has to be a real secret. No made-up shit. If we're going to get to know each other this weekend, let's do it right!"

Everyone looked around the room acknowledging the challenge. They couldn't turn back at this point. Renee ended up being the one to speak first. "Whatever is said here has to stay here," she proposed. "I'm in."

"Okay, me too," Nikki said.

"All right, all right," Lynda and Kay agreed finally.

"It's really not a big deal," said Angel. "I mean the tattoo and all. None of you have a tattoo?" They all conceded that they didn't. "Well, anyhow, my tattoo has nothing to do with playing pool," Angel explained. "I was a stripper for about two and a half years."

"What?" Kay asked, choking on her drink.

Nikki sat up on the edge of the couch. By this time all of the girls had a nice buzz going on, and the giggling and laughter were becoming contagious. Renee started laughing so uncontrollably, all of the girls stopped and looked at her.

"What are you laughing at?" Kay asked.

"At you!" said Renee. "You don't even know your own friend."

Kay glared at Renee, who was biting down on the remnants of ice that had settled in the bottom of her glass.

"It's not her fault," Angel said in Kay's defense. "Very few people actually know this about me; I've kept it to myself for a long time. But I've come to terms with it, so I'm cool talking about it now. It's not like it's really a big deal. I just went through some things that I'm not too proud of and choose to leave it in my past."

"Well, good . . . because I have a ton of questions for you—" said Nikki, gearing up to grill Angel.

"Okay, back to the eight-ball tattoo, which started this whole thing anyway," interrupted Lynda.

"Oh, that's right, my eight-ball tattoo. Well, it's a trick I was well known for." Angel looked around the room and could tell by the looks on all of the ladies' faces that their wheels were spinning, trying to figure out what in the world Angel would have done with an eight ball other than the obvious. "I used to come onto the stage after being announced and, once I stripped down to nothing, would do a split. When I rose up on my feet, I would leave an eight ball on the stage."

Silence filled the room.

"Damn!" Kay blurted out.

"So you mean to tell me you were holding an eight ball in your coochie?" Nikki stumbled on her words.

"Yes, that about sums it up." Angel laughed, amazed that no one in the room had heard of it. "You ladies don't get out much, do you?"

"Angel, that's gross!" Renee exclaimed. "Didn't that hurt?"

"Well, it's the truth." Angel shrugged. "And no, it didn't hurt. When it was time for me to leave the stage, I would do my split on top of the eight ball, suck it back up, and walk off. Men are so nasty; they absolutely couldn't get enough of it."

"Wow! How in the hell were you able to hold that inside you that long?" Kay asked inquisitively.

"It took a lot of practice. I used to use weighted golf balls that I would put inside me every morning. For me it was just like putting on my bra and panties. All day long I had to constantly flex my muscles down there to keep the balls from falling out."

"So you have a super pussy, basically," Nikki remarked, barely able to contain herself.

Angel laughed. "That's one way to put it."

"So you've been with women onstage before?" Lynda asked.

"Oh yeah, all the time. That's where the money was—girl-on-girl shows."

"How about outside of stripping, though?" Kay asked, not sure she wanted to hear the answer.

"There's no point in lying. Yes, I've been with a few girls back in my day," Angel admitted freely, "but it's not my preference; I love men."

"Okay, you know what we want to know now?" Nikki asked.

"But of course," Angel said. "You want to know what really happens in the VIP rooms you hear about. Let me just put it like this, ladies—you do not want your man in the VIP room. The things that go on in there are no joke."

"Have you ever done a VIP show?" Kay asked.

"Of course."

"So you've had sex with men in there before . . . obviously," hinted Renee.

"And women," added Angel, shamelessly.

"We see," Lynda said, appreciating Angel's honesty. Angel didn't owe the girls a thing but was coming clean, which meant that in return they would all be expected to do the same.

"What is the nastiest thing you've ever done?" Nikki asked.

"Well, let's see—" Angel looked up in the air, in an attempt to recall all kinds of sordid acts she had performed in the past. "I can name a few, and you decide. I've let a guy pee on me before. The sick thing about that was that he really got off on it. I mean it was like he was having sex; he loved it so much. I guess there's just something about treating women like animals that men secretly love. But the nastiest thing I've probably done was what they call a 'dildo show.'"

"Okay—wait, wait—this is too much," said Renee. "You mean there's something nastier than peeing on someone?"

"No, no, I want to hear this," Kay and Nikki said.

"Me too," Lynda chimed in. Renee, meanwhile, took two more sips and settled in to get an earful from Angel.

"The dildo show was actually for this one guy's bachelor party. Me and the girl that did the show with me came to the bachelor's house with these silver suitcases that looked like something 007 would carry. Inside the cases were like twenty different dildos—of all different shapes and sizes. After we stripped and did lap dances and all kinds of other things that you could probably imagine, me and this other girl both got on all fours in the middle of the living room floor on a blanket while all of the men lined up. Each guy got to pick a dildo out of the suitcase to put inside me and my girl. That was the first time I felt dirty and totally degraded. These guys were trying to kill us, man; they were merciless—and loving it. That was the easy part. At the end of the show, the soon-to-be-married guy picked the dildo of his choice. He stuck it in my ass while his boys cheered him on."

"Stop, stop!" Renee screamed. "I can't take it anymore; this is sick." Renee was definitely the "good girl" in the group.

"Just let her finish," Nikki demanded. "Dang! Let the girl finish."

Angel paused and waited until there were no more objections before she decided to finish her story. "So anyhow, he stuck it in my ass and then his best man stuck the other end in my girl's ass."

Renee was appalled, her eyes wide as half dollars. Kay had her legs crossed, her hand on her forehead, wondering how she never knew this side of Angel, while Lynda and Nikki pretty much were able to maintain their composure.

"Then," Angel continued, "they stood in front of us so we could give them some head."

Nikki stood up and took a deep breath.

"Whoa! Okay. Is that the type of shit that happened at Chris's bachelor party?" Nikki wondered. "My goodness!" Angel shot Nikki a look that gave the answer to her question.

"Probably," Kay guessed. "Men are freaks!"

"Why are men so nasty?" asked Renee.

"Women are nasty, too, though," added Lynda. "It's not all on men."

"True, but why are they so damn nasty?" repeated Nikki.

"Hey, you have to remember I was the one that let it happen; I didn't have a gun to my head. I just didn't care too much about myself back then. I was so damn broke and hurt from past relationships, I just decided to use men the way I had been used in the past."

All of the girls got quiet for a moment.

"But it's cool now, ladies. Really. That's a part of my past. I'm not sorry it happened; it's made me a stronger person. Besides, some of that shit was fun." Angel chuckled. "I won't tell a lie."

The rest of the girls started to laugh to lighten the moment. Renee was still looking a little unsure.

"So why did you stop stripping?" Kay inquired.

"Well, one night near the end of my 'career,' I came out on the stage with a mask and wig on, something I would do from time to time—"

"And you saw your dad, didn't you?" Renee gasped.

"No, but close enough," Angel said. "My uncle was there with some of his and my dad's college buddies. I had to go through the entire act knowing that he was going to be looking at me like he looked at the countless other naked women that would cross that stage—with lust in his eyes. It was gross; I wanted to throw up. But the crowd was calling my name, and I had to go through with it. My set was almost over when the deejay announced, 'Give it up for your girl, Eighttttt Balllllll.' Everyone clapped for me, and then the unthinkable happened—my uncle rose from his chair and started to make his way toward the stage."

"Oh shit!" Lynda exclaimed. "That's awful!"

"I tried to hurry up and pick up my clothes and act like I didn't see him coming, but the deejay stopped me. He was all loud over the microphone saying, 'Don't leave just yet, girl; you have an admirer who wants to show you some love.' I turned around, butt-ass naked, and was staring into my uncle's eyes. Then I had to kneel down in his face while he came as close to me as he could get and put his head as far between my legs as he possibly could without violating any club codes. Then he made me lean down so he could tell me something."

"What did he say?" asked Nikki.

Angel cringed. "He asked me when he could eat my pussy."

"Oh no! I can't believe he didn't recognize you," said Kay.

"Well, remember, I was disguised."

"You're tripping," Renee said. "I would have run my ass right off the stage. There is no way—"

"I know," Kay agreed, gearing her question toward Renee. "Can you imagine Uncle Byron asking you some shit like that?"

"No way!" Renee protested. "Ewwww."

"What did you say to him?" asked Lynda.

"I didn't. I just scooped up my money and ran off the stage. I was pretty much done after that."

"Wow!" Nikki stood up and gave Angel some dap. "You're the woman; I don't think I could have done it."

"Well, I didn't feel like the woman that day. That gave me the creeps—for real."

"Do you ever miss it?" Lynda asked.

"Well, sometimes. The money was great, but the life was too fast. I'd done all kinds of drugs—except heroin—and was really destroying my life."

"You're so pretty," observed Nikki.

"Thank you," Angel said shyly, glad that her turn was over for now. "So you ladies don't think I'm some big ho'? You don't want me to leave?"

"Hell no! You're cool with me, but I don't plan on ever leaving my husband alone with you," Nikki joked, pushing Angel on the shoulder to let her know she was only kidding—sort of.

Angel just smiled and shook her head. "So that's my secret. Who's next?"

No one spoke. Eyes wandered all around the room, everyone hoping that her girl would be the bigger woman and go ahead and step up to the plate, but it didn't happen.

Angel was getting ready to get hyped up, but before she got a chance to start in on the girls, Kay stood up, barely able to steady herself as a result of the alcohol she had been drinking. "I'll go," she volunteered, to the relief of Renee, Lynda, and Nikki.

Chapter 8

Club Suede

"I want to get mine out of the way; besides, it's really not that big of a deal," Kay said.

"Ummm, we'll be the judge of that." Lynda smiled deviously at Kay over the rim of her glass.

Kay rolled her eyes and held her stomach as if it was aching. "I feel sick," she said. "I don't want to tell mine."

"You have to," Nikki insisted. "Too late to back out now."

"Okay, okay, okay!" Kay relented. "I fantasize about Chris on a regular basis," she blurted out, covering her eyes as though she were trying to miss a gory scene in a horror flick.

Nikki was giggling; obviously, she hadn't understood what Kay said. "Wait! What did you say?" Nikki asked. "All I heard was Chris's name."

Renee, looking in Nikki's direction, did the honor of translating on Kay's behalf. "She said that she fantasizes about your husband on a regular basis."

The room fell silent—except for a small cough from Nikki as she tried to quickly process what she'd heard and still come off looking cool. "Girl, stop playing; that can't be your secret. We've all probably had a fantasy, here or there, or a thought that's crossed our minds about each other's men over the years," said Nikki, crossing her legs and smiling, trying to brush off Kay's confession.

"No, I like think about him when I'm having sex with Kevin sometimes," Kay told the group. She gritted her teeth, not sure of what Nikki would say.

"What in the hell—"

"Calm down," Lynda urged.

"I'm cool," Nikki said, reverting to the old-school, pre-motherhood Nikki that was down for whatever. "I just need more details, I suppose."

"This was a bad idea," said Kay.

"Kay, no, it wasn't; it's me. It's all good. You just kind of caught me off guard for a minute, that's all."

Kay knew that Nikki didn't truly mean what she was saying but realized she had to finish what she started. "It started about two years ago, I guess. I always thought Chris was cute, but he was always just Chris to me, you know . . . like a big brother. When we started talking about having the key party, for some reason I found myself praying that he would get my key."

"Dang! Praying?" Renee added, making things worse.

"Yeah, praying?" Lynda joined in.

"Anyway, one night before the key party I had a dream that Chris and I were alone in my bedroom and that we had the most amazing foreplay session that lasted for hours. I just remember not wanting it to ever end. I awoke the next morning feeling as if I had really been with him. It was to the point where I was kind of embarrassed to even look at him. After that, I kind of used him in my thoughts and my daydreams to . . . umm . . . you know . . ."

"Yuck!" Nikki spat, standing up and hitting Kay over the head with a pillow.

"At least I'm being honest. But it was just a dream. I would *never* take it any further than that," she promised, peering at her sister Renee intensely, who pretended not to notice.

"Are you finished?" Nikki asked. "Please say you're finished."

"Yes, that's all I've got," Kay confirmed.

"Phew." Nikki was relieved.

The girls didn't bother taking a break before the next person decided to reveal a small part of herself that no one knew about.

Nikki decided to go next. "I want to get this over with," she said, sliding back on the couch and resting comfortably against the pillows.

"There is no telling what you have to say," Lynda predicted.

"You're right," Nikki agreed. "Too late to get scared now. My secret really isn't all that relevant to my current life."

"Most secrets aren't, but we still want to hear it," insisted Angel.

"Absolutely!" Kay said. "You definitely need to come clean."

"All right, all right. I was a member at Club Suede." Nikki searched the room, expecting gasps and shocked looks, but nobody stirred.

Renee asked the million-dollar question on the tip of everyone's tongue. "What's Club Suede?"

"I've heard of it." Angel had a know-it-all look plastered across her face.

"How shocking," Renee said sarcastically.

"Whatever!" Angel said mockingly to Renee.

"It's a sex club." Lynda spoke up, putting it out there for everyone to hear.

Nikki looked up, feeling some sort of bond with Lynda for knowing about Suede. *At least I'm not all alone,* she thought; *there is another freak in the house.*

"Of course, it's one of those freaky clubs," Renee said, rolling her eyes.

"You know what?" Nikki said in frustration. "It's not always about being freaky or being nasty; sometimes people are just trying to be themselves."

"Whatever that means," Renee cut in, with an attitude.

"Calm down, girls," Kay said.

"Naw, I'm sick of always looking like a freak of nature for putting parties together or suggesting that we go to new spots, places that aren't your run-of-the-mill, everyday type of joint," protested Nikki. "Of course, now that I have the baby I don't do much of that old stuff anymore, but when I was doing it, I always felt like there was something wrong with me."

"Just relax," Lynda said. "Nobody is trying to make you feel alienated. Tell us about Suede . . . please."

"Sorry, Nikki," Renee said.

"Yeah, your bad," Kay reminded her. "Before you shoot it down, hear what it's all about first." Renee's silence acknowledged that she would at least hear Nikki's story before making any judgment.

Nikki had collected herself and was finding her words again. She was ready to talk to the girls. "Suede is a really cool place. Before I get into the hard-core details, just try to remember that people just like you and me work there."

"Yup," added Angel. "Just like women like us are the ones out there making that cash shaking their asses." They all started to laugh, lifting the cloud of seriousness that had threatened to overtake the room.

Nikki continued, "Suede is much more than your typical nightclub, girls. For those of you who haven't heard of it—it's an erotic city, a place where you could make your sexual fantasies come true . . . or watch while others do. Walking into Suede is like stumbling upon an underground community of people who only come out at night to party—harder than most people can imagine. The environment is primitive and animalistic in many ways. People are there for one reason and one reason only: to fulfill their desires and to get off in whatever way they see fit. As weird as it may sound to all of you, I felt right at home there—that is, when I was going. This was before the baby, let me remind all of you."

"Does Chris know?" Kay yelled.

"Just let me finish," Nikki replied, appearing worn out.

"Okay," Kay said, ducking her head apologetically for the interruption.

"There was a bouncer there named Bruce. He was like six seven, but as sweet and soft as any of the teddy bears you used to have in high school. He loved me in a sisterly kind of way and I always felt safe around him; he was my boy. I even kind of miss him, since I haven't been in so long. So anyhow," Nikki related, "the walls of Suede made you want to lie down on them bare and naked like a newborn. I watched people high on Ecstasy and lost in a haze of drugs and alcohol stand against those walls for hours simply talking and touching them, tripping on the sensation of the soft fuzz against their fingertips. Once I went to this event called a paint party where everyone in sight was naked and had glowing paint all over their bodies in all kinds of wavy and flowing designs. You could easily tell that the designs were made by fingers. It was such a sensual experience, ladies."

"So did you get painted?" asked Kay.

"Yes, that's probably the one time I was naked there. It was hot. Erotic. It's a night I won't ever forget. Most of the time I was only there to observe, to get a rush off other people's courage . . . or false courage brought on by the drugs and alcohol they were using. That's what I liked about Suede. I never felt pressured to be an active participant in what was going on around me. Watching had its own benefits, and I thoroughly enjoyed it each and every time. There were times I had seen a couple having sex not more than five feet away from me against a wall. It was so intense to be in the presence of people who were so open and free with their sexuality." Nikki paused to observe all of the girls staring at her. She felt kind of uncomfortable going on, so she stopped.

"You've got me crossing my legs over here," Angel remarked.

"Me too," added Lynda, leaning over to give Angel some dap.

"I can't even lie," Renee confessed. "Either you tell a good story, or I just haven't had any in a while."

Nikki then felt she had the reassurance she needed to continue, Kay being the only one who hadn't spoken up. But her eyes were fixed on Nikki, so she figured it was cool to go on. "In order to gain access into all of the different corridors and rooms in the club you had to wear a color-coded wristband that was issued from a window. One thing I don't miss is the tramp that worked behind the glass," Nikki recalled. "Ugh, she was such a trick! She looked crazy as hell with this awful weave sticking up all over the damn place and she would always ask, 'What can I do for you?' smacking her tacky-ass gum and flashing her gold tooth. I would say the same thing every time, so you would think she would have had it down. I would tell her I was going to be a voyeur that night—I was only going to watch. The end of our interaction was when she passed me a green wristband through the small hole in the glass and wished me a fun night. I did hit it off with one of the bartenders there, an Asian chick named Jenny, who always flirted with me."

"So did she like you?" inquired Renee.

"Oh yeah. She propositioned me several times to join her in one of the rooms after she got off work. I just never did."

"Wow!" Kay and Renee said together.

"So what's the wildest thing you've ever done at Suede?" Kay asked.

"That was definitely my next question," Renee chimed in.

"Hmmmm . . . I would have to say the time that I masturbated in front of a looking-glass room while I watched a couple inside the room having really rough sex. The rush it gave me can't even be explained."

"So you mean to tell me you did that in front of a bunch of strangers?" Kay asked.

"Damn! I'm barely able to do it alone," Renee confided.

"I don't have that problem," Angel boasted, with a look that assured them all she knew what she was talking about.

"Were you on drugs?" Lynda asked.

"Well . . . no . . . I . . ." Nikki stuttered, struggling to answer the question.

"You did drugs there?" Kay exclaimed.

"No . . . I . . . not that time."

"Okay, so you weren't on drugs when you did that particular thing, but you've done them there before," Lynda inquired.

Nikki shot Lynda a look that thanked her for coming to her rescue. "Yes, I tried Ecstasy once when I was there. Damn! I must be drunk. I can't believe I'm telling you guys this."

"Hey, look what I came with—and I don't even know you ladies." Angel's speech was slurred now. The ladies were definitely past the point of being buzzed.

"Actually," Nikki asserted, "I think it's easier to tell a roomful of strangers your deepest, darkest secrets than it is to tell your closest friends; strangers tend not to judge you as much." She was searching for acceptance in her friends' eyes.

"Nikki, come on, we have all been through way too much to be judging you now," Kay said, stumbling as she got up to give Nikki what seemed like a much-needed hug.

"Well, thank you, girl," Nikki said, returning Kay's hug.

"And I know you're not thinking I'm tripping," Lynda chimed in.

Then all eyes fell on Renee. "What? I'm not judging her. Really. I'm not. I wanna hear the rest of the story. Damn!"

"Okay, cool. I just had a moment. Sorry. Okay, remember that bartender Jenny I was telling you all about? Well, she convinced me to try it, and I really trusted her after getting to know her."

"So how did it make you feel—the Ecstasy?" Kay asked Nikki.

"I never liked the stuff, myself," Angel said. "I was into coke for a minute, though."

"Cocaine?" asked Nikki.

"Well, how about you and your Ecstasy?" Renee reminded Nikki.

"Okay, wait—I'm friends with a bunch of nuts," exclaimed Kay.

"No, you're friends with a bunch of people who have done things that you didn't know about," corrected Lynda.

"Isn't life crazy?" Nikki said. "The fact that you never really know what's going on in people's lives."

"Yeah, you just never know," Renee said.

Kay shook her head in agreement and Angel didn't say anything more.

Lynda yawned and finished the last of her drink. It set off a chain reaction and everyone started to yawn and stretch, getting up one by one and heading off to their respective sleeping arrangements for the night.

If the things they learned about each other on the first night were a precursor for how the rest of the trip would be, it was going to be very interesting.

Chapter 9

Smitty

Kay slid out of bed, awakened by the sound of running water coming from the downstairs bathroom. She knew it was probably Renee. She was dragging herself down the stairs as Renee came out of the bathroom looking wide awake.

"Good morning," they said to each other.

"You want to help me start breakfast?" Renee asked.

"Sure, I'll do the eggs and sausage," said Kay.

"Cool, I'll get everything else going."

The twins had always enjoyed cooking together from way back. After their mom died, they found themselves having to take care of their dad, and so they had to mature quickly.

"Are you putting on *Chocolate Factory*?" Kay asked. Even with her back turned cracking eggs, she knew that Renee was searching for a CD to put on.

"Of course," Renee said, happy to know that they still had the same taste in some things.

R. Kelly is enough to motivate me to do anything, she thought.

Breakfast was coming along just fine as the other girls

began to drag into the kitchen one by one. Angel immediately poured a big glass of orange juice and took two Tylenols. "Cures hangovers, girls," she said, popping the pills. "I always take two before bed if I've been drinking and two when I wake up."

Lynda and Nikki were the last to say their good mornings to everyone. They immediately took their places in the kitchen, putting themselves on "paper plate and fork" duty. Angel handled getting everyone's glasses together, filling them up with ice and juice. By the time the table was all set, Kay and Renee had the food ready and started passing platters over to put in the middle for easy access. Everyone sat down and started filling their plates with biscuits, eggs, sausage, and grits. Angel bowed her head, leading everyone in grace, so they could get to it.

"How did you all sleep?" Nikki asked.

"I slept great, believe it or not." Renee smiled.

"I don't think Angel and I changed positions from the time we hit our beds," said Kay, indicating that she, too, had slept fine.

"So we're going horseback riding today, right?" Angel asked, full of anticipation.

"Yes, and I'm so excited; I've never been," said Lynda.

"I don't think any one of us has," Nikki observed. "It should be fun—let's hope!"

The girls ate pretty quickly, so they could arrive on time at the stable where their guided tour was scheduled to take place.

"How much time do we have?" Kay asked.

"We need to leave in about thirty minutes to get there," Nikki stated. "We're supposed to be there at ten o'clock."

"Perfect," said Lynda, swaying to the sounds of R. Kelly's "Woman."

"So did we let Lynda and Renee get by without telling a secret?" Nikki asked the rest of the girls.

"I guess." Kay wondered what Renee would have had to say anyway; she was always so secretive.

"Thanks." Renee smiled at everyone around the table. "All of your secrets were plenty for us all, I think, but I owe you one."

"Me too," added Lynda.

The girls all raised their juice glasses, toasting the fact that in some way they had all truly enjoyed the night before.

"Okay, since we cooked, you ladies clean. You know the drill. We're going to get dressed," Kay and Renee said. They made off toward their rooms to take showers and get dressed.

The time it took to clean the already spotless kitchen wasn't even long enough to spark a conversation. Before they knew it, Angel, Nikki, and Lynda were finished and headed off to get dressed as well. Nikki spied Angel's tattoo briefly as she bent over to put a pan in a cabinet underneath the kitchen sink, and felt envious for a brief moment—Angel's free-spiritedness reminded her a lot of her own wild and reckless self of years ago. She wouldn't trade the life she had—ever—but sometimes, just sometimes, she missed that "thing" that she used to have, that she used to feel. Angel had that "thing" and, you could tell, was enjoying it thoroughly.

Kay was coming out of the shower next door to Lynda's and Nikki's room when she and Lynda bumped hips as they passed each other. Renee was coming back down the stairs, fully dressed for the most part, only needing to put on the belt that she was threading through her jeans. Her cell phone rang as she plopped down on the couch. Knowing who it was on the other end, Renee stood up and decided to take her call outside. Her relationship with her new man, Derrick, was at that stage where it was embarrassing to talk in front of people—that cute stage where everything makes you smile instead of suck your teeth and roll your eyes.

Before long, the girls had all filed into the living room

dressed like modern-day African-American cowgirls. Kay and Renee had on belts that looked almost identical—with big silver buckles on them . . . for the western look.

"Glad to see that no one wore their best jeans," Nikki observed.

"I'll just go ahead and say this," Angel confessed. "I'm nervous; I've never ridden a horse before." She read everyone's minds. "Okay, I know what you guys are thinking, but just because I've taken all kinds of risks in my life doesn't mean I don't have the right to be scared of horses." She laughed.

"You'll be fine," Lynda told her as they all walked out of the cabin, locking the door behind them.

The stables where Nikki had arranged for the girls to have their first horse riding lesson were less than five miles from the cabin. On the way out, they waved to John and Mary as they were tending to the grounds. The couple seemed so happy to be working in the yard, sprucing up their property; it was quite apparent that they took pride in Cavender Creek.

All of the girls spotted the stable at the same time and started pointing and motioning for Nikki to turn right up ahead. "Okay, ladies! Do y'all think I'm crazy? I see all those horses up there. I'm not blind!" Nikki shook her head.

"I think we're just a little excited," Kay said.

"And nervous," Angel reminded everyone.

Nikki parked the truck and walked over toward a makeshift office area. Kay led the group, opening the door. A cowbell hanging from the doorknob set off a chime that let the staff know that someone needed assistance. After a few moments of waiting in the lobby area, Renee rang the bell on the counter. Four or five rings later a teenaged boy came out of the back room and looked surprised as hell to see all of the women standing in front of him. "Um, hello, ladies, my name is Lance. What can I do for you?" he asked with a surprisingly deep voice and a great smile. He didn't look like he was any older than nineteen if that. Angel noticed his forearms and was ashamed to be admiring them the way she was but couldn't help it. He was pretty healthy for a kid his age. Close to being a man but not quite there yet. *He'd probably had a taste of pussy here and there,* she thought. Nikki's voice brought Angel back to reality.

"Hi, there," Nikki said, stepping up to talk to Lance. "I called and made a reservation for a group of five under the last name Reynolds. We're scheduled to go out today at ten a.m."

Lance looked at the reservation log in front of him, and his finger traced its way down the page until it stopped at Reynolds. "Okay, we've been waiting for you, Mrs. Reynolds." He smiled. "We're just about ready; follow me."

Lance led them to an area where several horses trotted around on their own behind a low dingy white fence. In the distance they saw a horse that looked like something out of a movie. It had to be a Clydesdale. Angel laughed and spoke nervously, pointing off in the direction of the immaculate horse. "That one looks like it could jump right over this fence if it wanted to," she said.

"It could," Lance said, walking by her, barely leaving room for air to pass between them. "I'll go get your tour guide," he told the girls. "His name is Smitty and I'm going to help him take good care of you."

Angel wasn't sure but it seemed as if Lance was flirting with her. It was kind of sexy and he was good at it too. It was more of a turn-on than it should have been.

Several minutes later a handsome black man came walking over to where the girls had formed a small tight-knit circle.

"Is this the Reynolds party?" the man asked.

"Umm, yes, it is. That's us," Nikki said.

Smitty turned his head to the left and spat out a stream of brown-colored liquid. Then with self-satisfaction, he adjusted himself, grabbing his groin and twisting whatever was inside his jeans all over the place. The girls were mortified by this, but Smitty just smiled. "Looks like you ladies are ready to ride," he said. He was a real live cowboy. The only thing missing was a piece of hay sticking out of his mouth.

Smitty was probably around fifty years old but looked to be in great shape underneath his button-down shirt and jeans. He wore cowboy boots, which automatically lost him several points.

"So who's done this before?" he asked, surveying the women.

"This is the first time for all of us." Lynda sympathized with Smitty, apologizing for the burden of five inexperienced riders.

"This is going to be extra fun, then," he predicted, looking each of the women up and down with one clean sweep of his eyes, undressing them with the finesse of a true veteran.

Smitty slightly tilted his cowboy hat upward so he could see all the women. "I need one of you to come with me." He walked away, obviously intending for someone to follow. Kay was volunteered by Renee with a shove in the small of her back and had to trot to keep up with Smitty. The others stayed behind chatting. About five minutes later, Smitty and Kay returned with enough saddles for all of the women.

"You and you," Smitty said, pointing at Nikki and Lynda, "you're first; come on." The group followed closely behind them. They all stopped at a beautiful chocolate-brown horse. "This one is yours, sweetheart," he said to Nikki, motioning for her to take his hand in a quick lesson on how to mount the horse.

Nikki did pretty good and got up on her first try. "You sure you've never ridden before?" Smitty said with a sneaky grin on his face.

Right behind Nikki's horse was Lynda's. It looked just

like Nikki's, except it had a big white spot on its right hind leg. Lynda had a little more trouble than Nikki getting on her horse but did so eventually. Smitty gave a quick lesson about the basic commands the girls would need to know to keep the horses in line. It seemed simple enough.

Lance went behind Smitty, double-checking things. Finally he jumped on his horse and Smitty gave the cue for them to file in behind him.

"Ladies, listen up," Smitty said in a serious tone. "I'm going to give you a few pointers on how to get back here in one piece."

This announcement made all of the girls sit up straight ready to hear what he had to say. He told them that everything was going to be fine and that they would have an enjoyable time as long as they followed his rules, which he spelled out for them one by one. "Number one: If you fall off, always mount on the left side of the horse. Number two: Hold your reins in your hands. Number three: Do not jerk on the reins; this will hurt the horse's mouth. Number four: Pull your reins in the direction that you want to go, such as left to go left and right to go right. And, most importantly, number five: Do not—I repeat, do not—get too close to the horse in front of you or attempt to pass a horse; this will upset the horses and then we'll have a problem." Smitty took a look around at each of the women's faces and saw the uncertainty in all of their eyes. He smiled and rode off ahead of them.

For the first fifty yards of their ride all of the girls were pretty quiet, trying to keep their emotions under control and get familiar with their horses. Smitty had kept them going in a straight line, which all of the girls had mastered so far. Just when they were all feeling like they were getting the hang of things, Smitty decided to have them turn left to do some sightseeing.

"Okay, ladies, remember what I told you: Pull lightly on your reins in the direction you want your horse to go."

Angel went first and successfully turned toward the left. Surprisingly all of the girls were able to follow Smitty's lead with Lynda bringing up the rear as they continued along with their ride. Smitty started to give them some background on the land they were traveling on.

"I'm sure by now you've noticed all of the weeping willow trees."

"It's my favorite tree," Nikki hollered from the middle of the line.

"They're really pretty," Kay and Renee both agreed.

Lynda kept quiet, trying to stay focused on not busting her ass.

Smitty knew a lot about the place. He had been working there for seven years, he'd told them.

"The weeping willow is probably one of the most symbolic trees in the United States," lectured Smitty. "Sitting under it is supposed to provide you with protection and comfort, contrary to popular belief."

Up ahead the girls could see a small stream and a line of little ducklings making their way across their path.

"We're going to stop up here to let these little ones go by," Smitty cautioned, turning sideways so the girls could hear him. As they all neared the line of ducks, they couldn't help but notice how cute the ducklings were. There was one in particular that was stumbling far behind the rest, trying to keep up. Seeing the little one go by made Nikki think about Corey back at home with Chris. She missed them and would be happy to see them when she got home. The ducks made their way across, and Smitty let the horses grab a quick sip of water before continuing the ride. They crossed over the stream and continued into the woods.

Lynda turned around to look behind her and was greeted by young Lance smiling right back at her. By the time Lynda turned back around she realized she had made a big mistake. Her horse was right on Angel's horse's heels. Before she could do anything it was too late. Angel's horse got spooked and stood up on its hind legs, rising up to about thirteen feet in the air. Angel screamed, doing all she could to stay on the horse. All of the girls started screaming as their horses became agitated and started to act up, too. Smitty quickly trotted over to the dramatic scene. Angel's horse rose on its hind legs once again, finally managing to throw Angel off its back instantly. She hit the ground with a hard thud and didn't move.

Lance rushed over to assist Angel. She looked like she was in shock but quickly curled up on the ground to protect herself in case the horse came down on top of her. Smitty grabbed the reins of Angel's horse and led it off to the side to calm it down. Lance got off his horse and helped Angel up. She brushed herself off and suddenly felt embarrassed realizing everyone was looking at her.

"You're bleeding," Lynda said, pointing at Angel's hand.

Lance reached over, taking a hold of Angel's hand. "We should go clean this up; you don't want that getting infected."

"I'm fine, really," Angel told Lance.

"No, really, let me clean that up for you, please," Lance said, asking nicely.

How could Angel resist?

"Smitty, we'll meet you back at the stables," Lance said confidently.

"Okay, we won't be much longer, take her on back."

Angel was too afraid to ride her own horse back, so she got on behind Lance while he led the other horse back beside his own.

When they got back to the stables Angel felt an eerie silence in the air between herself and Lance. He told her to have a seat on the couch in the break room area while he got the first aid kit. They had gotten acquainted somewhat on the ride back. Angel learned that he was in fact seventeen with a birthday coming up in a few months. When he came back he took a seat next to Angel on the couch.

"You're very pretty, Mrs. . . ."

"It's Angel, please just call me Angel." She interrupted Lance's attempt at being polite.

Lance smiled at her and then continued to clean Angel's wound. He finished it off with a Band-Aid and then leaned down and kissed her hand gently. Angel got heated almost immediately. She looked up at him as he gazed deeply into her eyes. At this point, she realized she was staring into the eyes of a child, but her body was telling her different. And her body never lied. Was this young boy really attempting to seduce her? She had a million different thoughts going through her mind at that moment, and none of them were good. The rational side of her told her that she needed to put a stop to what appeared to be happening, that it was her responsibility as the adult in this situation to tell Lance that he should stop. But the part of her that was winning was already too heated to do anything but go with it. Lance continued to gaze into Angel's eyes and found permission to lean over and kiss the side of her neck. His light kiss burned through Angel. She wasn't quite sure what it was about him that made her feel out of control.

Angel finally spoke up. "Lance, wait, stop, we can't do this. You're much too young. This is crazy."

"It's okay, Angel. I'm a *man*. Trust me. Besides, you're not that much older than me."

"I'm ten years older than you, Lance."

"Shhhh. That's okay. Just concentrate on how old I feel," he said, placing her hand on the huge hard-on in his pants.

Angel had to admit that he definitely felt like a grown-ass man. She was so turned on now that she felt out of breath.

He started to kiss her passionately. His tongue met hers as he began to unbutton her shirt and squeeze her breasts.

"Mmmm. Are you getting wet for me?" Lance whispered. But before Angel could answer he unzipped her jeans and whispered, "Let me check and see."

Angel gasped in delight as he slid his fingers deep inside her. She could not believe the pleasure he was bringing her. She realized that he was more aware of what to do than she imagined.

"Damn, you're so fucking wet," he moaned and then laid her down on the couch. Lance's hand was inside Angel's pants, exploring her deeply, all the while working her nipples with the tip of his tongue. Angel wanted sex at this point and couldn't control her urge to get off the couch onto her knees, unbuckle Lance's pants and start pleasuring him.

"Yeah . . ." Lance let out a brief sound that let Angel know that he was ready for her. She was straddling him on the couch now while his hands remained on the sides of his body as if he were afraid to touch her. It was at that moment that she realized that this was his first time getting a blow job. Angel looked up at Lance and said, "It's okay, I don't bite; you can touch me." She felt in control now, which turned her on even more.

"Can I touch your hair?" Lance asked.

"You mean can you pull my hair? Like they do in those movies that you and your friends watch when your parents aren't home?" Angel asked.

"Yeah, like that," Lance said, reaching out and grabbing a handful of Angel's hair. Although her hair was short, he managed to grab what he could between his fingers, pulling it hard.

Angel continued to bring him to the point where he couldn't take it anymore. She stepped back and looked at him. What had she done? This kid had no idea what he had gotten himself into. She was enjoying the fact that she was in complete control.

"You taste so good," Angel said as she took all of him in her mouth. Lance was shivering and then looked up at her. Angel knew what he wanted next but decided to make him say it.

"Tell me what you want!" Angel said sternly.

"I want . . . I want to . . ." Lance stammered just a bit.

"Say it! You want to what, Lance? You can say it . . . You want to fuck me?" Angel spoke for him.

"Yeah, I want to fuck you," Lance said, finding his confidence.

Angel got up, looking quite disheveled as she walked toward the door to the break room and locked it.

"How would you like me?" Angel said as she slid her jeans down for easy access, walking back over to Lance. He was now sitting up, looking as if he were about to explode at any minute.

"Get on your knees on the ground and just bend over," Lance said, clearly back in control.

Angel was damn near ready to come at that point. She did what he said and felt the initial thrust and yelled out slightly.

"You didn't think I knew how to fuck, did you?" Lance asked, holding Angel by her tiny waist with both hands. He started to pound her wildly and she loved every inch of him inside her. "Tell me you like it!" Lance said. "Tell me you like this teenage dick!" He then grabbed her by the neck with one of his hands and kissed her hard in the mouth, twisting her head around to meet his. "I'm going to pound you some more and then I'm gonna come inside you," Lance told her.

Angel gathered herself then and told Lance he had better pull out when it was time. She felt a difference in his movements and realized he was losing control, getting ready to release. She managed to push him backward and out of her just in time. Lance held himself and finished things off in his hand, breathing heavily and looking at Angel with a smile on his face. She got up, pulling her pants up quickly and fixing her clothes. She looked at Lance, not sure if this was an extremely low point in her life or not.

"Are you okay, Lance?" Angel asked him as she helped him clean up with a wet paper towel she retrieved from the kitchen area.

"Never better," Lance said with the widest grin he could muster up.

Angel just smiled and then kissed him on the cheek and walked out of the office, heading toward the truck to wait for the girls. She wouldn't tell them, she wouldn't tell anyone other than her sister maybe. That was the only person who knew almost all her secrets.

Moments later Angel heard leaves crunching nearby and realized the girls were only a couple of feet off. She hoped she had her poker face on and that she was wearing it well. They would no doubt have questions. Especially Kay and Nikki. The girls were chatting loudly about how the rest of the ride had gone but had looks of concern on their faces as well.

"Where were you, girl?" Nikki asked. "We saw that kid, Lance, and he didn't know where you went. We asked him and he said you must have gone to the bathroom or something. Are you okay?"

"Oh yeah, I'm cool. He cleaned my hand up and then I rested for a second until I figured you guys would be on your way back. I just came out here to wait for you guys. I guess I should have said good-bye to him at least. It smelled too bad around there and I was hoping the truck would be open so I could wait inside, but it wasn't."

The girls looked at Angel, slightly confused, but let it go. Except for Nikki. She knew Angel was up to something. What had gone down since Angel and Lance had separated from the group? Nikki knew she had a wild imagination, but even for her, the possibility of what she was thinking had happened seemed too far-fetched. She felt bad for considering that Angel would do something as crazy as that, so she let it go.

Renee stepped up and handed Angel a handful of Band-Aids. "Lance told me to give you these."

Angel took the Band-Aids and smiled. "Oh, thanks, he was really nice. I think he had a little crush on me maybe. Sweet kid."

The ride back was pretty quiet. Every now and then the girls would bring up something to talk about, and Angel would chime in here and there, pretending to listen. Eventually she laid her head against Kay's shoulder and closed her eyes, thinking about what had happened. That had been a new experience for all of them, but for Angel most of all.

Chapter 10

Second Chances

It only took about ten minutes to get back to their cabin. The girls filed in one after the other and plopped down wherever they could find an empty seat.

"I'm a little worn out," Renee said.

"Yeah, me too," added Kay. "I'm gonna take a little nap before we go."

"We have to pack and get ready to get up out of here, ladies," said Nikki, getting everyone back on track.

"I packed before breakfast," bragged Renee.

"Me too," Kay chimed in.

"So," Angel said jokingly, "I guess I'll head up and get my things together."

"Need any help?" Kay called out, to avoid being alone with Renee.

"No, thanks, girl," said Angel. "You wouldn't know what to do with this mess. I'll be down in a little while."

The room suddenly fell silent as Kay joined Renee in the living room. The moment was awkward for both of them. This was literally the first time that they had been alone together in years. No Nikki to lighten up the mood. No Lynda to break the ice.

"So have you spoken to Dad lately?" Renee started.

"Sure. I spoke to him a few days ago. He seems happy with his new girlfriend. What do you think? Have you met her yet?"

"Of course," Renee replied, taking offense. "I met her a while ago. I spent a lot of time with Dad last year."

"Yeah, Dad told me that you stayed there with him for a few months. How did you swing that—with work and all?"

"I just took a leave of absence. I needed some time away after my breakup with Jason; it was really hard on me."

"I'm sorry I couldn't be there for you," Kay said.

"I'm sure," Renee said sarcastically.

"Why did you say it like that?" asked Kay.

"Like what?"

"Like I'm full of shit, that's what! Renee, I'm not about to go there with you."

"Go where, Kay? I mean, first you accuse me of having sex with Kevin, then you cussed me out—and this was after you attempted to beat my ass."

"Oh, I did beat your ass, Renee, and you deserved it, too. Do you think you didn't deserve it? Is that what I'm hearing?"

"Hell no, I didn't deserve it; I'm your sister—your twin. You didn't even give me the benefit of the doubt. You just barked out your accusations and then put me in my place. You never asked me once if it was true or not."

"Well, was it, Renee? Did you or did you not have sex with *my* man the night of the key party?"

"I didn't. I did not have sex with him!" Renee screamed.

"Whatever, Renee. I don't believe you. I don't."

"Why? Because Jason told you? Do you know how fucked up Jason was that night he saw me and Kevin together? He was drunk. Jealous. Pissed. He wanted to believe it so he could have an excuse to beat my ass. I did not have sex with him, Kay. I didn't."

"Well, why don't you tell me what happened, then?"

"Oh, so now you want to know what happened. I've called you and left messages for you for the last two years, Kay. You refused to talk to me. Then when you did, it was only to appease Nikki. How could you shut me out like that?"

"Renee, didn't you think for a minute that I was hurt, too? How do you think it made me feel to find out that you and Kevin had sex?"

"We didn't have sex, though. And even if we did, you told him he could participate in the key party. And Jason did, too. So if you ask me, you and Jason were the ones that couldn't deal. I mean, didn't you have sex with someone that night?"

"That's not the point," Kay said, backing down.

"Kay, I really don't want to fight about Kevin anymore. I mean, it's been two years since all of this happened. You married him, so obviously you forgave him. So how the hell could you not forgive me, your own sister, your twin?"

"Because I was hurt, Renee. I mean—my God!—how could you do it? How could you have sex with him . . . I mean, even if it was a part of the key party and we all agreed? Didn't you think even once about not doing it when he showed up at your house that night? No, you didn't, and I'll tell you why you didn't—because you wanted him, Kevin, my boyfriend, my husband, ever since the first day you met him."

Renee was speechless. She knew that what Kay was saying was true. She knew she had sex with Kevin because she wanted to, because she loved him, too. She could have chosen to turn him away that night to honor her sister's relationship but chose not to. She never really realized how wrong she was until this very moment. She wanted to confess everything. She wanted to tell Kay that even though she didn't have sex with him the night of the key party—she did six months later—she still felt justified having sex with him after the way Kay had shut her out, doing it to punish her somehow, but the words wouldn't come. She just started to tear uncontrollably. She felt awful for what she had done to Kay and wanted to take it back but couldn't.

Kay saw that she had broken Renee down and wanted to reach out to her, to stop her pain, but she was feeling pain, too. The pain of that time came rushing back to her in one brief moment.

"Kay," Renee cried, tears streaming down her face, "I'm so sorry. I really am. You are right; I should have turned him away. I regret that I didn't, but I do want you to know that it is over. Whatever Kevin and I felt for each other, it's over. It has been for a long time. Can I ask you something, though?"

"Sure," Kay replied, shifting in her seat.

"Why did you marry him? If you thought we had sex, how did you forgive him and then end up marrying him?"

"Kevin doesn't even know. I never told him that I found out he picked your key. To be honest, I was scared to tell him. I thought if I told him, he would run straight to you."

"My God! Kay, how did you hide your pain? Didn't he notice you being upset?"

"He noticed, but I just blew it off. I told him I wasn't feeling well or I was tired. I made up any excuse I could until I got over it."

"Did you get over it?"

"No, not really, but the pain of seeing you two together in my head started to fade. And I loved him . . . unfortunately. I still love him more than anything in this world. I didn't want to be without him, and I couldn't bear the thought of him being with you. So I did the only thing I could think of: I married him."

"I don't know what to say to you, Kay. I mean, I understand that love can be deep as hell and can make you do crazy things—look at what I went through with Jason. Time and time again, I let him abuse me mentally and physically, but when he wasn't being cruel he was this wonderful, beautiful, powerful man that I admired and respected and loved. The good always seemed to outweigh the bad, so I blocked the bad out and just concentrated on the good."

"Did you speak to him much after that night he choked you?" Kay asked, regretting that she wasn't there for Renee when she was going through that time in her life.

"He tried calling me several times. He left really pitiful messages on my voice mail, pleading for me to forgive him, begging for a second chance. I never returned his calls. Then just a few weeks ago, he showed up at my job. He was in the parking lot. I was afraid at first; I didn't know what he was going to do. He looked really good. He was sober. He wanted to talk to me. He promised that he knew we were over but wanted to explain to me why he had treated me the way he did."

"Is that when he told you what his mother did to him?" asked Kay.

"You knew? How did you know?"

"Nikki told me. Jason had told Chris, and he, in turn, told Nikki. You know how it goes. Secrets can't stay secrets," Kay said, ashamed that she never took the time to call Renee to tell her herself.

"Yeah, I was really blown away by it. I mean, for a mother to make her sixteen-year-old son have sex with her to heal her own pain of losing her husband is sick. Really sick. We sat down and talked about it over dinner that night he showed up at my job. He told me that he was getting some help and apologized for not telling me sooner and for doing and saying the things he did to me."

"Wow! We have really missed a lot in each other's lives over the years," lamented Kay, scooting over to Renee and taking her hand.

"Kay, I want to tell you once and for all: I am so sorry about what happened with Kevin and me. It was wrong; I can admit that now. But you must know that I have moved on. I'm happy for you and Kevin and wish you well. I know that it will never be okay for me to expect to have the relationship we once had . . . especially since you are now married to Kevin. But I want us to start working our way back toward having a relationship that we both can feel good about. Will you give me a second chance?"

"Renee, I want nothing more than to put all of that key party stuff behind us, and I do want you to come by the house sometimes. I know it may be awkward at first, but we can get through this. We can."

Renee was hopeful for the first time in a long while. She decided to keep what had happened between her and Kevin to herself. There was no point in telling Kay that now. It would serve no purpose at this point—other than to take away the little bit of hope and trust that miraculously appeared on Kay's face. They hugged each other tight for the first time in a long while.

Chapter 11

Shay

"This sure did go by fast," Lynda said to Nikki as they finished gathering their things.

"I know. I can't believe you're leaving already." Nikki looked disappointed.

"Yeah, Shay doesn't like me to be gone too long," Lynda joked.

Shay was Lynda's girlfriend. She met her shortly after moving to L.A., but their love affair didn't begin for almost a year. Nikki had talked to Shay on the phone a couple of times and she seemed to be a really fun-loving woman. She was a thirty-six-year-old white yoga instructor. From pictures Nikki had seen, Shay was really pretty, her long blond braids and great physical shape reminding Nikki of Bo Derek in the movie *10.* Overall, it seemed to be a happy, healthy relationship for Lynda.

"Tomorrow is our one-year anniversary," Lynda informed her, "so I have to get back. We have dinner reservations at this restaurant called the New Yorker on the Upper East Side of L.A. Shay has been talking about it all year, so I'm taking her there. It's a surprise. After that we're going to take a drive to Vegas and hang out there for a few days. She's never been and neither have I, so it should be fun."

"That sounds so nice." Nikki smiled. She was happy for Lynda. It had taken Lynda a long time to admit that she was a lesbian. Her ten-year marriage to her husband, Rick, ended pretty abruptly when she found out that not only was she gay but he was too. Shay was just what Lynda needed. When she moved to L.A., she was confused about her sexuality and what had happened with Rick. Then she met Shay, out of the closet for almost fifteen years and one of the most confident women she had ever met. Shay embraced life about as much as being a lesbian, allowing Lynda to understand that being a lesbian was only one small part of her.

"Wow!" Nikki observed. "I haven't seen you this happy in years."

"I know, Nikki," Lynda replied. "I think she may be the one. We'll see, though; there's no rush. But so far, so good."

Just then Kay peeked her head in the door. "We're ready," she said.

"Cool, so are we," said Nikki and Lynda, ending their conversation on that note.

Angel came racing down the stairs with her purse and her bag. The girls locked the cabin up and placed their keys in the lockbox outside the front door. On the way out, Nikki remembered that they hadn't signed the guest book, so she ran back in, turned hastily to a page in the middle, and wrote:

We leave your cabin today knowing a little more about ourselves and a lot more about each other. Thank you for the wonderful stay.

Nikki, Lynda, Kay, Renee, and Angel
Oct. 2003

The ride back was uneventful. It was pretty silent most of the way home. Everyone eventually dozed off in the car. Nikki changed the CD to Vivian Green and got comfortable in her seat for the fifty-minute ride to her house, where her beautiful husband and baby anxiously awaited her.

Chapter 12

Frankie's

Nikki was sad to see her friends go and had mixed emotions when she said good-bye to the girls. Her getaway turned out better than she expected. Kay and Renee had survived it and even talked things through a bit. That alone made the trip worthwhile.

Lynda was the last to leave and was running a little late for her flight back to L.A. "Give Chris and Corey a big kiss from me. I've gotta run; my flight is at five." She gave Nikki the tightest squeeze before jumping in the cab that was waiting for her.

"I will, Lynda. I'll miss you, girl. I love you. Call me when you get in so I know you got in safely."

"I will, Nikki. Bye. I love you, too."

Though Nikki was sad to see all of her friends go, she was anxious to see Chris and Corey. The house was dark when she got in, no sign of Chris or the baby anywhere. *Surely, they couldn't be asleep this early,* she thought to herself, turning on the lights in the living room and placing her red Coach duffel next to the couch.

"Baby, I'm home," she called out. "Chris?" she called again, heading upstairs to the baby's room.

"Shhhhh!" Chris whispered. He was lying down with Corey on the daybed next to the crib. Corey was fast asleep. "I heard you come in, but I couldn't yell; I didn't want to wake him." He continued to whisper, "He's been cranky all day. It took me forever to get him to sleep. He must have known you were coming home."

Nikki smiled at the sight of the two loves of her life lying down together side by side. "Here, let me take him and put him down," she said, happy to be back at home attending to her little man. Chris tiptoed out of the room and waited patiently for Nikki to put him down.

When Nikki walked out of Corey's room, he grabbed her swiftly and spun her around. "I missed you," he said, gently releasing the bear hug he had on her.

"I missed you, too, baby. I missed you so much." Nikki led him to their bedroom.

"So tell me all about it! How was it? Did you ladies have a good time?"

"Not now, babe. Come here first; give me a kiss. I've missed those beautiful lips." Then they made love, taking advantage of the fact that Corey had fallen asleep early.

When Chris got to work the next morning, he was greeted by an angry voice mail message from Grant Reister, the COO of Marketing Zone, Inc., wanting to know why he hadn't met his deadline to launch the new Web site for one of their biggest clients, Greybar. Chris had never missed a deadline in the five years he had been working at Marketing Zone—until now. His assistant, Penny, tried to warn him that it was an impossible goal to have it launched before the end of the year, but Chris insisted that he could do it. Grant requested a few months ago that it be launched by October 1, and it wasn't even close to being complete.

"Have you seen Grant today?" Penny asked as soon as she saw Chris enter his office. Penny, Chris's loyal assistant from the beginning, was a plump, middle-aged white woman—still grieving the loss of her husband, who had died over ten years ago in a freak accident involving a school bus and a drunk driver. All the same, Chris was very thankful to have her.

"Penny, I'm not sweating Grant today. It's bad enough that I missed the deadline, but now the client has changes. I mean how am I supposed to feel bad about missing a deadline when obviously I wouldn't have made it anyway?"

"I know, I know. I'm not going to say I told you so, I promise. But, Chris, what were you thinking? You know how this works."

"Right. Penny, don't you have some work to do?" Chris joked.

Penny laughed "Okay, I'm going. Hey, are you coming tonight?"

"Coming where?"

"Frankie's. Most of marketing and, I think, a few people on the finance team are heading there tonight after work."

"Nah. Nikki just got home from her trip to the mountains; I'll have to be home tonight."

"Chris, she was only gone for one night. Come on, Nikki will be fine with it. You never come."

"I'll have to see, Penny."

"Okay, I'll leave you alone. I'll get those changes Greybar requested down to communications immediately."

"Thanks, Penny." Chris knew she was right. He didn't even know half the people on his floor by name, though granted it was a pretty big floor. He had the reputation of being a workaholic. He was well respected by his coworkers, but that's as far as it went. None of them really knew what he was all about. Other than at the annual Christmas parties, his co-workers never really saw him outside the office. He figured he would just play it by ear, feel Nikki out and see what she thought about him going out on a Monday night.

Chris found Frankie's, a little bar in downtown Atlanta, pretty easily using the address Penny gave him and MapQuest. He'd had a rough day and was grateful that Nikki signed his permission slip to go out. Penny and the whole gang pushed a few small tables together by the time he joined them, reintroducing himself to folks he had met and forgotten over the years. Penny was much louder than he ever imagined she could be. *Funny what a little alcohol can do to people,* he thought. She looked so happy. It was nice seeing her like that. She was always in an upbeat mood, but Chris knew that she had struggled with depression for many years.

By the end of the night, Chris's promise of a one-hour stay turned into damn near closing the bar, most of the gang having left. Penny was one of the last to go. "You coming, boss?" she said, grabbing her coat on her way out.

"I'm right behind you, Penny. See you tomorrow. Oh! And thanks for talking me into coming; I had a good time."

"You're welcome, boss."

Chris noticed that the music was no longer playing in the background, the smoky haze that filled his head all night beginning to fade. Frankie was busy washing glasses, carefully cleaning those stained with lipstick.

Chris observed on his first visit that Frankie's was an accommodating place for the lonely hearts of Atlanta. Whether you wanted to pick up a one-night stand, or drown your sorrows in alcohol and laughter before going home to your wife and kids, Frankie's was it.

Chris was on his fourth vodka gimlet by the time Frankie yelled, "Last call."

"I'll have one more for the road," Chris said, raising his glass, which held only a twisted, lifeless lime. He decided that he would take his last trip to the bathroom before heading out. When he returned to the bar he couldn't help noticing a new addition to the remaining party of four—a woman sitting in the stool he had kept warm all night.

As he began to approach her from the back, she spun around and faced him. He was taken aback by how pretty she was. Her skin was the first thing he noticed. It reminded him of the Caramel Macciata he drank at Starbucks most mornings. Her hair was short, jet-black, and glistened under the overhead light. Her slender eyes were slightly slanted, and her lips pouted and full, her tiny frame almost lost in what appeared to be a man's suit jacket.

"Are you just going to stare, or are you going to buy me a drink?" she said with confidence, spinning herself around to face the bar.

Chris was in sort of a crazy daze when he walked over to the bar and sat beside her. He wasn't sure if it was the gimlets that had done it to him or the sweet perfume she was wearing.

"Hey, actually I think Frankie is finished serving for the night. And I apologize for staring; that's not usually my style."

"Well, I'm flattered, then," said the exotic-looking woman, extending her hand. "My name is Mina—Mina Simone."

"Chris Reynolds." He took her tiny hand in his. He wanted to kiss it, but then, realizing that the liquor had definitely taken its toll on him, he politely shook it instead.

"Well . . . I can't believe you didn't make a 'Nina Simone' crack; I get that all the time."

"I figured you did, so I decided to spare you this time."

They both laughed.

"Interesting. Okay, well . . . now that we got that out of the way—where did you come from? I thought Frankie closed up for the night."

"He did; you just didn't notice me. I have been here for a few hours now. I was sitting right over there." She pointed to the velvet red chaise longue on the other side of the bar near the telephone and restroom area. "I came with a few of my coworkers."

"Yeah? Where do you work?"

"Ha! You're really starting to give me a complex now. First, you tell me you didn't notice me, and now this—I work where you work, silly: Marketing Zone." She smiled.

"Really?" Chris said, perturbed. He couldn't believe that he had never noticed her before . . . and her most incredible smile. "What department?"

"I'm in the travel department. On the fourth floor. I just started about two months ago."

"Oh, okay. That makes more sense now."

"What?"

"Why I never noticed you before."

She smiled again.

"Well, I have to get out of here. I'm *way* past my curfew." Chris pulled his wallet out to close his tab.

"It was nice meeting you, Chris. I hope to see you around. Maybe we can do lunch one day." Mina was having a little trouble taking off the suit jacket she was wearing, so he assisted her—deliberately ignoring her comment to do lunch.

"Thanks," she said. "I borrowed this from Frankie. It was freezing in here."

"You're welcome. Let me walk you out," Chris told Mina, holding the door open.

He and Mina were the last to leave. He walked her to her red Lexus coupe before heading home—late. He noticed two missed calls on his cell phone from Nikki. He had some serious explaining to do when he got home. This was highly unusual for him, which he hoped would help him with his explanation, something he wasn't looking forward to.

When he got home, Nikki was fast asleep. He reeked of smoke, so he took a quick shower. Then he checked on Corey, before snuggling up to Nikki and drifting off to sleep.

Chapter 13

Mina

It was about 6:00 a.m. when Frank Ski greeted Mina with his inspiration of the day, but all she felt inspired to do was roll back over and bury herself under her covers. She pondered over hitting the snooze button just one more time before taking that long trip to the shower but decided not to prolong the inevitable. It was time to get ready for work. Her usual routine included getting up at 5:00 a.m. and going on a two-mile run, but she just didn't have it in her this morning after her late night at Frankie's. Just as she started to step into the shower she heard the phone ring. She knew it had to be her sister, Selma. She was the only one who would call her this early. She was either calling too early or too late. Selma was Mina's older sister by four years and had just given birth to Mina's second niece, Leeann.

"What's up, Selma?"

"Hey, sis. You on your way to work?"

"Not quite. I was just about to jump in the shower. I had a late night and I'm in bad shape this morning. What are you doing up? Leeann keeping you awake?"

"Of course. Why else would I be up at six o'clock in the damn morning?" Selma fired back.

"Okay, okay . . . Don't sound so hostile. It's not my fault you and Paul can't keep your hands off each other."

"No. Correction. That would be my husband that can't keep his hands off me."

"Yeah, yeah. You give as good as you get. Speaking of husbands, I met this married guy last night. Selma, he was so ridiculously beautiful."

"Really? What did he look like?"

"He was tall as hell, maybe about six-three or six-four even. He had a mustache and goatee . . . ummmm, a gorgeous smile. He was just fine, girl . . . just fine as hell."

"What complexion? Dark skinned? Or light?"

"He was medium. Kind of like mine. He was just right. Perfect."

"Except for the fact that he's married. Hello?"

"Well, I know. That's not what I meant. I just meant his looks. Oh, and I think he's paid too. And he was a gentleman. He walked me to my car. I mean, who does that anymore?"

"Yeah. True that. So . . . he wasn't flirting with you, was he? I mean . . . you're not trying to start any trouble, are you?"

"Nah. He seemed really nice. A perfect gentleman like I said. Besides, I'm not trying to go down that route again."

"Thank God!"

"Shut up, Selma. Just because you've been married damn near your entire adult life doesn't mean that the rest of us aren't over here struggling trying to find our mate too."

"Girl, please. You haven't struggled to get a man *your* entire life. Period."

"Oh yeah. What kind of man, though? I mean, I'm just so sick and tired of these men out here. And, Selma, let me tell you something. If you thought I had it bad in New York, it's much worse here. The men are all either married, country as hell, or gay. I've never seen so many gay men."

"Aww, sis. That's awful."

"Check this out, though. This guy I met. His name is Chris. He works at the same company I do. He's on a different floor so I've never seen him. Isn't that crazy?"

"Oh no. So that means you'll be seeing him again, then?"

"Well, I told him we should go out for lunch sometime. But I doubt he will. He kind of blew me off when I said it. It was pretty embarrassing actually."

"It's probably a good thing. It doesn't sound like any good is going to come out of you spending time with a man that fine and married."

"Yeah. You're right. Not that I couldn't control myself if I did. I mean, I have standards and morals. Contrary to popular belief."

"I know, sis. I know."

"Whatever. Are you patronizing me?"

"Nope. I just know you very well. You love a challenge."

"Oh, Selma, please. I don't need a challenge anymore. I really don't even want a man in my life right now. I'm sick to death of them."

"Right. Remember Rob? Do you remember how strung out on him you were?"

"Now, why did you have to do that?"

"What?"

"Throw Rob in my face. That was so long ago."

"It wasn't that long ago. And he still calls Mom looking for you every once in a while. Did I tell you that?"

"Yeeeees, Selma. You did. Look, Rob was during my weak phase. When I was trying out that whole thug thing."

"Right. And he was a challenge because A, he was married, and B, he wasn't into you because you were not his type. He liked those ghetto girls. And what did you do? You decided that you were going to show him what he was missing."

"Oh, Selma, I did not. I was young and naive and Rob was sexy as hell and great in bed."

"Yeah. But you didn't find all that out until *after* you seduced him."

"No. I knew that from just looking at him. A woman knows these things."

"Yeah, but I bet you didn't know he would beat your ass, did you? Did you also count on that?"

"Ooooh. That was low, Selma. Even for your righteous ass. Besides, he didn't really beat my ass."

"Oh, really? And what would you call it, then?"

"Forget it, Selma. I'm not talking to you about this anymore. I have to go to work. I'm already late as hell standing here messing with you."

"That's right. That's what I thought."

"*Good-bye*, Selma. I'll call you later."

"Be good, sis. And tell Chris I said hello."

"Whatever. Bye!"

Mina knew Selma was right about Chris. She felt as if she was in trouble from the first moment she laid eyes on him. But she did know one thing. She was not going down that path again. She refused. Rob was enough.

Chapter 14

Sushi

Lunch was all Chris could think about by the time he got out of his 11:00 a.m. meeting with Grant. He got his ass chewed out for missing his deadline but scored points for taking it like a man. Grant told him that he had been there before and that "it happens to the best of us." He was impressed with Chris's confidence and candor. Chris didn't make excuses for what happened; instead he turned the tables on Grant by coming up with a new approach for the site and strategically laid his plan out step by step. He let Grant know that he had already spoken to the client and apologized, telling the client that it was a good thing that they missed the deadline so that they could jump on board with the new changes. It was all bullshit in the end, but Chris knew it would work. He knew how to push Grant's buttons. He always did. Grant was the typical manager who liked to see initiative and communication with his clients. Chris had won the GEM award at Marketing Zone three years in a row. The GEM award was given to employees who always "go the extra mile" for their clients or coworkers, etc. Everyone in the company had the opportunity to nominate one of their coworkers. There was a debate around the office on whether Chris could be nominated again this year. Chris couldn't deal with all of the drama and pulled himself out of the running. Nikki wasn't too happy with him since it meant missing out on a ten-day trip to Jamaica, but she understood that her husband happened to be one of the few genuine people in the world who liked to give everyone their fair share in life.

"Great meeting, boss," Penny said, catching up with Chris on his way to his office.

"Oh, thanks, Penny. You know how it is with Grant. You have to always make it about the clients. He lives for that stuff."

"Yes, I do know. Did you hear that his wife is in the hospital?"

"No. Why? What for?" Chris asked, concerned.

"Not sure, but the rumor is she has cancer."

"Damn! I'm sorry to hear that. He didn't even mention it to me."

"Yeah, when my husband died I didn't want to talk to anybody. I was just in denial. I figured, if I didn't talk about it, it wasn't happening. You're a lucky man, Chris. Don't ever take Nikki for granted. It is a lonely world out there when you don't have that special person to share your life with day in and day out."

"Oh, I hear you, Penny. Trust me, Nikki and Corey are the center of my universe. Believe that. Speaking of which, I owe her a phone call. I don't think she was too happy with how late I made it in last night. She and Corey were gone by the time I got up this morning."

"Uh-oh. So, what was up with that, boss? You went from one extreme to the other. First, you never hang out with us; then you were the last one to leave. I take it you had a good time."

"Yeah, it was cool. I don't know what happened. It was kinda nice being out spontaneously, you know. It was nice to break up the routine for a change, and it was a cool and comfortable spot."

"Well, you're welcome to come with us anytime. We try to go every Monday since it's three-dollar pitchers. And Mondays are usually stressful days. It actually makes you look forward to them instead of dreading them each week."

"Yeah, that's a cool trick, I guess. Well, I definitely won't be able to make it every Monday, especially with my performance last night. Let me call Nikki before I forget. I know that's all she's thinking of. You heading to lunch?"

"Yes . . . unless you need me for something else."

"Nah, take off, Penny. Thanks for getting everything put together so quickly this morning; I know it was a rush job."

"Anything for you, boss. I'll see you in a bit."

Chris wasn't looking forward to calling Nikki. He knew her extremely well and knew that if he didn't get a kiss this morning that that meant trouble.

"Hello, this is Nikki."

"Hey, baby, how are you doing?"

"I'm cool. A little busy. You need something?"

"Aw, don't be like that. Can we talk?"

"About?"

"I'm sorry I got home so late last night. That was crazy."

"No. What was crazy was the number of times you chose not to answer your phone."

"I didn't hear it ring! It was loud as hell in there."

"Whatever, Chris. You know how to put your phone on vibrate. Don't try and play me. You know I'm not one of those wives who trip when their husbands go out. I just ask for simple respect. I expect you to answer your phone when I call. I mean, what if it was an emergency?"

"Was it?"

"No, it wasn't, but that's not the point. It could have been. Corey could have been hurt. You need to be more responsible."

"Come on, Nikki. I mean, I haven't gone out in—shit! I can't even remember when. So I was out of practice. I didn't think about putting the phone on vibrate. My bad."

"Are we finished?"

"Oh, so it's like that? Do you accept my apology? Or do I have an attitude to look forward to when I get home?"

"You know what, Chris? You don't have to come home."

"Nikki, you're being ridiculous. I don't deserve this shit, and you know it. Why don't you tell me what's really bothering you?"

"Nothing, Chris. Nothing. I have to go; I have work to do. I won't be cooking dinner tonight, so you may want to pick something up if you plan on coming straight home tonight."

"You're tripping."

"Bye!" Nikki hung up.

Chris couldn't believe what he had just experienced as he walked frantically to the elevator on his way to lunch. He knew she would be a little salty, but he had no idea she was going to be this angry. He was puzzled. Nikki never really acted that way. That's the one thing he could always count on. Something else was definitely up, but he was too pissed to care at the moment. He didn't feel like he deserved that treatment. He had always prided himself on being a great husband, always very supportive. In fact, this was the kind of thing that Nikki used to do in the past—stay out late and not call or answer her phone—and he was always so understanding. He couldn't believe that the one time in God knows how long he decided to go out and stay out late, she decided to go off. Chris was so wrapped up in his own thoughts, he didn't even notice when the elevator stopped on the fourth floor. He was startled to see Mina walk in.

"Well, hello," she said, flashing that sweet smile of hers.

"Hey, how're you doing? Mina, right?" He was trying to hide the scowl Nikki had put on his face earlier.

"Yep, I'm doing good, Chris. Thanks. Just hungry."

"Yeah, me too. Starving," Chris said as they both focused on the numbers at the top of the elevator as it slowly descended.

"So where are you going?" she asked.

"Not sure yet. I think I'm in the mood for some sushi."

"Mmm . . . mind if I tag along? I love sushi; it's my favorite."

"Well, I . . . I'm not sure. I'm just not in that great of a mood; I'll be really bad company," Chris warned, feeling a little awkward. "Besides, I'm married."

"Oh, well, I'm glad we cleared that up. I'll go ahead and put the idea of getting a hotel room out of my head," she said sarcastically. "Come on, Chris." She gave him a little shove. "Are you kidding? I noticed your wedding ring last night. I just want to eat—food!—and I'm great at cheering people up! You look like hell. Come on, I'll drive and everything."

S*hit!* Chris said to himself, embarrassed about using the old "I'm married" line. He really didn't want to get this started; he just wasn't in the mood. All he could think about was Nikki and what could be wrong. But he didn't want to hurt Mina's feelings, so he accepted.

They ended up at Rusan's on Piedmont Road. The place was bright and noisy as usual. Chris gave dap to a few coworkers he saw on the way in before being seated at the only booth available way in the back corner.

"Are you getting the buffet?" Chris said excitedly, grabbing his plate.

"Ewww, no. I usually order off the menu. I try to stay away from buffets." She laughed. "I'll go order. I'll meet you at our booth, okay?"

"Yeah, okay." Chris had about three people ahead of him.

By the time he finished loading his plate up with California rolls and chicken wings, Mina had already gotten her food and was waiting patiently for Chris to return.

"I should have pegged you for a raw-fish-eating kind of girl," Chris said, sliding into the tiny booth. "How the heck do you eat that?"

"It's maguro. It's delish. Wanna try it?" Mina said, extending her fork of flesh to Chris's mouth.

"No. No, thanks. I'll pass on that; I'll stick to the cooked stuff."

"Awww, that's not real sushi. And are those chicken wings you have on your plate? Come on, Chris. That's ridiculous."

"Hey, these wings are good; it's the main reason I come here."

"I bet."

"What the hell is maguro, anyway?"

"It's just tuna. One day you'll venture out and try it. It's good . . . I promise. At least I got you to smile," she said, reaching across the table to stroke Chris's chin. Their eyes locked for a brief second. "So how are you doing? Have you had a busy day so far?"

"Yeah, you could say that. I was in a meeting all day pretty much. It was grueling, but I got through it."

"So what do you do, Chris?"

"I'm in marketing, so I do a little bit of everything. I'm mainly responsible for keeping our clients happy. I act as a consultant for the sales team whenever they go out and try and get new business. I give the clients ideas, et cetera, and then manage implementing them. I like it. What about you? What do you do?"

"I'm in the travel department. I'm the one in charge of getting travel packages put together. It's a lot of fun, actually. I get to dream about all the great places I want to visit one day."

"Sounds good. So where are you from? Are you from Georgia?"

"No, Manhattan, baby! I miss it so much. I just moved here like four months ago. My mom and dad recently separated, and she wanted to get out of there. She begged me to move here with her."

"Sorry to hear that. Separation is rough. So you live with your mom?"

"*No!* She's in a condo in Midtown; I have a studio downtown. I love it. It's the closest I could get to New York life anyway."

"Yeah, those studios downtown are sweet as hell. One of my partners lives down there. It's really nice."

"I like it a lot. My dad came down when we moved and helped me move in. He has been great. I'm still feeling my way around, though; I haven't met too many people."

"That's hard to believe—a pretty girl like yourself."

"Well, thanks, Christopher, but pretty girls have it hard, too. I seem to scare most men away, and the women all look at me with daggers in their eyes."

"Nah, that's just your imagination. You gotta be aggressive, forthright. You need to meet my wife. You and she would get along great."

"Really? So what's her name? Tell me about her."

"Her name is Nikki, and she's the most beautiful, sexy, intelligent woman I've ever had the pleasure of meeting."

"Wow! Lucky, too, I would have to say." Mina admired the glow that came over Chris's face when he mentioned Nikki's name.

"Yeah, she's not feeling too lucky at the moment."

"Uh-oh . . . trouble?"

"Well, she wasn't too happy with me last night."

"Why? Didn't she know you were going out?"

"Oh, most definitely, but I never really hang out that late, and then I missed a few of her calls."

"Oh no. Yeah, you have to answer the phone now. That's a must. Women don't play about that."

"Well, I didn't intentionally not answer it; I didn't even see the calls until I got in the car." Chris's bad mood was starting to resurface.

"It's just so impossible for us to believe that you didn't do it on purpose. She'll cool down, though. That's a mild fight, I would say."

"Well, hey, let's get out of here. Are you finished with yours?" Chris reached in his back pocket for his wallet.

"Yes," Mina said, leaving a tip.

"Let me take care of lunch today," Chris offered.

"Well, thanks, Chris. I'll get lunch next time. Deal?"

"Deal," Chris said, impressed with Mina's confidence.

"Come on, let's go," Mina said, walking through the door Chris so politely held open for her.

"After you."

"Thanks," she said, winking at Chris.

When Chris got back to his office, the only thing he had on his mind was Nikki. He couldn't stop thinking about her being so upset. He buzzed Penny and told her that he was taking off for the day and asked her to call him on his cell if she needed anything. When he arrived at Channel 2 he was anxious to surprise Nikki with the twelve somewhat tattered red roses he picked up from a hardworking man on the corner of West Peachtree Road.

Nikki was busy talking on the phone when one of her coworkers motioned her to get off. When she came around to the receptionist area, she saw the red roses sitting on the receptionist's desk.

"Where did these come from?" Nikki asked Carla, bringing a handful of roses up to her nose.

"They're from your husband. He just dropped them off."

She ran to the elevator to see if she could catch Chris before he left. She couldn't find him but instead felt two big strong hands creep up around her waist. Nikki's body instantly went up in flames. When she turned around she looked up at her husband and held him tightly.

"Thank you, baby. They're beautiful."

"You're welcome," Chris said, placing her face in his hands and kissing her lips gently. "I'm sorry about last night, Nikki. I'll make sure I have my phone on vibrate next time."

"Next time? Who said there's going to be a next time?" she asked sarcastically. "I'm sorry, too, babe. I overreacted. You were right; you didn't deserve that."

"So what's going on with you? Are you okay? That really wasn't like you."

"I know. I'm just being unreasonable, I guess. Who knows? Let's not talk about it anymore, okay?"

"Can you get out of here early today?" Chris asked with puppy dog eyes.

"I'm sorry, babe. I can't. I actually have a long night ahead of me. Can you get Corey from day care?"

"Sure. I'll wait up for you."

"I was hoping you would," said Nikki, getting one last kiss in before walking away. "I love you."

"I love you, too, Nikki."

Chapter 15

Pride

Nikki was exhausted by the time she left work. As she pulled onto the freeway she imagined taking a long hot bath and jumping right into bed. Since it was after nine o'clock she prayed that Chris was able to get Corey to sleep. He was definitely a mama's boy when it came to bedtime. Nikki would often end up sleeping with him in his room just to soothe him. Chris hated it when she babied him. He didn't understand that that's what it took just to keep her sanity. When Corey slept she slept and that's all she came to care about since she'd had the baby—sleep! When she pulled into the driveway she was happily surprised to see all of the lights off upstairs. That was a good sign for sure. As she walked into the house, silence welcomed her. She swung her coat on the coat hanger in the foyer, dropped her shoes on the shoe rack, and headed up the stairs. By the time she hit the last step toward the bedroom she smelled a familiar scent. Her favorite rain-scented candles were burning, which could only mean one thing. Chris was in the mood for sex and she was devastated.

"Hey, babe." Chris greeted Nikki in his boxers. He had a few candles burning on each nightstand and the water running in their master bathroom. "I figured you would be tired when you got home, so I drew you a warm bath. You up for it?" he said, pleased with himself.

Nikki was so grateful that she had such a wonderful husband who would go through the trouble of being so romantic on a Tuesday night, but at the same time she wanted to slit her wrists. She was so tired and all she really wanted to do was jump in the shower and into bed and go right to sleep since she had to get up and go to work in the morning and start the day all over again. The last thing she had on her mind was sex, and she knew that it was exactly where her night was headed.

"Oh, babe, you shouldn't have gone to all of this trouble," she managed to get out, hoping that Chris would catch on to her desperate cry for help.

"Not a problem, hon. I knew you would be tired so I wanted to do something special to help you relax. Come on. Let me help you with your clothes."

"No! I mean, I can do it," Nikki snapped.

"What's wrong? You okay?"

"I'm cool, Chris. I'm just really tired. Exhausted really." Nikki was trying harder than ever not to hurt Chris's feelings. She knew his intentions were good, but she really was not in the mood for a romantic night. She just wanted to crash. Him taking her clothes off was the start of his seduction, and she just wasn't up for it. Not to mention, she hadn't been that comfortable being naked around him ever since she had the baby. But she held it together. She went into the bathroom and stripped away her work clothes and slid into the Jacuzzi. The swirling hot water massaged her body just right as she closed her eyes and enjoyed the moment. She had to admit that it was exactly what she needed. If only this could be enough she would be happy. Her peacefulness, however, was quickly interrupted by the splashing of Chris's tall body slithering his way into the tub along with her.

"Chris! What are you doing?" she asked, reluctantly making room for him in the tub.

"I'm joining you, hon," Chris said, clueless. He then started to massage Nikki's thighs, working his way up to her spot.

Nikki wanted to cry literally.

"Chris! Okay, stop. Just stop!" she said bluntly.

Chris sat up and asked, "What? What is it?"

"Okay, this is the deal. Babe, I really just feel like relaxing and then going to bed. I'm not in the mood to have sex tonight. I'm really not. Can I get a rain check?" Nikki pleaded.

"Oh. Yeah. Sure. That's cool. I didn't know. My bad," Chris said, disconcerted. He then rose up and carefully stepped out of the tub, snatching his towel on his way out to the bedroom.

Nikki wanted to die. She felt so awful. How could she be this selfish? She hurt his feelings bad and there was no taking it back. She'd been doing that a lot lately. Sex was really just not what it used to be for her, and she didn't know how to fake it. It wasn't Chris's fault. He was still the same gorgeous, romantic man she'd ever known. It was her. She just couldn't get herself together. It started with her job at Channel 2, and then having the baby was the icing on the cake. She found herself depressed a lot of the time because she felt so drained every day. She felt empty at times, a shell of the person she used to be just a few years ago. She knew it was taking a toll on her marriage, but she didn't know how to stop it. Kay had advised her to seek some help, but she was too proud to go to a therapist.

When she finished washing up, she put her sleep shirt on and slid into bed next to Chris, who appeared to be sleeping.

"Babe? Are you up?"

"Yeah. What's up?"

"Are you mad at me?"

"Nope!"

"Come on, babe. Seriously. I'm sorry. I didn't mean to hurt your feelings. Can we talk about it?"

"What's to talk about, Nikki? It's the same ole, same ole with you lately. I'm all out of options."

"I know you're frustrated, but it's just so hard. I'm so tired all the time and I just can't seem to put you first."

"Nikki, I don't want you to put me first. I want you to put *you* first," Chris said, sitting up in the bed. "Look. I've been trying to give you your space. I know you're tired. That's why I did this for you."

"I know but you wanted to have sex too. If you only wanted me to relax you wouldn't have gotten in the tub. You wouldn't have the candles lit."

"What? So you're saying that this all would have been okay if I didn't want to make love to you? Nikki, I don't even know what to say about this."

"I know . . . I know. Chris, I'm just not in the mood today, that's all. Can't we just leave it at that?"

"Sure. Yeah. That's cool, Nikki."

"No, it's not. You're mad. I can tell by your tone."

"Well, shit, Nikki. What do you want from me? If you want me to say that it doesn't matter that my wife doesn't want to have sex with me, I'm not going to say it. Because it does matter. We have sex like once a month . . . if that!"

"That's not true, Chris. We just had sex last week when I got back from the cabins."

"Oh, so you're taking count now? So that was it for the month?"

"You're killing me, babe. It's not that deep. I was just really looking forward to chilling tonight. I didn't expect all of this."

"All right, Nikki. My bad, then. You don't have to worry about it the next time."

"Oh, here we go. So what's that supposed to mean? So you're never going to do anything romantic again?"

"That's not what I said. Let's just squash this. Now *I'm* tired."

"Well, can we talk? How was your day?"

"You're tripping. Now you want to talk about my day? I thought you were tired."

"I am. I mean, I planned on taking a shower and jumping into bed and then we could talk. I just don't want to have sex. God! Why does that have to be such a big deal?"

"It's not. My day was cool," Chris said coldly.

She knew that he was pissed, but she didn't know what else she could say. The night was ruined now. It was not like she could turn it around and have sex with him after what she said, but she wasn't ready to go to bed mad either, so she just went along with the conversation.

"So how was your meeting? Did you get in trouble for missing your deadline?"

"Nah. Not really."

"Well, that's cool," Nikki said. "So how was lunch? What did you eat today?"

"I went to Rusan's and had some sushi."

"Did you and Penny go?"

Chris pondered Nikki's question for a second. He wanted to lie and tell her yes. That would have been easiest, but he decided to stick it to her instead.

"Actually, I met this chick when I was at Frankie's last night. Her name is Mina. It turns out she works at Marketing Zone. She's on the fourth floor in the travel department. I ended up going to lunch with her." Chris wasn't sure what Nikki would say, but he didn't care at the moment.

"Really? Interesting. So why didn't you tell me about her on Monday night?"

"Well, you were asleep and then you weren't talking to me today, remember?"

Nikki felt as if he'd just kicked her in the stomach. What could she say to this now? She knew he was already mad at her for the disaster that had just taken place, and now he was throwing going out to lunch with other women in her face. She felt like she was being tested, so she answered accordingly.

"Yeah. You're right. I was pretty mad earlier. So who is this chick? Is she married? What's her story?" Nikki pretended to play along.

"No, she's not married. She just moved here from New York a few months ago and lives downtown. We just bumped into each other in the elevator. It wasn't planned or anything."

"I know. I didn't say it was. That's fine. I was just asking."

"So you're cool with me going to lunch with women?"

"Is there a reason I shouldn't be?"

"Nope. I was just making sure. So what if I did plan it?"

"What are you asking me, Chris?"

"Nothing. I'm just saying, what if I call her up one day and ask her to go to lunch? Are you cool with that too?"

"I'll ask again. Is there a reason I shouldn't be?"

"You're funny. So you have absolutely no problem with me befriending another female. Is that right?"

"Chris, why are you playing games? Is this some sort of test or something? I'm cool with you having a female friend if that's what you're asking. I've never had a problem with it before. Why should it bother me now?"

"Well, I've never had a female friend before, so I figured I should ask."

"I mean, it's not like I haven't had male friends in the past, so who am I to say you can't have a female friend? Do you want to be friends with her? I'm not understanding where all this is coming from. You just had lunch with her, right?" Nikki asked, perturbed.

"Yeah. No. I was just sparking up conversation. You said

you wanted to talk, right? So I thought I would get your take on this. I mean, you never know. Since we work together, it's possible that I'll see her again."

"You're funny, Chris. Whatever. I'm cool with it, if that's what you want to do."

"What do you mean by that?"

"Nothing. I'm just saying that I'm cool. Do your thang."

"I will!" Chris said, rolling over.

Nikki was struggling but was trying desperately not to show it. On one hand she didn't have much room to talk. She'd had male friends in the past. But not for a long time now and certainly not since she'd had the baby. She felt like she was playing on a different field now but had no logic or rationale to back her feelings up, so she did the usual. She let her pride get in the way and she wasn't honest about how his lunch date had really made her feel.

"Good night, babe," she said.

She got no response.

Chapter 16

Renee

Kay and Kevin had been extremely sweet to one another since she had gotten back from the cabin. Kevin hadn't been able to keep his hands off her, and she had been pretty horny since the weekend. Sometimes good sex was all they needed to get back on track. And although their sex wasn't the kinkiest, it was definitely good; she was into it most of the time. Lately she had been initiating more than ever, and Kevin appreciated it when she did that.

She dialed the house to let Kevin know she was almost home. She had made a quick stop to pick up some catfish, fries, and hush puppies for them to eat. They usually ate that kind of thing on a Friday, but she didn't feel like cooking. She figured it would be the perfect meal for a Tuesday evening. Kevin didn't answer after the third ring, so she hung up and turned the corner into their subdivision. *Too bad if he wanted anything else,* she thought; *since he couldn't pick up the phone.*

"Hello?" Kay's voice echoed through the silent house. "Anybody home?" she asked, seeing her husband stretched out on the couch sleeping with the remote on his chest. Kay went straight to the kitchen to put the food down, then went back to her and Kevin's bedroom to take off her shoes and coat to get comfortable. She walked back out to the living room and started to shake Kevin to get him to wake up, but he wasn't budging at all—then all of a sudden he grabbed her and pulled her on top of him.

"You're always playing. You scared me!" Kay laughed.

"Hey, hon," Kevin said, letting Kay sit up. He sat up and gave her a kiss on the forehead.

"I brought home fish and fries."

"Oh, you read my mind," Kevin told her, hopping up to go to the bathroom.

Kay went to the kitchen to get the food together. "I have got to make time to clean this place up this weekend," she said to herself, looking around her kitchen and shaking her head. She grabbed two trays and piled all of the food on top of them.

Kay noticed the message light blinking on their phone. Kevin never checked the machine. "Anybody call?" she asked as he walked back out into the living room.

"Oh yeah, Renee. Renee called," Kevin said, passive as hell, as if he had never heard of Renee in his life.

"What did she want? Do you know?"

Kevin immediately shrugged his shoulders as if to say he had no earthly idea what Renee wanted, nor did he want to know. "She just said she'd call you back. This fish is good, baby," he fawned, in a pathetic attempt to change the subject.

"It always is." Kay sounded sad and solemn. She turned her attention back to the television, where Bernie Mac was going off on his kids.

"So how was your day?" Kevin asked.

"Pretty busy, actually. I have two closings this week, so I stayed a little late making sure that everything was in place for the first one tomorrow."

"Glad I've got me a working girl," he said, smiling at his wife.

Kevin could tell that Kay had something on her mind and that she wanted to talk. He knew it involved Renee in some way, shape, or form—and he didn't want to know what it was.

"Can I talk to you about something?" she asked.

Damn! Damn! Damn! Kevin thought to himself, nowhere to run. "Yeah, hon. What's up? What's the deal?"

"Renee and I had a long talk while we were up at the cabin."

"Really?" Kevin asked with a piece of fish hanging off his lip, his surprise obvious.

"I know you're surprised, and so was I. But it kind of just happened."

Kevin determined that the safest way to play this conversation was to not ask questions and to talk as little as possible.

"Aren't you surprised?" she asked, taken aback by Kevin's silence.

"I mean, yeah, I guess—sure, I'm surprised," Kevin said agreeably.

"Well, anyhow, of course the situation with you and her came up."

Kevin had just swallowed a huge gulp of tea. The timing couldn't have been worse—it went down the wrong pipe. He started choking uncontrollably, which made him appear nervous and guilty.

Kay waited for him to get it together, making no attempt to help him whatsoever. Once he quieted down, she continued, "I just want you to know that I'm not going to dwell on what happened between you and Renee anymore. It's making me miserable, and I don't want to feel this way anymore. There have been so many days that I've wanted to sit you down, look you in the eye, and demand that you tell me the whole truth . . . because I know there must be more to the story of you and Renee."

"Kay, listen. Nothing hap—"

"It doesn't matter anymore, Kevin. I married you, and it's time for me to let it go. All of it. I've decided that I want a relationship with my sister again. Can you handle that?"

Kevin could feel all sorts of feelings rising inside the pit of his stomach. He felt cornered and targeted by Kay's decision to patch things up with Renee . . . as if it were the two of them against him. He couldn't explain why, but there was almost a jealous feeling. He had become used to the distance between his wife and her twin; it certainly had its advantages. Everything would change now.

"Of course I can handle it." He grinned. "I mean . . . that's your sister; I want you to be happy, Kay. So if that's going to make you happy, then I'm all for it." Kevin held Kay's hand and stroked her fingers.

"So you can handle seeing Renee here at our home from time to time? Or even maybe doing dinner every now and then with her and her new boyfriend?"

"She has a new boyfriend?"

"Yes." Kay gave Kevin a look, letting him know he was skating on thin ice.

"Listen, Kay, this isn't going to be a problem for me. Maybe it will help our marriage now that you've decided to get past this."

Kay felt really angry all of a sudden at Kevin's righteous attitude. He was talking to her as if her anger and insecurity over the years had come from nowhere, as if she was just crazy and had conjured up all of this drama just for the hell of it. She couldn't keep it inside. "You've got a lot of fucking nerve, Kevin!"

"Here we go. Here we go again." Kevin rolled his eyes and threw his hands up in the air, only making Kay's anger escalate. "I'm tired of feeling like I'm under fire in my own house," he yelled.

"Well, whose fault is that, Kevin? Huh! Is it my fault that you had feelings for my sister? Huh! Do you really think I wanted it to be that way?" Kay started to cry. She was mad as hell that her husband had betrayed her—in ways she would never know—and had turned a pleasant conversation into a bullshit argument, as usual. "Fuck it!" she screamed. "I can't even talk to you." She struggled to get to her feet in an attempt to walk away.

Kevin saw their entire evening slowly going down the drain and wanted to try and save it. He tugged on her arm, pulling her back down toward the couch. "Wait, Kay, wait. Listen, I'm sorry, okay? Let's not fight about this anymore."

Kay wanted to get out of Kevin's grip, yet wanted just as badly to get lost in his arms and for everything to be okay. She wanted to tell him that she knew he picked Renee's key the night of the key party, that her insecurities were well founded. She buried her head in his chest and cried, and cried.

Kevin stroked her hair in silence. "We'll get through this, Kay," he assured her. "I promise, we'll get through this just fine." All Kevin could think about now was the fact that there was a secret that he and Renee shared that could never come out now. It would ruin everything, and he couldn't let that happen. Not now when Kay and Renee seemed to finally have come to terms with the past and agreed to try and move on. The night ended on a decent note, but it would never be completely right. He knew that. He always had.

Chapter 17

Girl Talk

Kay had two hours to tame the overwhelming amount of paperwork that had taken control of her office at home. She had a closing to attend in Buckhead and was still having a hard time concentrating on anything but the talk she and Kevin had had a few days ago. Even though they'd decided to focus on the future, she couldn't let go. She was so sure that she was starting to get over what happened between him and Renee, but for some reason she couldn't think of anything else. She didn't trust Kevin and his feelings for her. She never really did. It had been a battle from the first day they met. She was second choice the night they met, and she still felt like that today even now that she was married. She was so exhausted from being jealous and insecure, and she was tired as hell of that awful feeling. Before she could get too deep into her thoughts, she heard the doorbell ring. She trotted down the stairs toward the front door, anxious to see who it could be. It was 9:00 a.m., and she wasn't expecting anyone. Before she got to the door she noticed Nikki's truck outside. When she opened the door, she could tell Nikki was not in the greatest of moods.

"Hey, Nikki, come on in. What's going on? What are you doing here?"

"I'm sorry, Kay. Can we talk for a minute? Are you working here today? Or are you heading out?"

"Well, I have a closing in a few hours, but it's okay. What's wrong? You look upset."

"You know what, Kay? You're going to think I'm crazy when I tell you this. But I have to vent, and I can't tell Chris."

"What is it?"

"Kay, I'm losing my mind. Chris met a woman at his job."

"Okay. What are you about to tell me? Is he fucking around on you?"

"No. God, no! Just listen. He met this woman at his job; her name is Mina."

"Mina?"

"Yeah, like Nina but with an *M*."

"Oh, that's kinda cute."

"Could you let me tell you my story please?" Nikki snapped.

"Okay, okay, my bad. Okay, so Chris met this chick, Mina, and what?"

"Well, this is the thing. I'm usually cool with this kind of thing. I mean, I couldn't care less if Chris had female friends in the past. Not that he ever did before now, but I always told myself I would be cool with it . . . because I wouldn't want him to trip on me having male friends."

"Right. Okay, so what? Are you tripping?"

"Yes, and I don't know why. It all started after we got back from the cabin. Chris went out that Monday night after we got back and didn't come in until damn near three a.m. I pretended to be asleep, but I was fuming, not so much that he came in so late—even though that wasn't cool either. But I tried calling him like three times, and he didn't answer his cell."

"Whoa? That's not like Chris. That sounds like some shit *my* husband would pull."

"Right! And I gave him such a hard time about it, Kay. You wouldn't believe the way I was carrying on. I was tripping. I sounded like one of those lame, insecure, jealous wives who won't let their men out of their sight for a second."

"Yeah, you sounded like me." Kay laughed at the irony of it all.

"Kay, seriously, you know what I mean."

"Nikki, I am serious. Welcome to the real world. I never understood how you could always be so calm about that kind of stuff in the past."

"Because I trust Chris; it's as simple as that."

"So you're saying you don't now?"

"No, I still trust him, I think. Shit! I don't know what the hell is wrong with me. It's like, ever since I had Corey, I've felt different. I feel like Chris looks at me differently, like I'm not sexy to him anymore, not the wild, passionate, crazy Nikki he fell in love with."

"Nikki, that's just in your head. Chris loves the hell out of you, and quite frankly, I think he's happy you're not so wild and crazy anymore."

"But that's not true. I'm still wild. I mean, I went to that Club Suede, didn't I?"

"Yeah, that you did. So Chris doesn't know about that, huh?"

"Are you kidding me? He would lose it if he knew I went there."

"Yeah, especially if he knew you went more than once to the point where you were damn near a regular."

"Umm . . . Kay . . . you're not helping."

"Oh, sorry. Speaking of Suede—I'm thinking of trying it."

"What? You can't, Kay."

"Why not?"

"Are you planning on taking Kevin with you?"

"No way. Come on, do you really think Kevin would set foot in a place like that? I can't even get him to slap my ass during sex, much less take me to a sex club."

"Why are you going? I mean, really . . . why?"

"Nikki, why is it okay for you to go and not for me?"

"It's not. That's my point. It was wrong of me to go, and it was especially wrong for me to go without telling Chris; he would be so disappointed in me if he ever found out."

"But didn't you love it there? Wasn't it hot?"

"That's not the point, Kay. Oh my gosh! See what I'm talking about? Listen to me. I even sound like a mother! I can't believe I'm lecturing you."

"You're crazy, Nikki. First of all, you are a mother and there's absolutely nothing wrong with that. That's what couples do: They get married and have babies. Second of all, you're still sexy and all of those things you were before."

"Kay, did I tell you that I have stretch marks?"

"Uh, yes . . . you've shown them to me a million times. So what?"

"Oh, that's easy for you to say, Miss Perfect Size Six."

"Nikki, come on."

"Kay, I'm telling you it's so awful the way I've been feeling lately. No matter how hard I exercise, I just can't seem to get rid of this tummy that I have, and my ass is just not as tight as it used to be. And let's not even talk about my tits. Jesus! I can't even go braless anymore."

"Nikki, what's this really about? Is it Mina? Is she fine or something? Have you met her?"

"No, I haven't. Chris just told me about her briefly. I guess they went to lunch one day, and she supposedly just moved here from New York and doesn't know anyone in town, blah, blah, blah."

"Ooooh, Nikki. Yeah, you're right; you're tripping. This is definitely not like you."

"See? What am I going to do, Kay? I have to get a handle on this."

"I have an idea. Why don't you invite her over to dinner? That way you can check her out and see what she's about, and it will also win you some points with Chris. He'll be so impressed with you."

"Kay, you're a genius. That's it! That's what I have to do."

"Besides, you might even like her, Nikki."

"Doubt it."

"Yeah, that's true. And she's probably a hag, anyway. Ha, ha!"

"You need to stop. Okay, moving on to me now; so where did you say Club Suede is?"

"Kay, are you seriously going to go?"

"Yes. Yes, I'm going. I mean, I'm not going to have sex or take off my clothes or anything like that, but I just want to try something different; I want to see what it's all about."

"What are you going to tell Kevin? Where are you going to tell him you're going? It's not good until really late."

"Not sure yet. I'll work that out. Trust me, Nikki. You don't understand. Kevin couldn't give a shit what I do. He barely notices I'm gone these days."

"Now, Kay, that's ridiculous. You're being dramatic."

"Seriously, Nikki, check this out. I told him that Renee and I made up and that she may be coming over from time to time. He was acting all jittery and shit. She's still under his skin—even now."

"Wow! Really? He was acting nervous?"

"Yes, he started stuttering, trying to tell me nothing happened between them."

"So, Kay, what if nothing really happened? I mean, they

are both telling you it didn't. I mean, basically, you're taking crazy-ass Jason's word over theirs."

"Because I'm not blind, Nikki. I know how they felt about each other. I've seen him look at her, and it damn sure isn't the way he looks at *me*. And Renee is a trip; don't let her sweet demeanor fool you. She loved the fact that my man was digging her. All through high school, I was always the one with the boyfriends. The guys always chose me over her. She was so jealous of me, she couldn't see straight. The only thing she had to hold on to was Dad. She was definitely his favorite. She wouldn't miss an opportunity to steal my man."

"Kay, that sounds crazy. Renee just doesn't seem the type to take pleasure in doing something like that. Especially not to you—her twin."

"Deep down, she loved that Kevin was digging her more than me. She's been waiting for this moment all of her life. I still don't know what he sees in her that he doesn't get from me."

"Kay, why the hell did you marry him? You clearly still don't trust them."

"I don't know, Nikki. I ask myself that all the time, and the only thing I can come up with is that I was in love with him. I still am. He was my world then. I was truly devastated when I heard that he and Renee spent the night of the key party together. I wanted to claim him somehow, show him that I had no hard feelings, and at the same time, I thought it would make him forget her somehow if we were married."

"Kay, I think he has. I don't think you're giving him the benefit of the doubt. You have to let this go. You're going to push him straight into her arms if you keep this up."

"I know. I'm trying. I try *so* hard. Anyway, ever since the key party and my night with Rick, I've realized that there's a lot going on in other people's beds that I would like to bring into my bedroom. I'm embarrassed to say—he put it on me. He didn't seem gay that night."

"Stop it. He's not gay; he's bisexual. There is a difference," Nikki said in Rick's defense. "It's so funny how easily Rick's name rolls off your tongue now. I remember how devastated you were and all the drama you put me through dragging me to the clinic to get your AIDS tests."

"Whatever. That was so long ago. I'm cool now; I'm over that. But seriously, I've wanted to experiment more, and Kevin is just so straitlaced. He's so good in bed, but I want more. You're going to think I'm crazy, but I want to role-play with him. He thinks that's silly."

"Oh, yeah, me and Chris used to role-play all the time."

"See what I mean? Anyway, I figure going to Suede would be a good way for me to get some of these pent-up feelings out of my system."

"Well, just be careful, Kay. You don't want to mess around and lose yourself there. It's easy to do, trust me. It was a wonderful experience, but I do regret lying to Chris about it. This is what I'm talking about. Before the baby, I wouldn't have felt the need to lie to him about this, but now that I'm a mother, I feel like he would judge me, look down on me, even. It's weird; I can't explain it."

"You went there before you had Corey, though, right?"

"Yes, I went a few months after the key party, but Chris had asked me to tone it down a little, saying he wanted to start a family. So I didn't want to tell him, because I thought he would be disappointed in me."

"Ah, yeah, good assumption. And Kevin would not only be disappointed—he would kill me! Divorce me! Leave me for sure! And I don't know why. What's the harm really?"

"Well, it's dishonest, for one. And then, it doesn't sound like he likes that side of you. That 'sex kitten' side. Poor Kevin. He doesn't know what the hell to do with you. Well, it's downtown. I'll send directions to your Hotmail. Just be careful, please. Damn! I wish I could go with you," Nikki said, half joking.

"I'll be fine; I can hang, I promise. So are you going to ask Mina to dinner?"

"You bet. I can't wait to meet this chick."

"She's probably really nice. You know if Chris likes her she's nice," said Kay.

"Yeah, we'll see. I'll know instantly what she's all about. Hey, I'm headed to work. Thanks for listening, girl; I really needed to get this stuff off my chest."

"Anytime, Nikki, anytime. Don't forget to send me those directions. And I can find it on my own if I need to, so don't play," Kay warned, showing Nikki to the front door. Kay was happy Nikki stopped by. Ever since she and Renee had fallen out and Lynda had moved away, she and Nikki had gotten a lot closer. She was even more grateful for their friendship now.

Chapter 18

Corey

Chris walked in late from picking up Corey from day care, relieved that Nikki wasn't home. She would have been livid if she knew how long Corey had been at school. He and Nikki had a pretty tight schedule when it came to the baby. Nikki dropped Corey off to school every morning since she didn't have to be at work until 9:00 a.m. Every Monday and Wednesday, Chris had a 4:00 p.m. meeting that usually lasted too damn long. It was a status meeting that his boss, Grant, set up to get a handle on what the weekly deliverables for their clients were. On those days, Nikki picked Corey up, leaving Chris responsible for Tuesdays, Thursdays, and Fridays. Corey's school closed at 6:00 p.m., which meant that Chris always found himself pushing it to get there on time. They had even warned Chris on several separate occasions that school policy was to call the authorities and report abandonment if the lateness continued and the emergency contacts couldn't be reached.

Chris didn't think they were serious—until one day, upon his arrival at Corey's school at close to 7:00 p.m.—a police car and the school's director were standing there waiting for him. Corey had been taken down to the station with a female representative from DFACS. The school director explained that they had made several attempts to contact both Chris and Nikki and then Nikki's parents. Chris wanted to kick himself. Nikki had told him earlier that morning that she would be unavailable by phone and e-mail all day, and he knew that his in-laws were in Italy celebrating their thirtieth wedding anniversary. It was all his fault, but it all ended up working out—Corey was fine when Chris arrived at the station to pick him up. DFACS never even opened a file for Chris. The rep for them told Chris she didn't want to see him down there ever again and that he was too responsible a person to have let such a thing happen. He sheepishly walked out of the station and tried to think of hundreds of places to go other than home.

Nikki never wanted Corey to go to day care until he was at least one year old. (Corey was six months old at the time.) She had to make a hard decision and put him in early so she could get back to work. It was one of the toughest decisions she had ever had to make. Chris insisted that she didn't need to go back. In fact, he begged her to be a stay-at-home mom, but she couldn't do it. She was torn between wanting to be back in the workplace again and giving Corey up to strangers. When they discussed putting Corey in day care, she cried throughout the entire conversation, finally agreeing upon a schedule that worked for both of them.

Chris knew Nikki wasn't going to understand or want to hear his explanation about getting caught up in a crisis at work and literally forgetting their child. That wouldn't go over well at all. He was so scared of what Nikki was going to say. She would probably never forgive him. When he got home and saw Nikki he knew that she was already aware that he'd been late again. She probably checked the answering machine and heard the message from the school that they were trying to reach Corey's parents and that it was very important. After he broke down and told her the truth about what had happened, her eyes were filled with contempt. She didn't speak to him for the rest of that night and very little for two weeks after that. He had to work really hard to gain her trust again, as far as Corey was concerned.

It was about six thirty, and he knew Nikki would realize he had been a little late picking Corey up since Kids R Kids was within walking distance of their house.

"Nikki?" Chris called out, praying he wouldn't hear a reply. "Hey, little man, it looks like it's just me and you." He gave Corey a high five. Corey just chuckled, clueless as to what his dad was so excited about.

"Okay, what shall we eat tonight? What do you feel like, Core? Let's see, we've got macaroni and cheese, ravioli, and spaghetti. You've got a much better selection than your dad's got. Okay, let's just hook this macaroni up, and I'll give you some of this sweet potato and apple juice to wash it down. Is that cool?" Corey, drooling all over his high chair, looked at his dad and nodded his head as if to say yes.

Once Chris got Corey fed, he quickly bathed him and held him for a bit until he fell asleep. He walked upstairs and put Corey in his crib, then decided to do some work on the computer in his bedroom. Before he could get his browser up his cell phone rang. He assumed it must be Nikki assuring him she was on her way home. "Hello," he said, unsure of the number showing up on his caller ID.

"Hi, Christopher," a woman answered back.

"Hello? Who is this?" Chris asked curiously. He didn't recognize the voice on the other end. Other than his mother, no one ever called him Christopher—not even Nikki.

"Wow! Forgotten about me already?"

"Seriously, who is this?" Chris said, starting to get a little annoyed.

"Okay, I'm sorry. I'm tripping. It's Mina. Jeez! I can't believe you didn't recognize my voice."

"Mina?"

"How did you get this number?"

"It was on your business card. Did I do something wrong? Should I let you go?"

"No, it's not that. I'm just—surprised to hear from you. What's up? Did you need something? Is everything all right?"

"Ha! You're so funny, so polite. Relax . . . please. No, I don't need anything. I just wanted to see what you were up to, that's all. Is it a bad time?"

"Well—" Chris looked around his empty bedroom, which was quickly filling with guilt. "I guess not, but I guess it's cool. So what's up? What are you up to?"

"Nothing. I'm still unpacking."

"Still? Mina, that's crazy. You've been here over four months now."

"I know, I know. But it's so hard. I come home so exhausted from work, all I want to do is jump into bed. I can't seem to get motivated."

"Well, I hear you on that one. Sometimes I get home and there's just enough time for me to grab a granola bar, a glass of milk, and fall out."

"Granola bar? Ewww! Doesn't Nikki cook?"

"Well, yes, she does, and she's great at it. But her job is pretty demanding, and so is mine. We just don't really have time to cook dinner and sit down together and eat. She's not even home yet."

"Whoa. She's still at work? That is awful. Poor thing, she must be so tired when she comes home."

"Yeah, she usually is. But, you know, I hook her up with a

little massage, a warm bath, and some hot chamomile tea from time to time."

"There you go again, being the perfect gentleman," said Mina, a hint of jealousy in her voice.

"Come on, I'm far from perfect. Believe me. But I know she works hard and she hooks me up in other ways, so she deserves it." Chris knew he was full of shit, but he wanted to make sure he wasn't setting himself up. He didn't know what to expect from Mina.

"Ah . . . way too much information—thank you."

"What? What? See, your mind just had to go there. I wasn't even talking about that."

"Whatever, Christopher."

"Why do you call me that?"

"Call you what? Your name?" Mina chuckled.

"Well, no one really calls me that, other than my mom. I mean, she used to."

"Ouch! Should I take offense to that?"

"No, that's not how I meant it. It's just strange, that's all. I just haven't really heard anyone call me that in a long time."

"I thought you just said your mom called you that."

"Well, she used to. She passed away years ago. She and my dad are both gone."

"Oh my gosh! I'm sorry, Chris. I won't call you that again, I promise. I didn't mean to bring back sad memories."

"What? You're straight. It was a long time ago; I was a kid when they died."

"How did they die?"

"Car accident."

"I'm so sorry, Chris. Do you mind if I ask what happened?"

"Nah, it's cool. Um . . . it really wasn't much to it. My mom had a little too much to drink and ended up at the wheel. The rest is really a mystery. A few of my aunts and uncles told me that she was too intoxicated to drive but that my dad was straight, so they let them go. They were shocked when they heard that she was the one driving. The police said it appeared to be a struggle. My dad had a few scratches on his face that were proven to be from my mom. My mom ended up flying through the windshield and died instantly. My dad survived for a little while but didn't make it through the night."

"How tragic! My God! How old were you?"

"Ten."

"So sorry, Chris."

"Girl, will you stop saying that? See, now you got me all spoiling the mood. I didn't mean to get you all upset. It's cool. I mean, it was a long, long time ago. I've definitely come to grips with it. You just reminded me of her for a second when you called me Christopher, that's all. It's cool, really."

"Okay, if you say so. So . . . do you mind me asking who you grew up with then?"

"My aunt Ann: She was my dad's sister. She wasn't married and didn't have any children of her own. She was my favorite aunt, and so it was inevitable that I stay with her. She raised me."

"Well, she definitely did one hell of a job for being a single woman."

"Oh, girl, you're crazy."

"Seriously, Chris. I've only known you a short time, but you seem to be one of a kind. Nikki really is a lucky woman."

Chris was speechless, leading to silence on both ends of the phone.

"Hey, baby," Nikki said, surprising Chris literally out of nowhere.

"Oh, shi—Nikki? What's up, girl? Damn! I didn't even hear you come in."

"Who are you talking to?" asked Nikki.

"What?"

"Who are you talking to?" she repeated.

"Oh, damn! Um . . . hold on, Nikki. Hey, Nikki's home. I'll just hit you up tomorrow, okay?"

"Okay, Chris. Tell Nikki to enjoy that massage." Mina snickered. "Bye."

"That's funny. Peace," Chris said, hanging up and putting his phone on charge.

"So what's up, hon? How was your day?" he asked, hoping to distract Nikki.

"Who were you talking to?" Nikki asked again.

"Oh, that was Kevin," Chris said. He wasn't sure how Nikki would react to Mina calling him at the house, so his first instinct was to lie.

Nikki noticed Chris seemed a bit jumpy, but she didn't feel like dealing with why.

"Oh, okay. Babe, I'm so exhausted. I'm gonna take a quick shower and then jump in bed. How is Corey? Did you get him in time today?"

"Will you stop asking me that every day, please?"

"I don't ask you every day. Just Tuesdays, Thursdays, and Fridays." Nikki giggled.

"Oh, so now you've got jokes, huh?" Chris teased, grabbing Nikki and tickling her.

"Stop. Chris, quit it; you're going to wake him up."

"Me? That's you making all the noise."

"Will you please stop?" she whispered, still laughing.

"Make me."

Nikki smiled and looked deep into Chris's eyes and started to kiss his face all over. First, his eyes, then his nose, then his cheeks, and then his lips. They kissed passionately as Chris lifted her up and carried her to the bed.

"Wait, Chris. I've gotta take a shower; I'm all icky," Nikki reminded him, releasing the hold he had on her, and then she ran into the bathroom and locked the door.

Chris felt relieved that she seemed to believe that he was

talking to Kevin. As he climbed into bed he thought about Mina and wondered what made her call him tonight. She was a trip, he thought. Bold, that's for sure, and then he closed his eyes, waiting for his wife to get done in the bathroom, hoping she would let him make love to her so he could get Mina out of his head.

Chapter 19

Guy Talk

"Kevin."

"What's up, Chris? Where you at?"

"I just got on 285, man. It's a bitch, too. This traffic kills me. I've got to get the hell out of Atlanta."

"I hear you, man. It drives me insane every freaking morning. So what's up? How's the job?"

"Look, Kev, check this out. I've gotta come clean about something."

"Come clean? Oh, shit! Should I pull over?" Kevin asked, cackling.

"I'm serious, man, for real. Listen, I met this chick. Her name is Mina."

"Chris, wait. Hold up, hold up."

"Will you listen? It's not what you think, all right?"

"I knew it. You're such a chump, man. Okay, what's up with this chick—Mina?"

"Okay, it's like this. I met her a few weeks ago at Frankie's. She is so damn fine, man. Just picture Nia Long . . . but finer."

"What? Aww, you're trippin'. She's finer than Nia Long?"

"Man, I'm serious as hell. She was so damn fine when I first saw her I had to do a double take."

"Did she see you?"

"See me what?"

"Do a double take?"

"What?"

"Did she see you do a double take? Because that's a real punk move, man, that's all I'm saying."

"No, she didn't see me; I'm not that rusty."

"Okay, okay, so she is fine as hell. Then what?"

"Well, it turns out she works at my job. She's on like the fourth or fifth floor. I'd never seen her. Isn't that crazy? I don't know how I missed her."

"So, was she into you or something? What's up?"

"Well, yes and no. I mean, she's real cool. It's strange. I actually like her as a friend. I mean, we've gone out to lunch a few times now. And then a couple of weeks ago she called me on my cell while I was at home."

"Word? What time was it?"

"It was like after nine or something. Anyway, I was acting all stupid and shit, all tongue-tied. It took me a second to get myself in check."

"What did she want?"

"That's the strangest thing. She didn't want anything; she just called to talk—like you call me sometimes. I mean, she really just called to kick it on the phone . . . like we were boys or something."

"Whoa. So what's up? Are you feeling her or something?"

"That's the crazy part. I don't know. I mean, I will say this—I haven't met a woman this fine, who I kinda dig spending time with, since Nikki."

"Man, you're trippin'. What are you saying? Are you about to fuck around?"

"Hell no! I didn't say all that."

"Then, Chris, what are you saying? What are you tripping about?"

"Okay, here's the deal. I already told Nikki about her. I mean, she knows we're friends. But you know Nikki; she never really trips. I mean, she acted like she was cool with it. I think she was. Really. You know Nikki is no ordinary chick. She even mentioned inviting her over to dinner one day soon."

"Man, your wife is something else."

"I know. It's wild. Do you think it's crazy that I stay friends with this woman?"

"Yup!"

"Why? Nikki is cool with it. What's the big deal?"

"Shit! You can't be serious. Look, whenever you start off a sentence with 'she's fine as hell' you're in trouble. Now, if you don't give a shit about eventually messing around with Mina, then I say go for it, but if you're trying to front like you two can just be friends and nothing else, then you're fooling yourself, man."

"Well, I know one thing for sure: I would never cheat on Nikki."

"Chris, you sound ridiculous; you can't say that."

"Why not? I mean it. Mina is a beautiful woman who happens to be cool as hell to hang around, but that's it. I mean, she can't touch my wife. I don't think I would do anything to risk Nikki leaving me. I don't think I'd cheat on her, man—ever."

"Never say never, dog."

"I'm sayin' it right here, right now—never."

"I hear you. But listen, it's not about that. Look at me and Renee."

"Aw, man, you can't compare the two. You were in love with Renee; I don't have feelings for Mina."

"Yeah, but I didn't start out being in love with Renee. I mean, I thought she was beautiful when I met her. Then I thought she was cool to hang around with. Sounding familiar?"

"Hmmmm . . . well, yeah . . . but I still say it's different. You told me it was like love at first sight when you saw Renee for the first time. I was just physically attracted to Mina. So what's up with Renee anyway? You talked to her in a while?"

"Well, yeah. It's been a little crazy, man."

"What do you mean? What are you two up to?"

"Nothing. Nothing. Seriously. I'm just saying that we talk a lot. She calls me on my way home from work sometimes."

"Annnnd?"

"And I call her sometimes, too."

"Kev, what's up, man? Are you struggling with her again?"

"I don't know, man. It's just so hard at home sometimes. Kay is just always riding me about something. If it's not one thing it's another."

"What's she riding you about?"

"Like, for instance, sometimes when I come home from work, I just feel like chilling. And then she wants to have sex. When I tell her to give me a second to wind down she gets all defensive and starts saying I don't want her and shit. By then I'm so turned off I don't want to have sex. Then we both end up going to bed mad. She's just too hard on herself sometimes, and it drives me crazy."

"So why don't you want to have sex with her? I mean, whenever Nikki comes at me it's on. For real!"

"Yeah, but that's because Nikki doesn't come at you like she used to. Kay wants to have sex every damn day. I'm not feeling that."

"You're not feeling having sex every day? Or you're not feeling having sex every day with Kay?"

"I don't even know anymore, man. I just know that when I talk to Renee, it's such a relief. She's not nagging at me about anything. She just wants to know how my day has been. That shit makes me want to fuck the shit out of her."

"Damn! For real? So have you?"

"Nah, man. I'm not trying to go down that route again. Besides, she's still seeing that banker. She talks about him all the damn time to Kay."

"Yeah, I think I did hear Nikki mention that to me. So what are you going to do? You sound like you're trippin' on this new guy in Renee's life."

"No. Not at all. Man, I told you a few weeks ago that Renee and I are cool. Just friends."

"Okay. So why can't me and Mina just be friends?"

"Well, you can, but I'm just saying that you're opening yourself up for some real trouble. It took me and Renee a long time to get to this point."

"Yeah, I hear you. But like I said, I don't have feelings for Mina. I'm just kicking with her, you know?"

"Yeah—not yet—but if you continue to hang out with her, what the hell do you think is gonna happen? Chris, you're trippin', man, I'm telling you. You need to leave this girl alone if you don't want trouble."

"She's punking me, though, man. She's all about us being friends, too, saying shit like 'you can't handle just being friends with me?' "

"Oh, see, she's trippin' too; you both are. She's playing you, man. She wants you bad, though, I'm telling you. Women are devious as hell—especially fine-ass women—trust me."

"Well, I'm not stupid; I know she's baiting me. But that doesn't mean I have to eat the worm."

"She's gonna eat your worm in a minute. Mark my words. You need to leave this girl alone, Chris."

"Well, I was tripping out when she called. When I was talking to her on the phone, Nikki snuck up on me. I didn't even hear her come in."

"Oh, shit! What did you do? Did she know who you were talking to?"

"Nah. She asked, but I kinda blew her off and got off the phone quickly. I just told her I was talking to you."

"See? Here we go. The lies are starting already. That's crazy, man. Keep me out of your shit. I have my own mess over here. Okay, so let me ask you this. Why didn't you tell Nikki it was Mina . . . if she's so cool with you and Mina being friends?"

"Yeah, I know. I asked myself the same question. I don't know, man. It just happened so fast; I wasn't prepared. So I thought it would be less complicated if I left it alone."

"Hmm . . . sounds like guilt to me."

"What the hell do I have to feel guilty for? It wasn't guilt; I mean, it was just an awkward moment. I'm gonna tell Nikki she called me, though."

"And why would you do that, Chris?"

"Why not? I've got nothing to hide."

"You're playing a dangerous game, my friend. Listen. You got lucky with Nikki the other night by her not pushing the issue, but don't underestimate her, man. She may be playing you, too."

"Nigga, you always think somebody's playing somebody. You crack me up with that."

"All right, you've been warned."

"Seriously, though, Kev, I'm cool; it's just kinda trippin' me out. I've never had a girlfriend before."

"Girlfriend? Damn! Don't let Nikki hear you call her that, though."

"You know what I mean: She's a girl . . . and then she's my friend. That's all I meant. I'm at work now; I'll holler at you later. You working out tonight?"

"Yep. You? Or is it daddy day care night?"

"What the hell ever, man. No, it's Nikki's night to pick Corey up. I'll see you at the gym around six. Peace."

"All right, bruh. Later."

Chapter 20

Something's Gotta Give

Mina had been on Chris's mind all day after his talk with Kevin. He wondered if he was making a mistake continuing with the so-called friendship he had started to develop with her. He had a lot of questions but no answers. He thought the best person to talk to this about was Nikki. She was his best friend and his true love, and he felt he should be able to share anything with her. But for the first time since he and Nikki had been together, he wasn't sure if he could talk to her about something—Mina. He didn't want to make a big deal out of it because then maybe she would think that he had stronger feelings than he actually had for Mina. He was definitely attracted to Mina and he also liked spending time with her. She made him laugh and she was fun. That made his days at work much more enjoyable. In fact he found himself looking forward to seeing her each day.

"Hey, boss," Penny said, interrupting Chris's thoughts.

"What's up, Penny?"

"Not much. I wanted to let you know that First Step

Incorporated approved graphics, so we are ready to get moving with building their site."

"That's great. Damn! They were on it. Okay, cool. I'll get these to Paul right away." Paul was one of the twelve Web developers Marketing Zone outsourced to build all of their Web sites for their clients. He was the best, in Chris's opinion, and whenever he could utilize him, he did.

"You okay, boss? You look a little preoccupied."

"Yeah, I'm all right. Hey, Penny, can I ask your opinion on something? You got a second?"

"Sure. What's up?" Penny pulled up a chair.

Chris got up and closed the door behind Penny, who looked at him concerned. "Relax. This is a personal matter," he assured her.

"Okay, I'm listening." She breathed a sigh of relief and made herself comfortable.

"All right, Penny, you were married for—what?—twenty-seven years before your husband passed away, right?"

"That's right. Best years of my life," Penny expressed proudly.

"Okay, here's my question: How did you guys handle, or did you ever deal with—well, my question is, what do you think about having friends of the opposite sex while you're married?"

"Hmmm. Do you mean how I would have felt if Danny had a female friend? Is that what you're asking me?"

"Well, okay. Sure."

"I wouldn't like it, not one bit."

"Really? Why?"

"Well, I would have to ask myself why he wanted to be friends with another woman when he had me."

"Yeah, but what's the difference if she is just a friend? I mean, I'm sure he had other male friends outside of you, right?"

"Well, sure, but that's different."

"Why?"

"Well, I guess it depends on the woman. What if she were really pretty or something?"

"So then it's not the fact that he's friends with a woman, but a pretty woman. So if she weren't attractive, then you would be cool with it?"

"Nope. I still wouldn't like it, but it definitely helps if the woman isn't attractive," Penny said, smiling. "Does this have something to do with that pretty little thing you've been going to lunch with, boss?"

"Penny, come on. No, absolutely not. I just had a conversation with a buddy of mine this morning who is in this predicament and I told him that I thought it was okay to be friends with another woman as long as it's cool with his wife—which he said it was. But then I started thinking about it more and more and wanted to make sure I gave him the right advice."

"Well, I don't know, boss. I'm an old woman, so I may be old-fashioned. But as far as I know, married folks don't do that sort of thing."

"Okay, Penny, I hear you. And you're not old; you just feel old. You gotta stop saying that, I keep telling you. The more you say it, the more you'll believe it."

"So what is going on with you and that woman?"

"Nothing. She works here in the travel department. I met her at Frankie's that night you dragged me out. That's all. We've just gone to lunch a few times. She just moved here and hasn't really gotten a chance to make any friends, so I'm just being nice."

"Okay, boss. Well, just as long as you're not too nice—if you know what I mean," Penny hinted, winking at Chris.

"You're funny, Penny. She's harmless. You know I'm in love with my wife. Nothing can ever touch that."

"Yeah, I know; you're one of the good guys. I've always thought that about you. You remind me of my Danny—just as sweet as can be."

"Thanks. I'm honored. Now get back to work," Chris said, smiling.

"Okay, boss. I hope I helped."

"Yes, you did. Thanks. I'll be sure to let my buddy know that I have an incredibly fine woman at my job who was married to the love of her life and she says 'don't do it,'" Chris said, saluting Penny, who blushed as she walked out of his office.

Chris sent First Step's graphics to Paul and headed out for lunch. He still had Mina on his mind as he headed to Willy's to grab a burrito. As he stepped into his truck he heard Mina's voice and thought he was losing his mind.

"Chris, wait up," she called out.

Chris could see nothing but a tiny flash of turquoise and black in his rearview mirror as Mina approached. He leaned his head out of the window. "Mina, what are you doing?"

"I was trying to catch you before you left."

"Why? What's up?" Chris was acting as if he wasn't particularly happy to see her.

"Are you going to lunch?" she asked, walking over to the other side of Chris's truck, opening the door, and sitting down beside him.

"Damn, girl! Aren't you a bit presumptuous?"

"What?" Mina purred, faking innocence. Chris was struggling at this point. He had thought about Mina all day; now she was here in his truck and he felt a little uncomfortable. "I have a great idea," she said excitedly.

"What?"

"Let's go to the movies."

"What? What the hell are you talking about? Have you lost your mind?" Chris said in a playful tone.

"No, seriously. How much fun would that be right now? I

mean, aren't you tired of just going to lunch every day? Let's do something different."

"Mina, I can't go catch a movie with you right now."

"Why not? What's the big deal? Come on. We can go to the one right up the street. That's so close. C'mon, we'd be back in a few hours."

Chris was looking at her in disbelief. Who was this woman who had just entered his life out of nowhere and who excited him to no end? She was so full of life and energy, so refreshing to spend time with. He thought about how he had spent his lunches before he met Mina: eating takeout right at his desk or taking a nap in his car. She actually made it fun to come to work. *The movies,* he thought. It seemed like such a simple request, yet it was so complicated.

"Chris? Hellloooooo, earth to Chris? You are so funny. What is the big deal?"

"Nothing. Listen, Mina, we have to talk."

"Oh, goodness, not the talk. What is it?"

"I'm not sure, but I think we are getting a little carried away. That's all."

"Carried away with what? What have we done? Let's see: We have gone to lunch—"

"We have been going to lunch together for the last three weeks—every day. People are starting to talk," interrupted Chris.

"Okay, so? I mean, what's wrong with that?"

"I'm married, Mina—that's what's wrong," Chris snapped. "And now we're talking on the phone outside of work."

"Chris, you are killing me. I don't understand the problem. We aren't doing anything wrong. It's actually really interesting having a male friend who doesn't want to get in my panties for a change."

"Damn! Is it like that?" Chris chuckled, fascinated at her boldness.

"Yes. Loosen up. Chris, look, I know that you are married

to the love of your life, your soul mate, your best friend in the whole wide world. It's cool; I get that. And I completely respect it. I'm not trying to get in the way of that. I promise. I just like you. I like you much better than the other people in this office, and I think it's cool that we've become friends. That's it—friends. Just friends."

"I know. You make it seem so simple, and I don't know why it shouldn't be. But I just feel guilty."

"I thought you said that Nikki was cool with it."

"Well, she does want to meet you; we're going to have you over for dinner soon."

"See, that's so nice. I'd love to meet Nikki."

"Yeah, she's great; you two would get along really well."

"Okay, so do you feel better now? We're cool, I promise; I don't have a hidden agenda. I mean, the fact that you're sexy as hell and exactly what I've been looking for all my life is just a coincidence." She laughed.

"Funny. Real funny. So the movies, what do you wanna go see?"

"*Something's Gotta Give*."

"*Something's Gotta Give*? Are you kidding me? That's a chick flick."

"Well, the last time I checked I did classify as a 'chick,' " Mina said, batting her eyelashes.

"Right. Point taken. But how about we go see *Barber Shop Two*? Or what about *Spartan*? That looked good."

"I already saw *Barber Shop Two*; I didn't really like it that much. Come on, pleeeease. Can't we go see *Something's Gotta Give*? It's at the dollar show. And I love Jack Nicholson; he's my favorite actor. Please, please."

"Did you say 'dollar show'?"

"Oh, see? Is that all I needed to say? I can be a cheap date occasionally."

"Good. All right, we can see it. I like Jack, too. I still can't believe you got me going to the movies on a Wednesday in the middle of a workday. You're crazy."

"You're so sweet." She smiled at Chris, pinching his cheek.

Chris could hardly concentrate on the movie with Mina sitting so close to him. She made him feel like he was in high school again. Nervous and unsure of himself.

Two hours later Chris and Mina walked out of Parkway Pointe stuffed with popcorn and Raisinets. "That was so great. Didn't you love it, Chris?"

"It was good. Jack did his thing."

"I mean, the chemistry between them was incredible. I loved the part when he told her she was a woman to love. I mean, he was so smooth."

"You're funny. Don't start getting all mushy on me now," Chris teased, secretly enjoying her going on and on. He was watching her as they got settled and started to head back.

"I'm not; I don't cry."

"Yeah, right! All women cry; it's in their DNA."

"What? Is that what you men think? Please. I don't cry. I mean, not over movies and silly things like that."

"Really? Nikki will cry at the drop of a dime. She acts all tough and stuff—and she is—but she's a big baby; she can't help herself."

"See, you're so sweet. You do realize that you can't go not even one hour without mentioning Nikki's name."

"Really? Is that what you have observed about me? You women are funny. You always think you know everything."

"That's because we do," Mina asserted, shoving Chris. "I mean, take Jack and Diane in the movie. She knew exactly what she wanted the first night they made love; he was all wishy-washy, unsure—whipped and didn't even know it. How could he not know that she was the love of his life?"

"He did know, but he wasn't ready to make that commitment. That's all."

"Okay, so what's up with that? Why can't men just commit? I mean, what is so hard about just saying it right at the moment? Why do they have to figure stuff out first? Why don't they just know what they want right away like we do?"

"Not sure. I mean, I knew when I met Nikki that she was going to be the woman I married, but that didn't mean that I stopped dating and dropped everything immediately. I still needed to take the time to be sure."

"Why?"

"Why what?"

"You just said you knew right away. So why did you have to be sure if you knew?"

"Come on, you know what I mean. I still had to take the time to get to know her."

"Yeah, while you dated and slept with other women, right?"

"Well, yes and no. I mean, I dated other women until we made our relationship official."

"And after?"

"And after what?"

"Are you saying you've never cheated on her?"

"Never . . . not once."

"I don't believe you."

"What do you mean? I'm serious. I've never been unfaithful to her. Not even when we were just dating."

"I don't think that's possible. Come on, Chris, you can tell me; we've been friends for a little while now. It'll be our secret."

"Mina, I'm serious. I haven't. Why don't you believe it's not possible?"

"Okay, listen. I'm going to tell you a secret. Don't tell anyone, okay?"

"Ahh . . . okay. What is it?" Chris asked.

"Have you ever heard of a place called Club Suede?"

"Yeah, isn't that some sex club where people go and have sex with strangers or something?"

"Well . . . yes. That's not really all that goes on there, but that's about right. Well, I work there at night."

Chris pulled into the parking lot at Marketing Zone, put his car in park, and gave Mina the craziest look he could muster up. "What do you do there—bartend? Wait tables?" he asked, hoping that was all that she did.

"Nope. I'm a dominatrix."

"You're a what? What do you mean?"

"Don't you know what a dominatrix does?"

"Of course I do, Mina. Tell me something. You're tripping me out right now. What are you saying? Are you having sex with these people?"

"What if I was? Would that bother you?"

"No. I mean, it's none of my business one way or the other what you do. I'm just a little surprised. That's all."

"Why?"

"Not sure. I just am. That's all."

"You look disappointed," Mina remarked, noticing the instant change in Chris's mood.

"So what do you do? I don't get it. Take me through a night for you there." He wasn't sure why it made him uncomfortable, but he didn't like it.

"Okay, first thing you need to know is that I don't have sex with anyone."

Chris was relieved and now even more curious to know what this was all about.

"Men come to me to have their fantasies become a reality. Some want me to just talk dirty to them. They want me to tell them to do nasty things to me. They want me to order them to slap my ass or something."

"Do you let them smack it?" Chris adjusted in his seat.

"Sometimes; it depends on who it is. For the most part, I just tie them up or handcuff them. Then I'll get my whip out and hit them with it, or I'll tease them with it."

"So . . . so how long does this go on?"

"Well, I get paid in increments of thirty minutes."

"And you're not having sex with these guys?" Chris asked in disbelief.

"Nope, not once. That's all part of the thrill—them wanting me and not being able to have me; it drives them insane."

"So have you ever had a time when you were turned on and wanted to have sex with them?"

"Sure."

Chris gulped. He was surprised, in shock; he never expected this. "Okay, so why didn't you have sex with them?"

"Well, mainly for safety purposes. I mean, I don't know these men, and my point to this entire story is that they are mostly—if not all—married."

"Damn! Really?"

"Yes, I'm telling you. Most men are not to be trusted. Especially the married men. I've told you this from the beginning. I've never met a man before now who didn't want to have sex with me—married or not; you're a real change of pace for me."

"Is that why you like hanging out with me? Am I some kind of challenge for you?"

"No, not at all, Chris. I'm not going to lie to you—I do find you attractive, and I think you find me attractive, too. Don't you?"

Chris felt like he was being set up. He wasn't quite sure how to answer her question, so he chose the safe way out and avoided it. "What's your point, Mina?"

"My point is that you're one of a kind. You have proven

that there are true men out there who love their wives and can be trusted; I like that about you. It makes me feel safe around you. I can be relaxed. I don't have to feel like I'm being checked out or watched. It's like you're my brother or something."

Chris knew that Mina was full of shit, but he let her go on. She needed to tell herself something to justify Chris not making a move on her, and this was it. "Well, we better get back inside," he told her. "I knew you were going to get me into trouble today."

"It was fun, though. Right?" Mina prompted, jumping on Chris's back.

"Mina, get down. You're tripping. What if someone sees us?"

"Oh, sorry, my bad. I forgot we can't look like we're having a good time."

"You're crazy. You know that?" Chris joked, checking Mina out from the back as she headed for the stairs. "Hey, no elevator today?"

"Nah, I'm gonna walk off this popcorn I just ate. See you tomorrow?"

"Okay, sure. See you tomorrow," Chris replied as the elevator closed. He wasn't sure what had just happened, but he knew one thing: His relationship with Mina was getting more complicated and more intriguing each day.

Chapter 21

Dominatrix

When Mina got back to her desk, she felt she'd made a mistake telling Chris about her second job. She really liked Chris and she didn't want him to lose respect for her. The fact that that was important to her made her rethink their relationship. It made her ask herself what she really wanted from Chris. She knew that she didn't want to go down the whole messing-around-with-a-married-man route again, even though she was extremely attracted to him and knew he was attracted to her. He was definitely a hard one to figure out, though, because he certainly had been doing a good job of keeping his distance. As she finished up her work for the day and headed home she figured it was too late for regrets now. She decided to give her sister a call.

"Helloooo," Selma answered.

"Hey, sis. What ya doing?"

"Nothing, girl. Just getting ready to start dinner. What's up? How are you?"

"I'm cool. What are you cooking?"

"Oh, just some spaghetti. You okay? You sound a little funny. What's going on?"

"Nothing, sis. I'm just in a weird mood, that's all. I'm getting ready to go to Suede in a few hours."

"Oh, it's that time already, huh?"

"Well, yeah, but I'm actually dreading it tonight for some reason. I told Chris about it and it hasn't really sat well with me since."

"Why did you do that? He definitely doesn't sound like someone who would approve of that."

"Well, I think that was just it. I don't need his damn approval. I mean, it's not like he's my man or anything. He's just a coworker."

"He sounded like much more than a coworker when you told me about him."

"Well, he's not! And he never will be. Maybe I told him to turn him off. I think I need to leave him alone, Selma. He's no good for me. I really, really like him and it can't go anywhere so I think subconsciously I told him hoping that it would help me get rid of him."

"Why don't you just tell him you don't want to see him anymore?"

"I can't. It's so hard. I like him so much. As a friend more than anything, which is what is making it so hard. He's really a lot of fun to be around, and then it certainly doesn't help that he's gorgeous."

"But he's married, sis. Leave him alone. You have to."

"I know but I don't want to," Mina whined.

"Then why are you trying to push him away?"

"Oh, I don't know. Maybe I wanted him to know all of me. Not just the side he sees at work. Hell, maybe I hoped it would turn him on or something."

"Well, how did he react when you told him?"

"He was a bit shocked. It was hard to read him. At some level, he seemed a little jealous when I told him about the men. He wanted to know if I've ever slept with any of them . . . things like that. Like he was really struggling with me being with another man. I liked the thought of that."

"But why, sis? You're really sounding like you're falling for this guy. I think you need to take a step back. Really, I do."

"We went to the movies today," Mina said, gleaming.

"What did you go see?"

"Something's Gotta Give. I loved it!"

"Sis, what are you going to do? It's starting to sound serious. Did anything happen?"

"Anything like what?"

"Like did you two hold hands or kiss?"

"Nooooooooo. Not at all. It was completely innocent. His wife would have been pleased."

"Somehow I doubt that."

"Seriously, nothing at all happened."

"I'm not going to say anything else about Chris tonight other than this. Be careful!"

"I will. I'm okay. Really, I am. I feel better now that I've talked to you. I hope it's dead at Suede tonight. I'm not really in the mood for these pitiful-ass men today."

"Well, why are you going, then?"

"Selma, don't go there please." Mina knew that Selma hated the idea of her working at Suede.

"I'm cool. I'm not going to say anything. I still don't understand why a beautiful, intelligent, sexy black woman like yourself would sell her body for sex."

"*Selma!* Stop. Just stop. First of all, I don't sell my body for sex. You are so funny, always seeing what you want to see. I have *never* had sex with any of these men. It's just something I fell into and I really started liking the power trip, not to mention the money! I have the best gig up in there. It's easy money."

"It's dangerous as hell, that's what it is . . . and one day one of these men is going to stalk you or rape you or something awful!"

"That is not going to happen. The security is so tight in there. They wish they could rape me. Shit, that was one guy's fantasy last week."

"Okay. I'm done. I will talk to you tomorrow."

"Okay, okay. I'm sorry. I know you can't handle the nasty talk. I will spare you tonight. I'm home now anyway. I'll talk to you tomorrow. I love you," Mina said playfully.

"I love you too, sis. Please be careful, though. Seriously!"

"Selma, you don't have to worry. I promise. I'll be fine. I'll talk to you tomorrow. Bye."

When Mina hung up the phone she thought about what Selma said about Chris. She knew she should stop calling him and seeing him. But her body wasn't listening. It couldn't wait to see him tomorrow.

When Mina made it to Suede she went into the locker room and transformed herself into her dominating role. As she walked down the corridor to her room, she saw Drew waiting for her. Drew was a thirty-seven-year-old white man she had seen before on several occasions. He was actually one of her favorite customers and one of the cutest white men she had ever encountered in real life. He reminded her of Brad Pitt with his scruffy shadow and his spiked blond hair. His body wasn't quite as chiseled as Brad's, but she could tell that if he put the beer down he had potential to be physically fit.

Drew was surprisingly her only white customer. He actually found her by accident. She was taking a break one day in the lounge area in front of the bathroom when he walked up to her and asked her name. He appeared embarrassed when she told him she worked there and wasn't interested.

She then proceeded to ask him questions such as, what attracted him to her and what would he do with her if he had the chance? He stuttered as he answered each question and then politely asked her if she would do a show for him. She accepted and had enjoyed seeing him ever since.

When she saw Drew, she greeted him with a kiss on the cheek, took his hand, and led him into the Red room. The Red room was tiny and dark with the exception of a red lightbulb screwed in the top of the ceiling in an exposed fixture. It was characteristic of a room where one would be questioned or perhaps even tortured. The wrought-iron chair in the middle of the floor stood solo and was where Mina sat wearing black leather pants, a tight black leather bra that showed an unabashed amount of cleavage, and stiletto heels.

"Don't look at me," Drew commanded, standing about two feet away from Mina.

She quickly turned around, now with her back facing Drew. She completely transformed herself into his fantasy. He never liked for her to look at him. He said it made him feel guilty. She figured he was married. He never wanted to talk about it and she never pushed the issue. She always made it a rule not to discuss the personal lives of her customers. That could only complicate things, she figured. The room was completely silent when Mina heard the door close behind her.

"What's your name?" Drew asked, pretending not to know it.

"Angel. What's yours?"

"Drew."

"Can I turn around now?" Mina asked, knowing what the answer would be.

"No, I don't want you to look at me. Don't turn around."

Mina was kind of getting into it tonight. She felt oddly aroused by Drew's demands.

"What are you doing back there, Drew?" Mina asked. "Do you like what you see? You want me to touch you, don't you?"

"Yeah, real bad," Drew told her.

"One thing you've got to understand is that in here, Drew, I'm the boss," Mina said, turning around slowly, a little nervous as to what his reaction would be. Normally Mina would listen to Drew and never turn around until he asked. Today she felt like mixing things up a bit. She could tell that he was pleasantly surprised by the change. His eyes widened as she stood in front of him.

"Get down on the floor on all fours right now," Mina snapped at Drew. He didn't budge, which unnerved her a little. Every now and then the clients wanted to be yelled at harshly and abused; that was the turn-on for them. Although Drew stood there towering over Mina with his six-three stature, she was clearly the one making the rules.

"Get down on the fucking floor, Drew, or I swear I'm going to slap the shit out of you." Drew finally knelt down, looking almost afraid as to what Mina would do next. The fear in his eyes almost looked genuine. Mina loved it. She walked around him in circles like a lioness, as if he were innocent prey she planned to devour. She knelt down in front of him with her legs spread open wide and got really close to his face, grabbing his tie.

"You want me to treat you bad, don't you?" Mina asked. Drew did not respond.

"Answer me!" Mina yelled, jerking his tie downward.

"Yes . . . yes," he said, bowing his head down in shame.

"Awww, is little Drew ashamed?" Mina teased.

"No, I'm not, I'm not," Drew said.

"Get up off that dirty floor and take a seat in that chair," Mina directed.

Drew stood up and sat down in the red chair. Seconds

later he had his dick in his hand massaging it slowly. Mina slapped his face.

"Did I tell you it was okay to do that?" she snapped. "Do you know how dirty and bad that is?" Mina asked. "Put it back in your pants right now and don't you dare take it out unless I tell you to!"

Drew didn't listen this time, though. He decided to test Mina so he held himself stroking it up and down, watching Mina.

"Oh, so you think I'm playing with you, huh?" Mina asked. She walked over to Drew and warned him to put it away and then reared back as far as she could, swiftly slapping her hand against his face. His glasses flew off, sliding across the floor. When Drew stood slightly to attempt to retrieve his glasses from the floor she pushed into his chest with the tip of her boot and told him to sit down. He held his face, sitting back down, looking at her.

"Tell me what you want me to do!" Mina said. "You want me to come and sit on it, don't you?"

Drew didn't answer right away. Instead, he slowly rose and walked over to where Mina stood. The fact that he wasn't talking made her a tad nervous, but she didn't let on at all. Instead she used that energy to attempt to slap him again. When he grabbed her hand and in turn slapped her, Mina was in complete and total shock. Before she could gather herself from the sting of Drew's hand slamming against her cheek he was behind her holding her tightly, panting and grinding against her back, pulling her hair so hard it was lifting her chin up toward the ceiling. He whispered in her ear.

"Shhhhh. Don't yell, I am not going to hurt you. This is all part of what I want, part of the act," he said.

Mina felt compelled to call out for help, but at the same time she was partly interested in what would happen next. The thought of how turned on she was feeling disturbed her to no end. He had never grabbed her like that before. He wasn't supposed to touch her at all. Those were the rules. She knew she was sick for liking it but she did. Before she could think about it too long, Drew spun Mina around and had her pinned against the wall, peering into her eyes, trying to find his words. She then spat in his face and he quickly slapped her in the face again. This time Mina felt something wet on her lip. She was bleeding, she could taste it in her mouth now.

"You nasty bitch," Drew said. "Don't you ever spit in my face again."

"Fuck you!" Mina said, spitting on the floor next to Drew's feet.

"Yeah, I like it when you talk dirty to me. You're so fucking sexy."

Mina was able to get her hands free, catching Drew off guard, and started to choke him with all the strength she could muster. He broke free of her grip and pinned her down on the floor. She felt like the situation was seriously getting out of control now. She couldn't show fear, and she damn sure couldn't show him how turned on she was. She wouldn't allow herself to touch him sexually even though she knew that he wanted nothing more than to rip her clothes off and have his way with her.

"Sit in the chair and make yourself come," Mina said, trying to reverse roles.

He was breathing heavily from the struggle that had ensued between them. He let her go, taking a seat in the chair and letting his head fall back, trying to catch his breath.

"Don't look at me," Drew said between pants.

Mina turned around in order to keep the situation calm and listened as Drew moaned and groaned behind her. She closed her eyes, losing herself in his ecstasy, imagining that it was her own. When he finally came it was as if he was inside her. When she opened her eyes she heard Drew's zipper closing and it brought her back to reality. He thanked her profusely and started to apologize for the roughness, but she waved him off and told him she would see him soon. She wasn't sure why she had let it go that far. She was scared to admit that she had probably enjoyed the rush more than Drew even. What was happening to her? she thought to herself. She imagined having her way with Chris on her way home that night, but her fantasy kept getting interrupted by the thought of what a good guy Chris was and how disgusted he would have been had he seen her tonight. It was enough to bring her to tears.

Chapter 22

Confirmation

When Mina got home and into bed all she could think about was Chris. Her experience with Drew continued to fill her with so many emotions she didn't know what to do with herself. It was late, after midnight, but all she could think about was talking to her sister. After about half a bottle of wine later, she called her cell phone hoping she would answer.

"Hello?" a groggy voice answered.

"Selma?"

"Sis?"

"I'm sooooo sorry to be calling you so late. I know you're asleep but I had to talk to you about something. Is Leeann asleep? Paul?"

"What the . . . what time is it?"

"I know, I know. Can you talk for a second?" Mina begged. "I'm so sorry, Selma. I know you think I'm crazy for calling you so late but I needed to talk to someone."

"What's going on, Mina? Are you in some kind of trouble? What's wrong?" Selma said, concerned.

"You're not going to believe me when I tell you this. I'm okay. I just wanted you to confirm something with me."

"What? What is it?"

"Remember earlier when I told you that I told Chris I was a dominatrix at Suede?"

"Yes. Did something happen to you? Are you okay?"

"No. Nothing happened. I'm fine. Listen to me. Did you feel differently about me once you found out I worked there?"

"What? I don't understand."

"I know. I'm talking crazy. Sorry."

"Mina, what's going on? What happened?"

"I don't know, Selma. Chris happened, I guess. I've never cared about what a man thought about me more than I care how he does. I would die if he was ashamed of me or thought little of me now that he knows what I do."

"Mina, you're talking crazy. Why would Chris's opinion matter to you? I mean, who is he to judge what you do?"

"I don't know. I just really value our friendship and I want to make sure that he still respects me."

"Mina, are you drunk?"

"Yeah, a little. Seriously, Selma. Do you think it's disgusting what I do there?"

"Let's not worry about what I think, Mina, you just worry about yourself. I don't care that you work at Club Suede. I promise."

"Selma?"

"Yes?"

"I . . . I . . ."

"Mina, what is wrong with you? Do you need me to come over there?"

"No. I need you to tell me your honest-to-God, true feelings about me working there."

"Why don't you just take some Tylenol, drink a big glass

of water, and go to bed? I'll see you tomorrow, okay? I'll come and see you and we can talk."

"Selma?"

"Yessss?"

"I had a really crazy experience tonight."

"Mina, what happened?"

"I let a customer get to me."

"What do you mean?" Selma said, sitting up.

"I let this guy have his way with me."

"Mina, what are you saying? Did you have sex with him?"

"Would it bother you if I did?"

"Mina, did you have sex with him or not?" Selma fired back.

"No. I didn't. I told you, I don't have sex with my customers."

"Then what?" Selma said, sounding relieved.

"He was a bit rough with me and I liked it." There was silence on the other end. "Selma? Did you hear what I said?"

"Yeah . . . ah . . . why are you telling me this?"

"I don't know. Because I'm drunk."

"How was he rough with you?" Selma asked curiously. She was not happy with what Mina was telling her.

"I slapped him as part of his fantasy and he slapped me back. Then I choked him."

"*What?*"

"I know, I know. It sounds crazy, but I liked it. I really did."

"Sis, you're talking crazy. You mean to tell me that this stranger put his hands on you and you liked it?" Selma was appalled.

"I want you to know this side of me. I'm crazy, Selma. I've done some really crazy things."

"Like what, sis? What are you doing?"

"I can't even tell you half of the things. I'm too ashamed," Mina said as she started to cry, thinking back to the horseback riding incident with Lance.

"Please don't cry, sis. It's okay. Nobody is judging you. Least of all me."

"Selma, Chris is so great. I just can't believe how great he is. I have really never met anyone like him." Mina sobbed.

"It's okay. You just need to go to bed. You're not going to remember any of this in the morning. I don't know what has gotten into you tonight but it's okay. Just go to sleep." Selma felt helpless.

"I don't know what's wrong with me, Selma."

"Mina, let me ask you something before you go. Why do you do it? Why do you work as a dominatrix, really?" Selma asked since that seemed to be what triggered her mood tonight.

"I can't explain it. It's so frustrating being a woman who has everything but nothing all at the same time."

"What do you mean?"

"I mean that I come from a good home. Sure Mom and Dad are divorced, but they both love me and still love each other probably. I know I'm attractive, smart, fun to be with. I have good friends and a family that loves me. I make a pretty decent living. But there is something missing."

"What? A man?"

"Nooooooooo. Not a man. I know that's what you think but it's not that. It's like my life is almost too perfect. I constantly feel the need to shake things up."

"That's just crazy. How can your life be too perfect?"

"I mean it, Selma. It's like I'm bored all the time. I used to get so tired of always doing the right thing. That's how I ended up with Rob. He was such a bad boy. I loved it! The fact that he was married was so taboo and unforgivable it turned me on.

"I know it sounds crazy but I'm telling you the truth. It

made me so happy to piss Dad off. I didn't care about anything else other than making him mad. And then Rob was the first guy that I experienced rough sex with."

"What are you saying, Mina?"

"I'm saying that he wasn't abusing me. He was hitting me while were having sex and I liked it. It was hot. It turned me on."

Selma was flabbergasted. All this time she thought Mina had been in an abusive relationship. She thought about all of the times she cried for her, got angry for her, and she was just fucking some crazy guy who liked hitting her and she liked it.

"Selma, are you there?"

"Yes. I'm just not sure what to say to you right now."

"Please don't judge me, Selma. I can't take it. I'm so sorry I let you believe that he was abusing me. I was ashamed. I was afraid you would react the way you're reacting right now."

"I just don't know what to say to you, sis."

"I know. I just wanted you to know all of me. I am a mess. And now I think I'm falling for another married man and he would hate this side of me too."

"You need to leave Chris alone, sis. He's not what you want."

"No, it's different with him, Sel. I really like him legitimately. That's actually what's scaring me about him. He's the real deal. I've never really felt this way about another man before. It's always been about me with all of these other guys. What I want. What I can take from them. What they can do for me. But with Chris it's different. I really and truly like spending time with him and I think the reason I'm tripping so hard right now is that I'm scared that I fucked myself up. Like now, I'm not worthy of a good man."

"He's *married*, Mina!"

"I *know*, Selma!"

"Then what are you talking about? You're talking crazy. I mean, no matter how much I disagree with the fact that you like men hitting you to the point where you're having black and blue marks on your face, it certainly doesn't mean that you're not worthy of a good man. You need to go to bed. Sleep whatever this is off."

"Yeah, but that's not all I've done. You don't know all of it."

"Sis. *Go to bed!* I can't take any more tonight. We'll talk tomorrow, okay?"

"Okay, Selma. I'm sorry." Mina hung up and fell into a drunken sleep.

She would remember very little about her conversation with her sister the next day.

Chapter 23

Racquetball

The woman at the window had seen Chris's face a million times before, but she always greeted him with the same flirtatious smile and sparkling look in her eyes. He was surprised the first time she told him that he was cute. Nikki would tell him that as his mom had occasionally, but no one else ever used that term to describe him.

"Hi, Sheila," Chris said, passing her his license across the counter.

"Hello, Chris." Sheila smiled and adjusted herself on the stool she was sitting on. "I see you've got the court reserved for two today."

"Umm, yeah, I do have the court reserved for two today. Can I get a few towels?" he asked, realizing he'd forgotten his gym bag.

"Sure," she said, handing him a couple of generic white towels. "So, your friend, is he any good? And is he as cute as you?"

Chris was embarrassed. He wasn't playing with another guy; he was meeting Mina there to play. Sheila had caught him completely off guard. Before he could answer he felt a jab in his side that startled him.

"Hey there!" Mina said.

He turned around and saw Mina standing almost right under his armpit. *She is so tiny,* he thought. He turned and saw Sheila's smile slowly fade into a grimace that made him feel like total shit, never mind the fact that she had just been flirting with a married man.

"Have a good game," mocked Sheila, in a smart-ass disapproving tone.

"We will." Mina, clueless, smiled and waved back at Sheila.

Mina looked so happy to see Chris. He couldn't help but feel happy to see her, too. Everything about her was contagious. If she smiled it made him want to smile. If she laughed it made him want to laugh as well.

"So what's up, Mina? How've you been? I didn't see you at work today. Rough night last night?"

"Nah. The usual. I had a little too much wine once I got home and chatted with my sister until I passed out. No big deal."

"So how was work? Club Suede, I mean," Chris said sarcastically.

"It was fine. Can we concentrate on this ass-whupping I'm about to give you, though?" Mina said, making sure she changed the subject. The last thing she wanted to do was talk about her other job with Chris.

"Girl, please . . . I would be surprised if you lasted more than five minutes; I've got game. I told you me and my boy Rick used to play here all the time, so I guess you can take his place and get whupped like he used to," Chris bragged as he put on his headband.

"I know that's not a headband." Mina was making fun of how serious Chris was taking their match.

"Oh yes, it is, girl, and after this is done you can kiss it."

"So what's the deal? Are we going to fifteen or twenty-one?"

"Oh, check you out—with the racquetball lingo," Chris said, shaking his head. "Your serve."

He tossed her the ball. Mina caught it with one of her little hands and impressed Chris more than she knew with that move alone. He loved a woman with a little athleticism in her blood. The first match went by without either of them saying a whole lot; they were both concentrating on beating each other to a bloody pulp. Chris noticed that she had her "Z" serve down. She was taking no prisoners.

"So you're a little competitive, aren't you?" he asked as he returned her serve.

"You could say that." Mina delivered the ball to Chris off the far wall with nice backhand action.

"So what's your sport? Are you a Venus and Serena follower?"

"Yeah, they're great, but I'm not a huge tennis fan. Awww!" Mina exclaimed as the ball went past her. The score was now 3–2 in Chris's favor.

"Are you trying to distract me by asking me all these questions?" Mina squinted her eyes to focus on the ball.

"It's not my fault you can't do more than one thing at a time." Chris laughed.

They were both pretty winded and each was hoping that the other would call for a break. Mina gave in, saying she needed water. Chris watched as she walked toward the door where her water was and saw her bend over to grab her towel. He noticed a tattoo on her back, an eight ball, one of the oddest tattoos he'd seen. Before he could ask Mina about it she came and sat next to him on the floor, distracting him by her closeness. The beads of sweat glistening on her forehead turned him on—he wanted a taste.

"What are you looking at?" she asked.

"Oh, my mind was somewhere else. My bad."

"You're cute. You know that?" Mina told Chris.

"Cute?" Chris asked, surprised to hear Mina use his wife's description. "How is it possible for a grown-ass man to be cute?" he asked, loving the attention.

"You just are. I guess it has a lot to do with the fact that you're so nice, and of course being a married family man doesn't hurt. I keep telling you: All the good ones are taken."

"Yeah, right, and I keep telling you, as pretty and as smart as you are, your husband is right around the corner."

"Nah. You know what, Chris? I'm not sure I wanna get married."

"Really? Why not? I haven't met too many women who didn't want to get married . . . eventually. As a matter of fact, I don't think I've met any."

"Yeah, I know. I just really don't think I could deal with having to answer to just one person for the rest of my life. I definitely don't want any kids. I mean, I think I may be too selfish or something, not really willing to share my time."

"Wow! That's honest."

"Do you think that makes me a bad person? I mean, it sounds a little harsh when I say it out loud, but I'm serious, Chris. I've been proposed to a couple of times, but it just never went any further than that."

"So what happens? You just lead these men on, make them fall in love with you, get them to propose, and then say 'psych'?"

"No, it's not like that. I mean, it wasn't like that. I thought I was in love with them, too, but then when it came down to it, I realized it wasn't the course I was ready to take."

"Damn, girl! You're a trip. That's cold."

"Umm . . . did I say something to upset you? Because you're the one that's tripping."

"Nope. I just think it's crazy to never want to get married.

I mean, don't you get lonely? Don't you want a companion?"

"No, not really. I mean, I have you, don't I?" Mina asked.

"Whoa! You have me as a friend; I'm talking about much more than that . . . like someone to come home to every night, someone to make love to whenever you feel like it."

Mina threw her head back in laughter. "I can get all of those things without being married—especially lovemaking. Trust me."

"What the hell is that supposed to mean?" Chris stood up.

Mina realized she had hit a nerve but was curious to see how far she could push him. "It means that most married men complain about never getting enough sex from their wives, that's what."

"I guess no one's asked me that question."

"Oh, whatever, Chris. You can't tell me that you get sex whenever you want. Nikki is barely home, and when she is, I'm sure she is tired as hell. Besides, I know for a fact that after women have babies they don't feel as confident anymore."

"How the hell would you know that, Mina?"

"I have a lot of married girlfriends in New York, and they've all been through it."

"Well, they don't represent married women in Atlanta who have had kids."

"Now, how the hell are you gonna speak for a woman, Chris? Do you even ask Nikki how she feels since she's had Corey? I mean, you can't tell me that you haven't noticed a change in her since she's had a baby. You told me yourself that she used to be a little wild and has calmed down quite a bit."

"Right, but only because I asked her to; she didn't want to."

"See, that's what I'm talking about—men telling me what to do, how to be, how to act; I can't hang with that."

"Girl, please . . . I'm not buying this shit; you're just mad because you haven't found the man of your dreams, your soul mate."

"Chris, give me a fucking break," Mina snapped. "Of course I can get a guy, the man of my dreams if I wanted to. I've had the man of my dreams; I just chose not to marry him."

"I don't believe you."

"How the hell are you gonna tell me who I have or have not met?"

"I just don't buy it. You wanna know what I really think?" Chris walked toward Mina so close she could feel his breath on her face. "I think you wanted those men who proposed to you to be the man of your dreams. But they weren't, so you didn't settle. Which is cool. But I do think that you would appreciate a good man, your soul mate, if you were to meet him. And the fact that you haven't met him pisses you off, so you decided that it would be much easier to lie and say that you don't want to get married because that sounds better than not finding the right man."

Mina just looked up at Chris and became silent. She was so heated that she didn't know if she wanted to slap him in his face or kiss him. He was right; she did want to have it all—the husband, the baby, all of it. And she wanted it with him, and it killed her because he didn't even see it. He didn't see her, not in that way. The tension was thick between them. Chris wanted desperately to kiss her and Mina knew it so she started to move her lips toward his but he backed away. His eyes closed briefly as he tried to regain his composure. Chris knew that they were both getting a bit carried away. He felt uneasy. He knew he had entered forbidden territory. Mina looked frustrated and on the verge of being sad even. He desperately needed to switch things up to keep the mood light but couldn't come up with anything.

"So what's up with that tattoo on your back? What does it mean?"

"What? Tattoo? Oh, that. Ummm, it's a long story. I really don't want to get into it right now." Mina was crushed. She was frustrated and felt defeated. She had truly never met a man who challenged her to this degree. She could not understand how he could resist her.

"You okay?" Chris said, knowing she wasn't and why.

"Yup."

"You better perk up. It's time for me to whip that ass again," Chris said, continuing to try and lighten things up.

"Ha! In your dreams, Chris," Mina said, snapping out of her mood. "Hey, you're still gonna love me after I beat you, right?" she added with the most innocent expression on her face.

"Of course I will." Chris was spooked by her choice of the word *love*. He knew she didn't mean anything by it . . . but still. A slight chill went through him, and it may have been that he was more afraid that he was starting to have strong feelings for Mina. He'd never allowed himself to get close to any woman other than Nikki. So why now? And why Mina? Besides the fact that she was beautiful beyond words, it was becoming more than just a physical attraction; he really was beginning to feel a mental connection. Chris had a strange feeling in the pit of his stomach that he was trying to push away.

"Take that!" Mina yelled.

He had lost another match to her. He had the feeling he was going to lose a lot to Mina but couldn't put his finger on what exactly was at stake. He looked up just in time to see her bending over to get her towel. The outline of her thong was visible. He knew then it was time to bounce. "Hey, Mina, you win. I need to go. I just remembered that I need to make a few stops after I leave here."

"Whatever you say." She walked over to Chris and got really close to him and poked him in the chest. "Say it," she ordered.

"Say what?"

"Say Mina is the *woman*."

"Mina is the woman," Chris said, hypnotized, barely able to get a genuine smile across his face.

He had finally identified the feeling in his stomach: It was fear. He was afraid that, for the first time, there was another woman out there who had the potential to distract him from the love of his life and his family.

They gathered their belongings and walked off the court. He wasn't going to be able to spend any more time with Mina alone—as much as he wanted to; it just wouldn't be smart.

"So you owe me one next week," Mina remarked.

"You got it," he said reluctantly.

Chapter 24

Pillow Talk

The night air did Chris good on his way home from the racquetball courts. Mina was heavy on his mind as he pulled into his driveway and closed the garage behind him. He wondered if Kevin was right. He had fallen into a place he didn't feel he could get out of now. He was definitely developing strong feelings for Mina and, for the first time, was unsure of how deep those feelings went. He tried to analyze the situation in his mind. He envisioned Mina in his head, how beautiful and sexy she was, and so smart and witty. He thought about how much she made him laugh and about how much they had in common. The more he thought about her, the more he wanted to get back in his car and head downtown to her place. He had to pull himself together. The light in his bedroom glowed from all the way upstairs. He knew Nikki was up waiting on him and he dreaded facing her—he felt guilty and was afraid it would be obvious.

"Hi, honey," Nikki said, happy to see her husband.

"Hey, babe, what are you doing in bed so early? Is Corey asleep already?" Chris bent down to kiss Nikki.

"I know it's only nine o'clock, but I was so tired when I got home that I just quickly fed Corey and put him down in his crib. Surprisingly, he fell asleep within a half hour."

"Whoa! He must have had a rough day today." Chris chuckled.

"Are you hungry? I cooked . . . believe it or not," Nikki said proudly.

"Whaaat? I can't believe it. Yeah, I'm starving actually. I was out on the racquetball courts and worked up a serious appetite."

"Oh, so that's where you went."

"What do you mean? Were you looking for me? Did you forget I go to the gym on Wednesday evenings?"

"Well, yes and no. I was so excited about getting off early and tried calling you to let you know that I was going to pick something up for dinner and Penny said you left already. I assumed you were on your way home but remembered it was your workout day. I stopped by the gym but didn't see you."

Chris thought he would be sick. "Oh, I decided to play a game of racquetball instead. Kevin called and canceled on me, and I didn't feel like lifting alone." He was hoping she would just drop it now.

"That's cool, honey; no need to explain. So who won?"

"Won what?" Chris stuttered.

"The game, racquetball?"

"My bad, girl; I'm just tired. I won, of course."

"So who did you end up playing with?"

"Just Mina," Chris said confidently.

Nikki's mood changed instantly. Her smile turned upside down in the blink of an eye. "I didn't know she played," she said, trying to compose herself.

"Well, I didn't either. Turns out she's pretty good, but I still beat her. Hey, I'm going to head to the shower real quick. I'll be right back." Chris had no desire to talk to Nikki about Mina tonight, not with the thoughts that had been swirling in his head earlier. He wanted so badly to put her out of his mind, but she kept creeping back in even in the shower—he had to tame the hard-on that had started to rise. Just then he felt a slight breeze as the shower door opened.

"Hmmm, looks like I'm just in time," Nikki said, joining him. She stroked Chris up and down.

Mina instantly disappeared from his mind. He was now preoccupied with this dazzling, enticing woman who resembled his wife—he couldn't even remember the last time he saw Nikki completely naked, much less with the lights on. Beads of water trickled down the curve of her plump ass as she slowly slid her body up and down Chris's chiseled torso. He had no idea what came over Nikki, but whatever it was he liked it; in fact, he loved it. He was so turned on, he wanted to eat her alive. He turned her around swiftly and started to kiss her passionately. He lifted her leg and slowly slid his dick inside her, making sure she could feel every inch. The water rushed over their bodies and rejuvenated the lust they once had for each other.

Nikki and Chris made love for what seemed like hours. They took their excursion from the shower, to the bathroom countertop, to the floor, then to the bed before they were through. When Nikki slid from on top of Chris and drifted off to sleep, he couldn't help staring at her. He took his index finger and gently stroked her eyebrows, her cheeks, her lips, then kissed her softly on her mouth.

Nikki's eyes slowly started to flutter until she stirred. "What are you doing, babe?"

"You're so fine. You know that?" Chris said, gazing at his wife.

"Honey, what's going on with you? Are you okay? You're in a strange mood; you're being so mushy."

"Yeah, I know I'm tripping. You know I love you, right?"

"Of course I know," Nikki replied, unsure whether Chris was saying it out of love or reassurance. "Can I ask you something, Chris?"

"Sure. What's up?"

"Are you and Mina just friends?"

"Why would you ask me that, babe?"

"I don't know. I guess I'm having a hard time with your new friend. The girls call her your *girlfriend.*"

"That's ridiculous," Chris said, remembering when he referred to Mina as his girlfriend to Kevin recently.

"They were just joking, honey. Calm down. What are you getting so upset about? You're scaring me."

"How am I scaring you?"

"Because you're getting upset. Which would only mean that I hit some kind of nerve."

"I'm not upset. I just wish you hadn't brought her up, that's all; I thought we were having a great night."

"We were. We are, aren't we? Why would me bringing Mina up change that?" Nikki didn't like the way Chris was acting at all—guilty—which made her wonder . . .

"Chris, you never answered my question."

"What question?"

"Are you and Mina just friends?"

"Of course, Nikki. I mean, what the hell do you think I've been doing?"

"Well, up until a minute ago, I was pretty sure you were just friends, but now I'm not so sure."

"How can you say that when you were the one that brought her up? You were the one that asked if we were just friends. That doesn't sound like a woman who's sure of something. Nikki, we *are* just friends."

"Okay, Chris, that's all I wanted to know."

"So do you have a problem with us being friends? Because we talked about this and you said you were cool with me having a female friend."

"I am. Cool, I mean," Nikki lied.

"So what's this about, then?"

"Chris, just drop it; it's cool."

"Do you want me to stop seeing her?"

"No, that's ridiculous. That would mean that I didn't trust you—and I do. Can I trust *her?* Has she tried to make a move on you? Does she flirt with you?"

"Nah, Mina has plenty of men falling all over her; I'm just an old married guy she works with, that's all."

Nikki laughed. "Chris, do you hear yourself? You can't be that naive. You know good and damn well how gorgeous you are and that women love married men, so give me a break with that shit."

"I'm just saying that she's not interested. She's made that perfectly clear."

"What? So you two have talked about this?" Nikki snapped.

"Well, no, not really talked about it . . . I mean, she told me what her type of man is, and I'm not it: That's all I'm saying. She really is just a friend, Nikki. I mean, we talk about the same things that me and Kevin do; it's really interesting."

"Interesting how?"

"That a man and woman can be friends without there being any sex involved. You used to tell me that all the time, remember?"

Nikki wanted to crawl into a hole and die. She did tell Chris that. She was so sure of herself back then when she told him that garbage; she wished she could take it back. "Yeah, I remember."

"You burned that theory in my brain back in the day when you first met that guy Charlie and tried to convince me that he didn't want you."

"Oh, goodness! I can't believe you even remember Charlie; that was so long ago, Chris," Nikki acknowledged, knowing she had just gotten a phone call from him last week.

"Well, hey, I'm just saying that I can't believe how stubborn I was then. I was a trip, wasn't I? So stuck on that shit; now look at me . . . all grown and mature and shit."

"So what's this, Chris? Payback?" She couldn't help it. The insecure wife was coming out and had to be heard.

"Payback? I don't follow you."

"Chris, stop patronizing me. You know what I mean—are you friends with Mina now because of all the drama I put you through with Charlie?"

"Girl, don't be silly. You act like I picked Mina up in a bar or something; she works with me, babe. That's it. I mean, we went to a movie and played some racquetball. What's the big deal?"

"Movies? What the hell—you took her to the movies? When was this?"

"Oh no, I didn't really take her. We went to the movies on our lunch break one day, that's all. It was kinda cool, a nice change of pace."

Nikki wasn't sure how to handle this one. She was steaming, but she wanted to keep it together. She didn't want Mina to break her. She felt tonight like she had gained so much ground and didn't want to lose any. "The movies? Interesting. So what did you go see?"

"She dragged me to some chick flick, that Jack Nicholson movie."

"*Something's Gotta Give*?"

"Yeah, yeah, that's it."

"Really?" Nikki said, gritting her teeth. "So how was it? Was it good? I wanted to see that one."

"It was cool. Funny. We can go see it; I don't mind seeing it again."

"Yeah, right! When's the last time we went to a movie?" Nikki was bitter now.

"Well, we will just have to make the time. I mean, that's

what grandparents are for." Chris smiled. "Hey, don't forget that Mina is coming to dinner tomorrow."

"How could I forget? I can't wait to meet this *girlfriend* of yours," Nikki said, batting her eyelashes at Chris.

"Stop calling her that," Chris snapped, which only made Nikki more unsure of what was really going on between the two of them.

"I was just kidding, honey."

"Hey, you hungry?" Chris asked, changing the subject.

"Hungry? Chris, it's two a.m."

"I know, I know. But in the movie Jack and Diane had eggs and wine by candlelight. It was kinda cool. Wanna try it?" Chris said, dragging Nikki downstairs without even letting her put on her robe.

Nikki was still a little mad at Chris, but she really wanted to try hard not to ruin this moment the way she had so many others.

Chapter 25

Dinner with Mina

Chris got home from work, jumped in and out of the shower, and started to get dressed in a hurry. Nikki was downstairs doing her best to cook, while Corey crawled around the kitchen floor. Chris knew he had better get himself downstairs before Nikki got frustrated and the whole mood changed. Mina was expected to arrive at six thirty, only forty-five short minutes away. He was just about done when he heard Nikki call his name with distress in her voice.

"Coming, honey," Chris yelled ahead of him as he headed down the stairs. "The food looks great."

"Thanks, babe. Can you get Corey and keep an eye on him? I've got this."

Chris grabbed Corey, then took a seat at the kitchen table so they could keep Nikki company as she finished preparing the food.

"Oh, babe, I completely forgot to ask you—did you ever hook up with Jason?" Nikki asked. "How did that go?"

"Oh yeah, it was cool. It's so crazy that it's been over a year since I've seen him."

"Give me the scoop." Nikki put the final touches on the chicken Parmesan she had just taken out of the oven.

"Right, right. Um, he's actually doing really well. You would probably trip if you saw him, though; he's really thin."

"Thin?" Nikki repeated. "Since when?"

"Apparently he's a vegan now; he barely eats anything. He said he dropped like twenty-five pounds in two months when he first started eating the way he does now."

"So what's the difference between vegetarians and vegans?" asked Nikki.

"Hmmm . . . I'm not sure. I don't remember. I don't know what they eat, but I know what he doesn't eat."

"And that is?"

"I know they don't eat meat or dairy at all; he eats a lot of grains, beans, nuts, fruit, and vegetables."

"I wonder what made him decide to do that."

"He said that he was working on an animal cruelty case last year that changed his perspective on some things, and so he just decided he didn't want to eat animals or animal products anymore."

"Wow! What else is up with him as far as his life and his mental health go? Did he seem to be doing better with all the stuff he was going through? Is he finally getting some help?"

"Yeah, he found this counselor who has become his lifeline basically. He sees the guy weekly and he says it's the best thing that ever happened to him. He says that the majority of his therapy has involved writing a lot. He keeps this journal—actually, three of them: one for his dad, one for his mom, and one for his sister."

"He needs to buy another one . . . for Renee."

"True," Chris said, thinking back to all Jason had put Renee through. "It's hard to imagine that all of his family died; that's so terrible."

"His sister was like seven or eight, right, when she died in that car accident?"

"Yep, I think so," confirmed Chris.

"So, as far as his mom and what she did to him go, has he gotten past it some? Is he able to function in relationships with women better than when he was with Renee?"

"He says it's coming along." Chris got up to help Nikki start setting the table. "He has had maybe two relationships over the years that didn't work out all that well, but he says the main thing is that he's getting to know himself a little better."

"Well, I'm glad; I really like Jason. We should have him over for dinner sometime over the next few months."

"I think he'd like that," Chris said, checking his watch. "She'll probably be here any minute."

"I know. Okay, now it's Mi-*na,* right, not Mia?" Nikki asked.

"Yes, Mi-*na*."

"All right, babe, everything is ready. Let me just go and wash my hands and stuff, and I'll be right back down."

Just as Nikki was heading up the stairs, the doorbell rang. Chris offered to get it.

Nikki went upstairs and touched up her makeup a bit and made sure her hair was in place. She was feeling really nervous and unsure of what the evening would bring. When Kay suggested that Nikki invite Mina over to the house for dinner, it made perfect sense. It sounded like such a good idea—at the time—but now Nikki was having second thoughts and it was much too late for that. It wasn't like her to feel this way about a social situation, but it was the first time she had ever invited a female friend of Chris's to the house for dinner. Nikki wasn't really sure how she felt about it but was trying to be cool and just go with the flow. She felt like her hand had been forced in a way . . . due to the fact that Chris was dropping Mina's name way too much. She took one last look in the mirror and started downstairs.

Nikki smelled Mina before she saw her and recognized

the scent immediately. It just so happened to be her favorite—Donna Karan's Cashmere Mist. The only thing worse than the sound of another woman's voice in her house was her smell. When she rounded the corner she saw Chris and Corey standing in her kitchen with *Angel, Kay's friend from the cabin*. She was rendered unable to speak or think clearly. "Angel?" Nikki said. "What are you doing here?"

Chris was holding Corey, looking back and forth from Nikki to Mina, puzzled.

"No, honey, this is Mina," Chris said, looking at Mina as if to say . . . go ahead . . . tell her who you are.

"Um, no, this is Kay's friend Angel," Nikki said. "Where's Mina?" she asked out loud.

Chris put Corey down in his playpen in the living room.

Mina stood silently with a nervous smile on her face, just as confused and surprised as Nikki. "This is really weird . . . wow," Mina said. "Only me, something like this could only happen to me."

She looked at Nikki and realized she had better start explaining. "I can explain this. Really, I can. My name is Mina, but I go by Angel too. Angelina is my middle name and so I kinda got stuck with Angel growing up." She turned to Chris. "I met Nikki not too long ago for the first time when the girls took that trip to the cabin in the mountains. When I met Kay I introduced myself as Angel because that's what I go by outside of work. That's why Chris knows me as Mina and you know me as Angel, Nikki."

"And so you two work together?" Nikki asked.

Chris spoke for the first time. "Yes. *This* is Mina!"

"Yeah," Mina said, shrugging. "Small world, huh?" She wanted to leave at that moment. How could this be happening? What were the chances of Chris's Nikki being the same Nikki she had met a few months ago?

"You know what, guys, I can leave. It's probably best if I just go," Mina said.

"Why should you leave?" Chris asked. "I mean, there's nothing wrong. An uncanny coincidence, that's all. It's not like you lied or something."

Chris regretted making the statement before it finished coming out of his mouth. But it was true, Mina hadn't lied.

Nikki felt very weird about what was going on for some reason. She didn't trust Mina, Angel, or whatever the hell she was calling herself.

"So you didn't know that Chris was married to me?" Nikki asked suspiciously.

"No. Absolutely not. I mean, Chris told me his wife's name was Nikki, but it's not like it's an uncommon name and I never saw a picture of you, so the thought never crossed my mind."

"So you have *never* seen a picture of me? Chris has a picture of me on his desk, right, babe?" Nikki said, peering at Chris for an explanation.

"Yes. Of course I do, but she has never been in my office."

Nikki didn't know what to do with the sick feeling that had invaded her stomach. On one side she thought, *Okay, it's just Angel*, the nice, cool chick she had met at the cabin. This should almost be a relief. But then her mind revisited that moment at the truck after the horseback riding when it was clear that Angel and that young boy were up to no good. Maybe she didn't know Angel like she thought. And Chris definitely didn't know her as well as he thought he did. Men were so stupid.

Nikki realized that she would have to get through dinner somehow. She was just really anxious to tell Chris the truth about Mina. He was going to trip.

"Girl, what are you talking about, leaving?" Nikki asked. "You act like I don't know you. I just needed a minute. I mean, I was expecting to see a complete stranger and then it ends up being you. I'm straight now. Let's sit down and eat."

"Are you sure?" Mina asked, trying to look relaxed.

"We're sure," Chris said.

"Thank you so much for having me, or rather, for letting me stay," Mina said, smiling at both Chris and Nikki.

Mina began to unload the small bundle she had in her arms. "This is for you." She leaned down into the playpen, handing Corey a teddy bear that sang when its belly was squeezed. "And this is for the two of you," she said, handing Nikki a small gift-wrapped box and then giving Chris a bottle of wine with a bow on it. Nikki noticed that Angel had acknowledged her in the gift-giving before Chris. *Smart girl,* she thought.

"You didn't have to do this," Nikki protested.

"Yes, I did; I really appreciated the invite. And I know I'm little, but I do plan to eat. Chris says you can cook, so I'm looking forward to dinner."

Nikki thought to herself, *No, she didn't just point out how little and cute she was. The nerve.* "Well, let's eat," she suggested. "Everything is ready."

Nikki wasn't sure how to react to Angel. It was as if she was meeting her for the very first time. She couldn't concentrate. Her mind kept going back to when they were at the cabins. She revealed so much about herself that night; things that Chris didn't know about her. It was so damn weird. She didn't know how to feel about Mina turning out to be Angel. She wasn't sure if it was more or less of a threat.

They all headed toward the dining room, off to the left of the living room. Chris left Nikki and Mina alone and went to put on some music. He threw on Jill Scott's CD for background music. The girls and Corey were already seated by the time he got back. Their dining room table sat six people. Corey was at the head of the table in his high chair, Nikki was next to Corey, and Mina was seated right across from Nikki on the other side of the baby. Chris knew to take a firm seat right next to Nikki and did so, saying grace so they could get started.

Chris was a little leery of Mina. He didn't know what to think about her having met Nikki before. It seemed like something out of a movie. Like some fatal attraction shit. *Is it possible that this is just a coincidence? It has to be, right? I mean, what would be her reasoning in lying? What would she have to gain?* He decided to put it out of his mind for the time being. He would just have to feel her out from this point on more than ever. He was nevertheless impressed with Mina. She was acting just as he'd expected her to, showing Nikki and his home the utmost respect. That apart, she looked amazing. She had on a black skirt that came right above her knee and a pale yellow sweater that fit her perfectly, showing off all of her curves. Her breasts were bigger than Nikki's; they definitely stood out on her tiny frame. She was a "ten" all day long, and Chris was feeling more attracted to her than ever before. *I have to be careful not to mess this up,* he thought. He didn't want anything to go wrong—especially since Nikki had been so agreeable with the whole situation in the first place. And now with this added "coincidence," it could easily get very sticky.

Chapter 26

Satisfaction

"Okay, so you have to tell me all about yourself, Mina . . . I mean Angel . . . Well, what should I call you now? This is so weird," Nikki said.

"Oh, you can just call me Mina since that's how Chris knows me. I guess it would be too weird for you both to call me by a different name. This is so crazy. I'm so freaked out by this. Truly I am," Mina said, genuinely embarrassed.

"Okay. That's cool, Mina. I love that name, by the way," Nikki said, being fake as hell. She wasn't sure what her problem was exactly with the entire situation. She just knew she didn't like it. She wondered how much Chris knew about Mina. If he knew that she was a stripper. But most of all she wondered if he truly knew the person she was. The fact that Chris didn't appear to know about Nikki's past membership at Suede was the only thing that eased her mind. She figured if Mina truly had known that she was Chris's wife, and had bad intentions, Chris certainly would have confronted her by now. Or perhaps she told him not to tell her. She was going crazy. She knew she had to get Mina alone somehow and ask her straight up what the hell was going on.

"Yeah, Mina. Tell me about yourself, and I do mean Mina. I know a little bit about Angel but nothing about Mina. Chris probably left out all the good details. You know men." Nikki smiled. "You never mentioned where you worked or I would have known right off that you and Chris worked for the same company."

"I know," Mina said. "It just never really came up. If you remember, we didn't really talk about work all that much." She and Nikki smiled. Mina had managed to shut Nikki's line of questioning down. "But anyhow, let's see, I work at Marketing Zone, but not in Chris's department. I work in the travel department. I'm originally from Manhattan and just moved down here with my mother about eight months ago. I helped my mom get set up in a place in Midtown, and I live in a studio apartment downtown by myself." Mina took a bite of her food waiting on a response from either Chris or Nikki. The situation was really uncomfortable. She could tell Nikki wanted her to go.

"Oh, okay. I'm sure you won't be single long; you're so pretty." It really was hard for Nikki to take her eyes off Mina. Her beauty was one of those things that you could just get lost in. Somehow all of Mina's features came together in a way that made for an extremely exotic and beautiful look.

"Oh, thank you; so are you. I love your hair. I've been thinking about growing mine out," Mina replied.

Nikki could have done without the charity compliment, but she took it in stride. Not that Nikki didn't think that she herself looked good, but coming right after the compliment she gave Mina it just sounded forced.

"Do you like it?" Nikki asked Mina, referencing the highlights she had recently gotten done. "It's a new look for me."

"Yeah, it looks really nice. You didn't have highlights at the cabin, right?" Mina asked.

Nikki told her she had just had it done over the past week-end.

"Dinner is great, Nikki," Mina said, taking a sip of wine.

"Yeah, you really outdid yourself this time, hon," Chris said, breaking his silence.

"Thank you." Nikki smiled. "It's my first time doing chicken Parmesan, so I'm glad it came out all right."

"I could definitely use some cooking lessons," Mina said. "I spend way too much money eating out."

"It's so easy to do," Nikki said. "Just to grab something while you're out and bring it in to eat. Those days are over for us, though, with Corey here to keep us watching our spending."

Corey was sitting there looking adorable as usual, playing with his food.

"So have you been out much around town?" Nikki asked.

"Not really. I've been to maybe three spots since I've been here and they were okay."

"Let me guess, Visions, 112, and Havana Club?" Chris asked.

"Umm, no, none of those. Let me see if I can remember the names."

Nikki had that feeling in the pit of her stomach again. She had to know if Mina told Chris about her being a member at Suede. What would she do? Chris didn't know Nikki had gone to the club, and he would be pissed if he found out from someone he had just met . . . virtually a stranger. Nikki had to find a way to get Mina alone to talk to her. She could not let her leave without knowing.

"I did enjoy Taboo," Mina said. "The music and the crowd there were both great. Halo was okay, too. I can't remember the name of the other spot, but it was a salsa club, I think."

"Probably Tongue and Groove," volunteered Chris.

"Yeah, that's it, Chris," Mina said, her eyes lighting up. "I had a pretty good time there. It reminded me of New York; it kind of felt like a club from back home."

"So did you go to school in New York?" Nikki asked.

"No, I actually did my freshman year at a small private college in New York State."

"So what did you study there?"

"Well, I originally went in to study law but decided I just wasn't all that interested in it. I come from a family of lawyers and doctors, so I figured out pretty quickly that I was following my family's dream, not my own. I left there after the first year and then transferred to F.I.T. in New York City."

"F.I.T.?" Nikki asked, embarrassed that she didn't know what that was.

"Yes, Fashion Institute of Technology," Mina said proudly. "During my summers while I was in school, I would do some waitressing and then travel as much as possible. That's my true love: traveling."

Waitressing, my ass, Nikki thought. *You were stripping.*

Nikki loved the idea of Mina traveling; in fact the farther, the better. She thought it would be great if Mina would take her ass somewhere right at that moment . . . far, far away.

Now what was Nikki gonna do? She had a "perfect ten" sitting at her dinner table who was getting closer to her husband each day and she was screwed and she knew it. This was a bad, bad idea. She couldn't wait to talk to Kay and thank her for the advice to invite Chris's "girlfriend" over. *Speaking of Kay, how the hell didn't she know that Mina and Angel were the same person?* she thought. She couldn't wait to grill her about all of it.

Everyone had finished eating. That was Nikki's cue to get up and start clearing the table. Mina tried to help but Nikki politely refused the assistance.

"Chris, do me a favor and pour us some wine. You two go hang out in the living room while I get the table cleared off."

Mina smiled as she walked out of the kitchen with Nikki's husband and son.

Nikki quickly cleared off the table and considered calling Kay for some clarification but decided against it. There was really nothing to do at this point. This was one of those things she was going to have to ride out to the end. She walked into the living room to join Chris and Mina. Corey was sitting on the floor playing with toys, and Mina was sitting next to him in adoration. Nikki walked over to the table where the wine was and realized that Chris hadn't poured her any. He must have recognized his oversight because he reached for her glass at the exact same moment . . . but was too late. Nikki shot him a deadly glare and poured her own glass. She took a seat on their ottoman, and Corey left his spot near Mina to join his mother.

"Uh-oh," Mina exclaimed, "he has a spot on the back of his pants; I think he had an accident."

"I'll be right back," Nikki said, smiling and grabbing a hold of Corey's hand. Right at that moment she felt like disappearing and never coming back. She could hear Chris and Mina talking and laughing; it made her want to throw up. Things had changed so much since the baby had come, but it seemed like she was the only one affected. Chris's life had pretty much stayed the same. Nikki changed Corey's diaper and fought back tears. She felt like a shell of the person she used to be, like she wanted her old carefree life back. As she looked down at Corey she knew that he meant the world to her, but with that newfound life came many sacrifices that she wasn't always happy to make.

"This is so crazy," Mina whispered to Chris as soon as Nikki walked upstairs. "I'm so sorry about this."

"What the hell is going on, Mina? Did you know?"

"What? Hell no. How could I? Why wouldn't I tell you if I did?"

"I know. I don't know. It's just weird as hell, that's all."

"Tell me about it. It's crazy to think that I spent the weekend with your wife and didn't even know it."

"So then, aren't you and Kay friends? How is it possible that Kay didn't know that you worked at Marketing Zone?"

"She does know. I guess she just didn't think about it since Nikki told her my name was Mina."

"So how come you never told me you go by 'Angel'?"

"Chris, what's up with the third degree? Shit, it just never came up. Only my family and friends call me Angel."

"So I'm not a friend?"

"Of course you are, but it's different with you because we started out as coworkers."

"Yeah, but I met you at Frankie's."

"Right, and as far as I could tell you were neither my friend nor my family when we met, right?" Mina said, starting to get a little pissed at the questioning. It was apparent that Chris didn't trust her, and she didn't like it.

Nikki and Corey returned to the living room to find it empty. Chris was standing in the foyer talking to Mina. To Nikki's surprise, Mina had her coat on. Nikki didn't want to appear to be too excited about Mina's early departure, so she asked her if she was sure she had to go so soon.

"Yeah, I should let you guys enjoy the rest of your evening as a family."

Chris and Nikki walked Mina out to her car with Corey in tow. Nikki hadn't forgotten about wanting to talk to Mina privately. Corey was getting cranky in Chris's arms and wanted to get down. Nikki took advantage of the situation and suggested to Chris that he go inside and get Corey ready for bed while she said good-bye to Mina. Chris looked a little nervous as he walked away. He was actually proud of how Nikki had handled the situation. That's what he used to love most about Nikki: her confidence.

While they walked toward Mina's car Nikki made herself ask the question out loud. "Um, this is going to sound really weird," she warned, "but I have got to ask you something, Mina."

"Sure, what's up?"

"Did you mention to Chris what I told you at the cabins about being a member at Suede?"

"No, Nikki. As I said earlier, I had *no* idea that you were Chris's wife until I saw you."

"I know. I'm just being crazy. Listen," Nikki said, with a puppy dog look on her face, "Chris doesn't know about me and that place. I don't want you to think I'm out there like that. Please don't mention it to him. I would like to tell him myself when the time is right."

"Of course. I wouldn't think of telling him," Mina said, trying to hide the twinge of satisfaction in her face. She couldn't help but feel vindicated knowing that Nikki wasn't the perfect wife Chris always made her out to be, but nevertheless she had no intention of telling Chris about Nikki and Suede. Who the hell was she to judge? she thought. "Yeah, I won't say a word," Mina confirmed again. "Besides, Nikki, every marriage has secrets . . . from what I've heard. Right?"

Nikki felt forced to answer. "Yes, I guess every marriage does . . . and so does every friendship, right?" she said, letting Mina know that she had shit on her as well.

"Yeah, so I guess it goes both ways," Mina said. "What happened at the cabin stays at the cabin."

As Mina drove off, Nikki stood in her driveway with a feeling of regret. She knew at that moment that something had gone very wrong but couldn't appreciate how disastrous a mistake she had made by not only going to Suede, but by inviting Mina into her home and her life. She turned and went back into her house and tried her best to erase the look of devastation on her face.

* * *

Chris was in the living room when Nikki came back into the house closing the front door behind her, wanting to forget the conversation she'd just had with Mina. Nikki sat down in the living room looking at Chris longingly.

"We need to talk," Nikki told Chris.

"What's up?" Chris asked.

"Don't you think it's kind of weird that Angel and Mina are the same person? It seems like more than just a coincidence to me. Doesn't it to you?"

"Well, I thought it was a little odd at first too. I mean, it's definitely weird and ironic but I don't think she tried to hide anything if that's what you're asking. Am I missing something else?" Chris asked.

"Yeah, you're missing a lot. You have no idea who this person is you're dealing with," Nikki said.

"Who I'm dealing with? Why do you say it like that?"

"Did you know Mina used to be a stripper?" Nikki asked flat out.

The look on Chris's face gave him away completely. He was floored by the remark.

"A stripper?" Chris said, looking confused. Did she mean that she worked as a dominatrix? Was she just trying to be polite calling her a stripper? He decided not to spill that bit of knowledge until he felt her out more. "C'mon, babe, that sounds like something you and your girls came up with."

"We came up with? She told us herself at the cabins," Nikki said. "And that's not the worst of it. I would bet money that she hooked up with this teenage boy at the horseback riding spot we visited while we were there. He couldn't have been more than seventeen."

"What? You're tripping, Nikki. Why are you on her like this?"

"Me on her? Why are *you* on her like this?" Nikki asked.

"Like what? We're just friends. Calm down, you're making this more than it needs to be, seriously. Mina is my friend, that's it, no more, no less," Chris said.

"Yes, that may be true now, but you don't know her like you think you do."

"Well, I haven't had that much time to learn everything there is to know. Is that a crime?"

"No, I guess it's not but I just don't feel comfortable with this thing between you and her," Nikki finally said.

"Oh, I get it. So this is the part where you start telling me who I can and can't talk to? Is that where you're going with this?" Chris asked.

"Well, what do you want me to do, just stand by and watch you make this mistake? I'm not trying to control you; I don't trust her," Nikki said.

"This is classic," Chris said.

"Funny enough, you know who Mina reminds me of?" Chris didn't give Nikki a chance to respond.

"She reminds me of *you,* Nikki," Chris said. "Based on what I know about her so far, she seems like an intelligent, ambitious woman who enjoys meeting people and having a good time."

"Yeah, a real good time," Nikki said, crossing her arms.

"How quickly we forget about how to have a good time, Nikki. Have you forgotten your key party days? Your days of wanting to be all up in women's strip clubs with your friends, and who knows what else?" Chris remarked. "Since when did you start judging people like this?"

"Since they became a threat to my marriage and family!" Nikki said.

"A threat to your marriage and family? You're taking this too far . . . way out of proportion," Chris said. "And even if you don't trust Mina, what happened to you trusting me?"

"It's not like that, Chris. I do trust you, but women are sneaky."

"All women or just Mina?" Chris asked, taking a stab at Nikki.

"Fuck you, Chris," Nikki said. "I'm so sick of you and this thing. And I'm sick of sounding like a nagging wife. You're right, you're a grown-ass man, do what you want. But for the record, I'm asking you to stop seeing her." Nikki got up and walked out of the living room, going upstairs to be alone. Chris didn't even try to stop her. She hated him for that. For letting her walk out of that room in shambles. The tears came suddenly and wouldn't stop flowing. Nikki dialed Kay's number hesitantly and then got ready to hang up, but Kay picked up before she could.

"Hello? Nikki?"

"Hey, Kay."

"What's going on? How are you?"

"I'm cool, but listen, this is going to sound weird but you know that tonight was the night I had Chris's little girlfriend over, right?"

"Oh yeah, how did that go? Was she cool or do you hate her? Tell me how it went."

"It turns out that Mina is your girl Angel," Nikki said.

There was silence on Kay's end. "I don't get it. What do you mean?" she asked.

"Just what I said. When I came downstairs, your friend Angel was standing in my living room and Chris introduced her as Mina."

"Wait, wait, how could this be? Help me understand what it is you're saying," Kay said.

"She said she goes by Mina at work, which is why Chris knows her by that, but with close friends and family she goes by Angel."

There was silence on the line as Kay tried to process the information Nikki had just shared with her. "Damn, I don't know what to say. I mean, talk about coincidences," she said.

"Yeah, well, I don't understand how you didn't know, Kay. I mean, I told you Mina worked at Marketing Zone. Didn't you know that Angel worked there?"

"Well, yeah, I did, but I just never put the two together. I remember thinking that both Angel and Chris worked there, but I had no reason to think that Mina and Angel were the same person. Why would I?"

"I don't trust her," Nikki said.

"I don't think you have a reason not to trust her, Nikki, not yet," Kay said.

"Yeah, but do you even know her all that well?" Nikki asked.

"Do we ever really know anybody?" Kay asked.

"My point exactly, so there's no telling what this chick is all about."

"Well, I haven't talked to her that much since we got back from the cabin, just an e-mail here and there but nothing extensive, no real conversation."

"And she didn't mention befriending a married man?"

"Nope. She sure didn't."

"You don't think that's strange?"

"Not really, Nikki. Where is all of this coming from? It almost seems like you would be a little relieved that she turned out to be Angel. I thought you liked Angel."

"Are you fucking kidding me? Yeah, Angel seemed like a cool chick before I found out she could be possibly fucking my husband!"

"You think they're fucking?"

"Kay, I'm hanging up now. I can't talk to you right now. You're killing me."

"Nikki, calm down. Let me process this. I'm just saying that nothing has really changed just because you found out that Mina and Angel are the same person."

"What do you mean? Everything has changed!"

"Like what exactly?" Kay asked.

"Okay, first of all she was a stripper who had sex with random men for money. Second, she most likely fucked that boy at the stables. And third, she knows my fucking secret. She knows things that I haven't even told Chris about."

"Ah . . . okay. I see your point. I can see why you're a little concerned."

"A little? Kay, are you serious? I told Chris tonight that he can't see her anymore."

"Really? What did he say?"

"I didn't even wait for his response. I stormed up the stairs and called you."

"Stop tripping, Nikki, it will be fine. I can't wait to talk to her, though, and see what's up," Kay said.

"Well, you know you better call me as soon as you do. I want to hear how tonight went for her. I was as nice as I could be," Nikki said. "Under the circumstances I think I did great."

"I'm sure you did," Kay said sarcastically. "Get some rest. I know you're worn out, man."

"Good-bye. I'll talk to you later," Nikki said.

"Later, girl," Nikki heard Kay say faintly as she hung up the phone, lying back on her pillow. She closed her eyes, wanting the night that had just happened to go away, but instead visions of Mina laughing and smiling were stuck in her mind and kept swimming in her head. She wanted them to stop but they wouldn't. She wanted Mina and Angel both to go away for good.

Chapter 27

The Living Room

Nikki was thankful for her night out with Renee and Kay as she shut down her computer and headed to the Living Room. The Living Room was a spot Nikki had chosen for all of them to meet. The planner in her had been reawakened when Kay suggested that they get together. Nikki was on an e-mail list for new spots and events going on in Atlanta. The Living Room was supposed to be really nice. The thing that set it apart from other clubs was that the only seating in the entire place was couches and love seats. No chairs at all, except at the bar. It was the perfect setting for a few girlfriends to get together and chat. She was excited sitting there waiting for Kay and Renee to arrive. It was times like this when she missed Lynda the most, but she knew that she was happy with Shay in Cali. How uncomplicated their lives must be, she thought, to not have to deal with a man. As she waited, she thought back to her night with Mina and Chris and how grueling it all was. She hoped that Chris would do the right thing and stop seeing her, but at the same time she was afraid that he would resent her for trying to control his life as he so rudely said to her last night. Either way, she knew in her heart that she needed some time away from him and the baby. She couldn't wait for this time to chill out and have a drink.

The waitress brought her drink out just in time. "I love your shoes," the scrawny young girl told Nikki, who was psyched by the compliment. She paid almost 180 dollars for them—a black and peach pump with the cutest little bow tied around the heel—and had been holding out on them for a special occasion.

"Oh, thank you so much; they're my favorite."

"Yeah, very cute," the waitress said, leaving Nikki alone to twirl her ankles around, admiring her own shoes.

"No, you are not just sitting there smiling at how good you look," a familiar voice sneered. Nikki looked up and saw Kay and Renee standing in front of her. Kay had her lips twisted up at Nikki . . . like she was too much.

"No, I—"

"Whatever, girl; you are a trip," Renee said, scooting by Kay to give Nikki a hug.

"Nice shoes, girl," Kay remarked.

"Thanks."

"So what's up with this spot? It looks kind of cool. Nothing but couches, huh?"

"Yup, couches and living room tables," added Nikki.

"They're so comfortable, too; we could be here all night," Renee joked.

"That's the plan." Nikki winked at her. The waitress came back over, took drink orders, and asked if they wanted to see menus. The girls agreed that they were okay with just drinks for the time being. When the waitress walked away, they started in on their conversation almost immediately. "I've had the longest damn week," Renee complained. "This is just what I needed, Nikki."

"Meeee too," Kay said. "So how are you doing really?"

she asked, not sure if Nikki wanted to talk about what had happened with Angel in front of Renee.

"I'm here, Kay. I really needed to get out," Nikki said. "I've been feeling stressed out lately, especially since last night. I'm just not really like myself. I mean, every now and then I feel completely drained with Corey and trying to keep up with my wifely duties with Chris." Kay and Renee nodded in agreement, but Nikki knew they couldn't truly understand since neither of them had children. "But it's a different kind of stress," she added, "like I feel nervous that something bad is going to happen or something."

"Really? What happened last night? Does this have something to do with Chris and that chick you told me about?" Renee asked.

Kay put her drink down on the table after taking a huge sip. She knew what Nikki was going to say. She decided to help her out.

"Something really weird happened when Nikki met Chris's girlfriend," Kay said.

"She is not his girlfriend!" Nikki snapped.

"Sorry, Nikki. My bad. Chris's new female friend," Kay said, correcting herself.

"So what happened? Get to it," Renee said.

"I'll tell her," Nikki interrupted. "It turns out that Chris's little friend from work is really Angel. You know, Kay's friend Angel? Apparently, she goes by another name at her job, Mina. When Chris met her at work he was introduced to her as Mina. Kay was introduced to her as Angel. I was completely floored to find out it was Angel."

"What the hell is that all about?" Renee asked, looking at Kay for answers.

"Why are you looking at me?" Kay asked Renee defensively. "Nikki came to me and told me that about three months ago Chris came home and basically told her that he had a friend named Mina, that he'd met her at work, and that she'd recently relocated from New York. She said that they had gone to lunch a few times and that she was really cool—and harmless. How was I supposed to know that Mina and Angel were the same person?"

"So the fact that she was from New York and worked at Chris's job didn't clue you in a little, Kay?"

"Come on, Renee. I mean, why would I think that, if they had two different names? I never thought they were the same person."

"So no one knew her last name?" Renee asked, continuing to grill Kay and Nikki.

"I never asked what her last name was. Chris always just called her Mina, so that's all I needed to know about her. Shit, I didn't even know what Angel's last name was, much less Mina. Damn, this is weird. I still feel like I'm talking about two different people."

"So hold on for a second. I still say that's weird, Nikki," Renee observed.

"Which part?" Nikki asked.

"Well . . . the fact that he told you about her at all."

"Nah, that sounds like Chris," Nikki and Kay both agreed.

"Okay, so he's just so great that he wants to be open and honest with you about everything?" Renee asked, looking directly at Nikki.

"Well, I guess it does sound kind of weird but yeah, he always tells me stuff; he's a pretty good guy, I thought, or I think," Nikki said somberly.

Renee just shook her head in disbelief.

"Well, the story gets crazier," Kay cautioned. "She came to their house for dinner last night." She couldn't help but butt in.

"She came where?" Renee asked, looking at Nikki in total shock.

"Kay is the one that told me to invite her over," Nikki explained, pointing at Kay.

"Oh no, this is nuts," Renee conceded. "You never invite another woman into your house. Are you crazy?"

"Why do I have to be crazy?" Nikki asked.

"Well, Kay," asserted Renee, "maybe I should be asking you that question since you're the one that told Nikki to invite her over."

"I invite *you* over to my house," Kay said, taking a stab at Renee.

"What the hell is that supposed to mean? I'm your sister," Renee fired back.

"Oh God. Please don't start, ladies," Nikki said, breaking it up.

Renee cut her eyes at Kay, waiting for an apology.

"What? Okay, okay. Sorry. I'm just saying that I'm not crazy," Kay protested. "I thought it was a good idea. I mean, she was stressed out about this girl and wanted to know what she was all about, so I thought, what better way to feel out your competition than to meet them face-to-face?"

"Okay, so how did dinner go then?" Renee urged.

"Well, she came over, and all of us had dinner at the house: me, Chris, her, and Corey. It was just really weird because I was expecting to be meeting Mina and meanwhile I'm staring at Angel across my dinner table all night like she was a total stranger. I just wanted her to go home." Nikki got quiet, obviously pulling up memories of Angel in her mind.

"Okay, let's put the issue on the table," Kay proposed. "On a scale of one to ten, what do you think you are?"

"You mean like in terms of my looks?" Nikki asked.

"Yeah," Kay said.

"I'd say a seven—with my clothes on; probably a five and a half with them off these days."

"Nikki, you're being ridiculous and you know it," Kay said, shaking her head back and forth. She couldn't believe how low Nikki's confidence had gotten in such a short time. She used to be the most confident woman she knew. "And how about Angel, in your opinion what is she?" she asked Nikki. "Be straight up."

"Okay, okay, okay. With her clothes on, she's a fucking ten, and with her clothes off, she's probably a twenty!" Nikki griped, grabbing her drink and taking two more sips.

"She's right," Renee said, nodding her head.

"Yes, we have a major problem here," Kay agreed.

"So did you talk to her, Kay?" Nikki asked. "I'll assume no since you didn't call me."

"I tried to call her but she's not returning my calls. I left her like three messages today. I don't want to have anything else to do with her anyway," Kay said. "Not knowing that she's trying to diss my girl. Besides, she's the one that dissed me first, really. She hasn't really called me since we went to the cabins. I spoke to her maybe like once. I thought we were going to hit it off better than that, but I guess she got too caught up in *your* man to worry about me."

"I told him I wanted him to stop seeing her. Do you think I made a mistake?" Nikki was desperate. "Isn't it possible that Chris is telling me the truth about her?"

"I think you did the right thing. I mean, he had no idea what he was getting himself into," Kay said.

"So you don't think men and women can be friends?" Nikki asked.

"Nope, there's no way," Kay professed. "Not in my eyes."

"Well, I think it depends on who the friend is. I mean, I wouldn't want Derrick having a female friend who looked like Angel," Renee said. "But if he knew her before he met me, like if they grew up together or something, what can you do? It would be weird with her calling the house and stuff, but I would have to accept it. And in that case she would probably be more like a sister to him than anyone he would want to have sex with."

"Yeah, but I still think it's hard, even if they knew each other all of their lives. Men are no joke. They'll have sex with anyone." Kay was thinking about Kevin and how he didn't seem to mind that Renee was her sister when he fell for her.

"I have several friends from my past that I still keep in touch with," Nikki pointed out, "and that's all they are to me—*friends*. It can work . . . especially when two people love each other as much as Chris and I do. I mean, that's why I feel so hypocritical telling him that he has to stop seeing her just because she is a woman . . . but it's so much more now because I know what kind of woman she is. I didn't before. That's why I said he could initially, but now I'm dying! Chris knows a few of my male friends . . . and look at all the shit I've gotten Chris into in the past."

"Listen, Nikki," Kay said. "Chris is a great guy—we all know that—but when it comes down to it, all I'm saying is that men are naturally attracted to women . . . especially pretty ones. And under the wrong circumstances, they would probably cross lines that they shouldn't as married men."

"It just sucks," Nikki said. "This is not how I wanted my marriage to go. I never wanted to be that jealous, insecure wife who forbids her husband to be around other women. I'm just so screwed up, guys. I can't believe I'm letting her get to me like this. You should have seen the way Chris looked at me last night when I was whining and insisting that he stop seeing her. He was looking at me like I was a stranger. And then he had the nerve to tell me that she reminded him of me, like that was supposed to make me feel better or something."

"Yeah, but, Nikki . . . you have always been wayyyy too open-minded. I used to look at you two like you were from another planet."

"Great. And now we're like every other couple out there. Boring."

"See, that's your problem, Nikki. And it always has been. You can't have it all. Marriage comes with rules. Period! You just can't go out doing what you wanna do without expecting any consequences. You spoiled Chris with all of your talk about openness and trust. You gave him the key to bring Angel into your life," Renee lectured.

"Thanks, Renee. That's just what I needed to hear tonight," Nikki said sarcastically.

Renee just shook her head.

"So what now? Are you two going to be all right?" Kay asked.

"I don't know, Kay. First of all, I don't even know if he's told her to go to hell yet. Like I said, I haven't spoken to him since last night, but I'll just have to tell him that it's only because of what I know about her why I asked him to stop seeing her, not because she's a woman."

"So do you really believe that?" Kay asked.

"What?"

"That you're only upset because she turned out to be Angel?"

"Yup."

"You're lying. You were upset before that. You were upset from the beginning," Kay said. "I don't know why you can't just admit that you're human too and that it bothers you to see Chris with another woman. A beautiful woman at that. You always want everyone to think that you're so tough. But you know good and well that you were struggling from the start."

"Well, damn, Kay. Okay, yes, I was. Is that what you want to hear? But I'm saying I wouldn't have said anything if I didn't know she was Angel. It just sucks to me that now I'm sure Chris will look at me crazy when one of my male friends calls the house. I just left myself wide open."

"They can still call, you just don't tell him about it," Kay said, motioning the waitress over for the check.

"So is that why Kevin doesn't have a problem with you

having male friends? He just doesn't know about them?" Nikki argued.

"Yeah, well . . . what he doesn't know won't hurt him."

"Oh, I get it. So everybody just lies—is that it? That's so hypocritical," Nikki acknowledged. She had never liked the idea of lying to Chris. Not that she hadn't done it, but she didn't like it.

"Well, tell me this," Kay demanded, "whoever these male friends of yours are, do they just outright call your house? And when Chris answers, do they ask for you? Is that how it goes?"

"Well, not exactly. I mean—"

"I thought so," interrupted Kay.

"I'm just maintaining certain relationships that are important to me," Nikki informed the girls.

"So you're lying to Chris, then," charged Renee.

"Don't say it like that," begged Nikki.

"Well, if you're not telling him that you're talking to these 'friends' on your cell or at work, then it's lying," Renee stated.

"Whatever. They're just friends, platonic friends that I had before Chris and that, God forbid, I'll have after him. But I tell you what—I'm not going out with these guys. I mean—shit!—Chris is acting like this chick is Kevin or something. They go out to the movies, they play racquetball, and they go to lunch all the time together. I'm so sick of this bitch, I don't know what to do."

"He goes to the movies with her?" Kay asked, shocked. "What the fuck—Nikki, this has got to stop. I'm so glad you finally put your foot down."

"So I did the right thing, then, right? I don't know why I'm struggling so hard with this."

"I think you need to tell Chris that you're not comfortable with him hanging out with Angel outside of work one on one," Renee suggested. "But I don't think I would forbid him to see her. I mean, he does work with her. That's a bit much. It's so dramatic."

"I know. It really sucked to have to tell him that. I mean, I don't own Chris, and he doesn't own me. Who am I to tell him he can't have lunch with someone just because she's pretty? I'm telling you, he's going to think I'm insecure."

"Are you?" Kay asked.

"Yes, lately, I am."

"How do you know what Angel's intentions really are?" Renee asked.

"She doesn't know," Kay said. "I mean, even though we know Angel, that doesn't mean she can totally be trusted."

"I'm sure Chris likes her. Hopefully, he's not going to fall in love with her or something crazy like that."

"No way!" Renee said. "Chris loves you. But you do need to make sure you're doing your part in the marriage."

"Are you guys having other problems? In the bedroom or just in general?" Kay asked.

Nikki was ashamed to admit it. "Yes, we are and it's all my fault. I'm soooo tired all the time. Between Corey and work, I barely want to have sex. We had sex the other day for the first time since we got back from the cabins," she said, deflated.

"So how often are we talkin'?" Kay asked. "Once a month? Twice? What?"

"Um, I guess like twice a month or something," Nikki admitted.

Kay and Renee both took a drink from their glasses at that point.

"What do you want me to do? I work, I cook, I clean, and I take care of Corey; I'm tired!" Nikki said in an attempt to defend herself.

"Too tired to have sex with your husband?" Kay asked.

"Kay, you don't have kids, so you don't understand,"

Nikki lectured. "I'm so happy that you and Kevin are still at it like newlyweds."

"I didn't say all that," Kay corrected.

"So don't you think Chris probably misses that?" Renee asked.

"Yeah, no shit, Renee! But most times I'm too tired to care."

Renee didn't take offense to what Nikki had said; she knew her friend was just frustrated.

"I just—I don't know what the hell to do. Am I really just handing my husband over to this chick on a silver platter?"

"Yes, you are," Kay told her, "but it's not too late."

Renee scooted close to Nikki on the couch and reached her just as she broke down. "It's okay," she said, letting Nikki cry on her shoulder. Renee and Kay looked at each other, not knowing what to really say.

Nikki looked up and started wiping her tears, trying to get it together. "I think my main problem is that I'm just not as confident as I used to be: That's the bottom line. It sucks. Ever since I had Corey, my mind-set has changed. Instead of feeling like Chris's wife, I feel like the mother of his son. Mina reminds me of myself a few years back—so full of life and energy, I wanted to take on the world. Now all I feel like doing is sleeping when I get home. It's crazy. I do feel confident about one thing, though: I trust my husband."

"Yeah, but he's also a man, Nikki, and men just don't spend time with beautiful, sexy women without secretly wanting to hit it," Kay hinted. "So stop beating yourself up. You did the right thing by telling him to stop seeing her."

"So do you guys really think he's screwing her?" Nikki asked.

"Umm, maybe not yet, but it's inevitable, in my opinion," Renee predicted, barely able to look Nikki in the eye.

"Yeah, I mean, Nikki, he really shouldn't be spending this much time with any woman other than his wife," Kay warned.

"All I can say is that I understand where you're coming from as for not wanting to look jealous and insecure, telling him he can't see her anymore, but the consequence of that is that this girl is spending quality time with your husband. Quality time you should be spending with him," Kay reminded Nikki. "So again, you did the right thing. The ball is in Chris's court now. He's the one that's going to have to honor your request and stop seeing her."

"We're going to get you through this," Renee promised.

"Yup, we've got you, Nikki," Kay said. "We won't let Angel mess up anything between you and Chris. But a lot of this is on you. You need to find some energy."

"Yeah, you've got major work to do," added Renee. "You have to bring back the Nikki he fell in love with. For real!"

Nikki collected herself, wiping the tears from her face. She knew they were right. She had to get herself together before it was too late.

Chapter 28

Tough Choices

After a grueling day at work, Chris decided to take advantage of Nikki being out with the girls and hook up with Mina. He asked Kevin to pick up Corey and to watch him for a few hours. It was clear that Mina had avoided him all day. She usually called him on his way to work and then he would see her at lunch. His phone didn't ring once and when he tried to call her to see if she wanted to do lunch he just got her voice mail. He knew she was at work, though, because he did see her car in the parking lot when he pulled in that morning. He decided that the best thing he could do was wait by her car. She had to go home at some point, he figured. After about ten minutes he saw her weaving through the other cars in the parking lot to get to hers. Mina noticed him standing there.

"What's up?" she said glumly.

"Hey, stranger. How are you?" Chris said, nudging Mina's shoulder with his. Chris could tell that she looked down. Sad. It made him sad. He wasn't sure why she had been avoiding him. He didn't feel as if he gave her any reason to think that he didn't believe what she said last night.

"Stranger? I just saw you yesterday."

"Damn, girl. What's going on with you? It's obvious you've been avoiding me today. I haven't heard from you all day."

"Ohhhhh . . . poor Chris. Did I bruise your ego?" Mina said sarcastically as she proceeded to open her car door.

"Wait a minute now. Where is this coming from, Mina? Where are you going? Can we talk?" Chris said, placing his hand on hers in an attempt to stop her from turning her key.

"Talk about what, Chris? You and your wife made it perfectly clear that you didn't trust me, like I was some crazy bitch trying to run a game on you and your family."

"What? How did you come to that conclusion? I mean, it was definitely weird what happened. Don't you agree? But it's not like I blamed you or anything."

"Yeah, it was weird but shit happens sometimes. I don't see the big deal really, and then you started grilling me, asking me a bunch of questions like I had an agenda or something."

"That's not true, Mina. I mean, I was asking legitimate questions. I didn't know what else to think. It all just happened so fast. I didn't really have time to process it all."

"Well, process this. I'm not crazy. I'm not a stalker. When I met Nikki at the cabins I thought she was really great. We really hit it off. All of us did. I had absolutely no idea that she was your wife until yesterday."

"So when I told you my wife's name was Nikki, you didn't think to mention that you had just met a woman named Nikki a few months ago?"

"I thought it to myself. But I didn't say it out loud. I have no reason that I can come up with on why. It just wasn't that big of a deal. I never would have thought that that woman at the cabins was your wife."

"What's that supposed to mean?"

"It means just what I said. When I pictured your wife, the Nikki I met at the cabins is not what I came up with in my head."

"Why?"

"No reason."

"Well, you must have a reason. What? Did you think my wife was some tame, innocent housewife or something?"

"Don't be ridiculous, Chris. I knew she worked."

"Oh . . . but tame and innocent, huh?"

"Chris, what do you want from me? Why are you here?"

"I just wanted to talk to you, Mina. I was worried when I didn't hear from you this morning."

"Why? I mean, it's not like I'm your girlfriend or something. I don't have to check in with you every day."

"Come on. Don't be like that. You know what I mean."

"No, Chris. I really don't. I mean, what exactly are we doing, huh?" Mina said, getting a little choked up. She was tired of wanting Chris and not being able to have him. Meeting Nikki last night and seeing him with her and his son really opened her eyes. He was a family man. Married. Unavailable.

"I thought we were friends," Chris weakly replied.

"Okay. Well, *friend,* I have to go home now. I've had a long day and I'm not in the mood to chat it up with you this evening," Mina said, attempting to open her car door again.

Chris stopped her again. He held her face in his hands and wiped the tear that rolled down her cheek.

"What do you want from me, Mina? I don't understand what's going on here," he said, gazing into her tearful eyes.

"*I don't want anything from you!*" Mina screamed and broke free of the hold Chris had on her. "Just leave me alone, Chris. Please just leave me alone."

Chris knew that this was his free pass to let her go and never look back. She did what *he* came there to do. She ended their relationship. He should have been relieved but he wasn't. It made him sad. He didn't want it to go down like this. He didn't want her to walk out of his life hating him. Mad at him. Sad.

"Okay, okay, okay. Mina, listen to me," he said, blocking her entrance to her car door yet again. "Just hear me out. Please."

Mina wanted to sock him in his eye. She wanted to cuss him out. Tell him to go to hell. But she couldn't resist him. She was falling in love with him and it scared her because she knew he would never leave Nikki. Never.

"What is it, Chris?" Mina said, sounding defeated.

"Whatever this is, whatever is going on with you we can fix. I don't want you to go. Not like this. I really like having you around. It's been fun. Different. I enjoy spending time with you. I don't care if your name is Angel or Mina. I don't care what you've done."

"What did Nikki tell you?"

"That doesn't matter. What does matter is that I don't judge you. I'm not like that."

"Chris, what did she tell you?" Mina was steaming inside. She couldn't believe that Nikki told Chris her secrets but conveniently left out her own. She wanted to spill everything to Chris. She wanted to tell him that his wife was no better. That she was a liar and a slut who traipsed around naked in a sex club while her husband was at home trusting her every word. She was so pissed she couldn't even see straight. It made her rethink her entire plan of action. She had decided once she left Chris's house last night that she was going to leave him alone. Do the right thing for a change. It was one thing to try and seduce a stranger's husband, but when she found out it was Nikki she actually felt bad for all of the subtle, flirtatious things she had ever said to Chris. She decided that he was off-limits. She liked Nikki when she met her at the cabins. She would never want to break up her home. But when she realized that Nikki told Chris her secrets, secrets they all swore would stay at the cabin, she became vindictive. Spiteful.

"So are you going to tell me what Nikki told you?"

"All right. I do have a few questions."

"Oh, here we go. What?"

"Did you have sex with a kid while you were at the cabins?" Chris asked.

Mina paused. She was completely and utterly devastated that she had to answer to that. She wasn't sure how to handle the question. She could definitely lie. Nikki never really saw her with him. It was obvious as hell but she never really saw him. She couldn't prove it.

Or she could come clean and see how Chris would react. After all, she did do it and liked it and it was part of who she was.

"Yes."

"Wha . . . yes? You did have sex with a kid?" Chris stuttered.

"Yep. What else do you wanna know?" Mina said confidently.

"Why? Why would you do that? How old was he?"

"Oh, I don't know. I think seventeen going on eighteen or something like that. And why? Well, he was hot. He was into me. I was turned on by how innocent he appeared. How anxious he was to be with me. Should I go on?" Mina said with her hands on her hips. "What else did she tell you? That I was a stripper? That I did parties? That I got paid to have men stick dildos up my ass? What else?"

"Damn. Mina, look. You don't have to . . ."

"Don't have to what, Chris? I mean, you wanted to know, right? Nikki felt the need to tell you all of my dirty little secrets, right? So there it is," Mina said, turning away now in shame. She tried to put up a good front, but the truth was, she never wanted Chris to know that side of her. She never wanted him to know about any of it.

"Mina, stop crying. It's okay. Why are you crying?"

"Because I know what you're thinking. You're thinking I'm some sex addict or some nasty stripper who sold her body for money."

"Mina, look. I don't know what kind of impression I gave you, but I'm not some innocent guy who has never seen the world. Damn. You make me out to be some kind of saint or something. I'm far from perfect. Far from a saint. Trust me. I go to strip clubs. I know what goes on there. And I like it. So I'm not tripping on you for that. And the only thing I'm gonna say about the kid you had sex with is that you need to be careful on that tip because you could straight-up go to jail for some shit like that."

Mina looked up at Chris with tears flowing down her cheeks once again. She couldn't believe that he could be more perfect than he was until now. "Well, at least give me a chance to explain."

"You don't have to explain, Mina. And I told Nikki the same thing. It's none of my business what you did or do with your life."

"Oh, because we're just *friends,* right?" Mina said, smiling at Chris for the first time.

"Yeah. Something like that," Chris said, finally relieved that he had broken through to Mina.

"All right, Chris."

"So are we cool?" Chris asked.

"Yup. We're cool. So you missed me, huh?" Mina said. "That's kinda cute."

"I never said I missed you now. That's a bit of an exaggeration, don't you think?"

"Hmph. Whatever you say, Chris. Whatever you say. So do you wanna go grab a drink?"

"Nah. I can't. I have to go rescue Kevin from Corey. He's probably under the table about right now hiding."

"Okay. Well, I'm glad we talked. Cleared the air. So I'll see you tomorrow, then?" she said, giving Chris a hug.

She felt good in his arms, Chris thought to himself as he squeezed her tight. He couldn't believe that he didn't tell her that he couldn't see her again. It was harder than he thought it was going to be. He was starting to feel a little addicted to Mina. He was going to have to just break it to her another day. He would have to find the right time. He didn't know what had just happened. He just knew he didn't like seeing her sad and he didn't like her being mad at him and most of all he wasn't ready to let her walk out of his life.

Chris didn't realize how much time had passed by the time he picked Corey up from Kevin and Kay's and got home. He was devastated to find that Nikki had beat him home.

"What's up, Nikki? Early night?" Chris said, bending down to give Nikki a kiss.

"Yeah, Kay had some work she had to do and Renee dissed us for her new man so we all cut out a little early after some well-needed drinks. Here, let me take the baby. Where were you? Where did you take him?" Nikki said, heading upstairs to put Corey down.

"Oh. I didn't. I just asked Kevin to pick him up for me tonight. I ended up having to work later than I thought. I have another huge project on the table and I had to prep for a presentation I have in the morning." Chris couldn't believe how easily the lies started to roll out of his mouth. It was starting to scare him, the effect Mina had on him.

When Nikki came back downstairs she joined Chris on the couch.

"So how was your night out with the girls?"

"Are we going to talk about this at all, Chris?"

"Talk about what?"

"Mina."

"Oh. Her. Umm. What about her? I thought we said all we had to say about her last night."

"So you're going to stop seeing her, then?"

"Nikki, what do you mean stop seeing her? I mean, you make it seem as if I'm dating her. We're just friends."

"So what you're saying is that you are *not* going to stop seeing her? Is that what I'm hearing?"

"Nikki. She works with me. What do you want me to do. Avoid her?"

"Chris. Don't patronize me. You know what I mean. I don't want you going to the movies with her . . . to lunch. I don't want you playing racquetball with her. Period. Done."

Chris knew he was being ridiculous. He had no choice but to agree to what Nikki was asking. "Oh. Of course. Sure. I don't have to hang out with her anymore if that's what you want."

"Yep. That's what I want," Nikki said, pleased with herself.

Chris wasn't sure what his next move should be where Mina was concerned, but he knew he had to make things right with him and Nikki, so that's what he did.

"So do you wanna watch a movie? I got *Mystic River* on DVD yesterday thinking we could watch that," Chris said, scooting closer to Nikki.

"Sure. Let me run and put my pajamas on. I'll be right back."

Nikki ran up the stairs, leaving Chris to ponder on what he was going to do about Mina. He knew Nikki was right. And then he heard Kevin's words coming back to haunt him: *You need to leave this girl alone if you don't want trouble.*

Chapter 29

House Party

Nikki had really started focusing on Chris more than anything, taking the advice of Kay and Renee and trying to spice things up a bit in the bedroom, to turn his head back in the right direction. She had to admit she hadn't really given him much of a reason to be all that interested in her lately. She knew she was guilty of giving her husband every reason in the world to lose interest in her and their sex life. She had been coming to bed most nights in a T-shirt, shorts, and a scarf tied around her head. Sleep was so much more attractive to her than Chris ninety percent of the time, but she decided she needed to work hard at making herself more desirable to Chris. It had been a few weeks since Mina revealed herself as Angel and vice versa and turned her life upside down. Since Chris agreed not to see Mina again, things had calmed down a bit and she was looking forward to spoiling Chris like she used to back in the day.

Nikki was excited about the visit she had planned to her parents. When she was with them and the baby, it was the closest thing to a break that she got. She told Chris that she was going to go ahead and stay overnight at her parents', and he was more than okay with it. He could probably use the break himself, not having to worry about her or the baby for a change. She knew that Kevin had called, trying to feel Chris out to see what was up for the weekend. Chris surprised her by telling Kevin he hadn't been feeling all that great and that he was going to hang at home and get some rest. She kind of liked the fact that he hadn't planned some elaborate night out with the boys like he usually did just because she wouldn't be home.

Chris was kicked back watching some home improvement show, happy as hell to have the house to himself. A few times he jumped up thinking he heard Corey crying upstairs, then realized that he wasn't even there—his nerves were bad. The phone rang a couple of times, and he just let whoever it was leave a message. He didn't want to talk to anybody about anything. Period. His last couple of weeks at work had been hectic as hell, with all kinds of deadlines coming to a head. Penny stayed late three or four nights to help him in any way that she could. She was his biggest help. He welcomed the work. He was able to blow Mina off each time she wanted to do lunch or grab a drink after work. He missed hanging out with her, though. He couldn't believe how much. Now the weekend had finally arrived, and he didn't want to do a thing. Kevin had called and asked if he wanted to go grab a couple of beers at ESPN Zone and then maybe hit a club or something, but Chris turned him down, telling him he wasn't feeling well.

Chris took a nice long hot shower; he must have been in there for at least thirty minutes, twenty minutes to shower and about ten to complete his self-gratification. His right hand had been his lover for going on at least a year and a half now; sometimes he pitied himself for that reason. Ever since

Nikki had gotten pregnant he became secondhand goods. When she had gotten too big in the pregnancy he understood, but now since Corey was here, the sex still wasn't regular at all—most nights she turned him down. He would ask her about it every now and then, but he didn't bring it up too often because she reacted so defensively. In fact, it rarely fazed him anymore; he just hoped it would get better—real soon.

He realized he left his Adidas flip-flops in the bedroom. He hated walking around barefoot even around the house, one of his quirks. He scooted to the room and found them underneath their bed. With his head still at the floor he heard a buzzing sound. He had no idea what it was at first. He looked at his pants lying on the floor and realized his cell phone was vibrating inside his pants pocket. Initially, he walked out of the bedroom leaving it behind. *What if it's Nikki and there's something wrong?* he thought. *Or even someone from work?* He went back to the room and grabbed the cell phone out of his pocket. Scrolling through the text messages, he finally reached the last one that came in. It simply said *please call* with a phone number he didn't recognize.

His curiosity got the best of him. He took a seat on the edge of his bed and grabbed the cordless phone off the receiver. When the person on the other end picked up, all he heard was noise in the background.

"Yeah, did someone call Chris?" he yelled, trying to be heard over all the noise.

"Who?"

"Chris!"

"Oh, let me check. Hold on," the woman on the other end told him.

The next voice he heard was Mina's.

"You called!" she said, sounding really happy. "I didn't think you would."

"Where are you?"

"Why? Are you going to come if I tell you?"

"Maybe," he flirted, leading her on. He knew good and well that he had no intention of going out of the house.

"I want you to come. It seems like it's been forever since I've seen you."

"So what are you up to?" he asked, trying to take control of the sudden erection that overcame him.

"Listen, I know it's so last minute, but I wanted you to come to this party with me and just didn't know how to ask since you've been so busy with work and all."

"What kind of party is it?"

"Well, it's a party that they're giving my boss from my second job."

"Suede?" he asked.

"Yep! But I must warn you—you may see things you haven't seen before."

"Where is the party?"

"It's at this penthouse off Peachtree Street; it's called Scandinavian House. I know you're thinking of all kinds of reasons not to come. I'll have you home at a reasonable time, I promise."

"You act like I can't go out," Chris said, trying to reestablish his manhood in Mina's mind—and his own.

"Well, come on, then. I'll see you in an hour?" she asked, hopeful as hell.

"Cool. I know exactly where it is."

"When you park and come inside the lobby, just take the elevator all the way to the top and it's the door at the end of the hall."

"All right."

"Chris?"

"Yeah?"

"I can't wait to see you."

"I—um—I can't wait to see you either, Mina." When Chris

hung up the phone he couldn't believe what he had done. He was definitely out of his mind. Purposely and strategically going against Nikki's orders to not see Mina again. He figured, what was the harm since Nikki was out and about anyway? It was just a party. It's not like he was going out with Mina one on one. This was different, he convinced himself. He planned on hanging out for a quick second and then heading back to the house before Nikki even knew he was gone.

Around nine o'clock Nikki started missing Chris. The new attention she had been giving him had rubbed off on her, too, and she felt the void. She knew her parents wouldn't mind watching Corey and letting her go home and enjoy some quality time with her husband. She ran upstairs to go and ask permission, feeling like she was in high school again. She could hear the sound of water splashing and Corey squealing and found all three of them in her parents' bathroom. She started to explain and ask if it would be all right if she went home. They told her that it was not a problem at all and gave her a sly look . . . like they knew she just wanted to get home in bed with Chris. She pretended she didn't notice the look and gave them all hugs and kisses before leaving. Then she went back downstairs to grab her purse and was in her car in minutes.

As she turned off their street and hit the ramp for 75 North heading toward home, she smiled at herself in the rearview mirror, proud that she was still able to step up her game. *That's what it was all about,* she thought; *when someone comes along and threatens your territory, you have to be ready*. One thing that Chris would be surprised to see was the Brazilian wax she had gotten a few days earlier—she was bare as hell down there. He was going to love it. Renee and Kay were the ones who convinced her to do it, saying that he would really like it and would find her irresistible. Who would have thought that they would be the ones giving her advice? She used to be the one with all the tricks up her sleeve . . . but not so much anymore. The wax was something she promised herself she would keep up with because she loved how clean it made her feel. She was getting hot just thinking about Chris's mouth being down there on her skin as smooth as it was now.

Nikki could hardly contain her excitement when she pulled into her driveway. She didn't see Chris's truck and assumed it was in the garage. The house was empty. She looked at the clock in the kitchen and realized it was almost ten o'clock. She figured Chris must have made a run to the gas station to get a snack or something to munch on and hurriedly ran upstairs to change into her new black lace outfit that she had been saving for a special occasion. *This will be perfect,* she thought. She threw on a pair of three-inch black heels, just to add a little something. Sipping on a glass of Merlot and listening to Nora Jones, she waited for her husband to walk in so they could have mind-blowing sex. By ten thirty, she decided to call him. She dialed his cell phone number and left him a text message that read *I'm home; come and get me.*

A few minutes after she hung up the phone she heard the buzzing noise that she was so familiar with: It was Chris's cell phone going off in his pants pocket somewhere in their bedroom. *Where was he?* Now she was starting to get worried. Wherever he was, he didn't have his cell phone, which she knew was the only way she could get in touch with him if she had an emergency. Fear was turning to anger now. She was pissed as hell; she knew that something out of the ordinary was up but had no idea what. *There is just no way he wouldn't at least have called me if he changed his mind and decided to go out.* She tried to relax and get back in the mood but ended up drifting off to sleep.

Nikki woke up around midnight and realized that she was still alone. It was the worst feeling ever. She changed into a T-shirt and some shorts and went downstairs to wait for Chris. Her timing couldn't have been better—she heard the key turning in the lock of their front door by the time she made it to the last stair. When she saw his face, all of the emotions that had been building had turned to mush.

He looked scared stiff standing there looking at her.

"Hey, babe," he said, startled to see her at home. Nikki felt the fear and disappointment starting to set in. She wanted to know where he had been but was scared to ask questions, afraid she wouldn't be able to live with the answers. She knew he hadn't been with Kevin, because she'd overheard their conversation herself. He followed her into the kitchen and asked what she was doing home . . . as if she had broken a prior arrangement.

"Who were you with?" she asked.

"Who was I with when? Tonight?"

"No, Chris—yesterday! When the fuck do you think? Yeah, tonight!"

"Whoa! Wait a minute. Why are you so upset?"

"I want to know where you've been and who you were with."

"Listen, Kevin called me at the last minute and said he was going to this party and—"

Nikki floated off for a minute unable to hear Chris's words anymore, only seeing his mouth move and the desperate look in his eyes. She had been hoping, praying even, that he hadn't been with Mina, but she knew he was lying about Kevin.

"Are you fucking her?"

"What? Who?"

"Miiiiiina, Chris. Mina!"

"Hell no! Where did that come from? Why do I have to be fucking her, Nikki?" At that point he walked over to Nikki and put his hands on her shoulders to reassure her, trying to reel the situation back in. "Babe, I love you so much; I wouldn't do that to you—ever."

"You don't love me, Chris, you love your fucking self! If you loved me you would stop seeing that bitch! What choice do you leave me, huh? You see how much pain this causes me and you still sneak off and go see Mina?"

"Nikki, I didn't sneak. Stop making this out to be worse than it is."

"I hate you so much right now I could scream! I know you weren't with Kevin. Stop lying to me. That's all you've been doing is lying to me ever since you met her. What's happened to you? What has she done to you?"

"Nikki. Okay, listen. I was at a party, that's it."

"You know what, Chris, fuck you and fuck Mina. Fuck both of you! You can both go straight to hell together."

Nikki was finished. Done. She wanted so badly to believe him but wouldn't allow herself to. She wanted to tell him about the special night she'd had planned for them; instead she looked at her husband and just walked upstairs to her bedroom. On her way up the stairs she barked, "I hope it was worth it." She wanted the words to burn—in the event that he was fucking Mina. Chris didn't say anything. All Nikki heard was the fridge open, followed by a beer tab popping open. She just wanted him to stay away from her for the rest of the night. For the rest of the month for that matter. She was devastated and sickened as she crawled into bed, feeling totally defeated.

Chapter 30

Rick and Lynda

Nikki woke up the next morning in a bit of a daze. After the fifth ring, she realized that the phone in her house really was ringing and that she wasn't dreaming. She lurched across Chris's side of the bed, which was empty, in an attempt to catch it before whoever was on the other end hung up.

"Hello?" Nikki answered, sounding totally winded.

"I didn't catch you at a bad time, did I?"

"Lynda?"

"Hey, girl!" Lynda replied.

"No, you didn't catch me at a bad time."

"All right, don't have me on this phone while Chris is banging you."

"Whatever. Not a whole lot of banging going on around here these days," Nikki confided, the drama from the night before flooding back into her memory. Chris had finally come upstairs last night and forced Nikki to talk through the situation. He was so sappy, never wanting to go to bed angry. He tried to get her to believe that he just went to the party because he knew she was going to be at her parents' house all night, that he left his cell phone by accident, and that he didn't think it was a big deal. He turned it around on her and brought up her insecurities about Mina and tried to reassure her that he was finished with Mina. He promised her again that nothing happened between him and Mina and that their friendship was truly over. She believed him in a strange, crazy, hopeful kind of way, so she let it go and they went to bed.

"Nikki, you need to stop blaming your lame-ass sex life on my godson," Lynda joked, interrupting Nikki's flashback. "Everything isn't Corey's fault."

"No, you're right, it doesn't have anything to do with the baby this time. It's Mina."

"Oh no, you haven't nipped that shit in the bud yet?" asked Lynda, surprised that Nikki was still going along with that whole deal.

"No. I told him to stop seeing her. And I thought he did. But now I'm not so sure. He went to a party with her last night. I don't know. Maybe I've lost my touch, Lynda. You think that's what it is?"

"Maybe so, girl."

"Thanks, Lynda. Damn!"

"Look, girl, I didn't call to talk about you . . . for real; we'll come back to that later."

"Don't tell me you're marrying Shay or no shit like that—it's just way too early in the morning, Lynda."

"No, no, no. I'm not marrying Shay. Not even close. Check this out, though. Rick called me last week and wanted to meet me for dinner while he was out here in L.A. on business."

"Rick called you . . . your ex-husband Rick?"

"I know, right. That's what I said."

"I thought you two hated each other."

"Yeah, me too."

"So what happened? Did you meet him?"

"Well, of course I had to talk to Shay about it and see what she thought of me hooking up with him."

"Damn! So even chicks get jealous over that type of stuff; fraternizing with ex-lovers is just taboo all across the board, I guess, huh?"

"Yep. But Shay didn't mind at all; she told me it would probably be good for us, that it might give me some closure to that part of my life."

"So where did you two meet?"

"Okay, let me tell you what happened," Lynda said, floating off into storytelling mode. "Okay, so I met with him last night at the Four Seasons. It's a really nice spot for dinner and drinks. So, I'm sitting there at the bar waiting to see Rick walk in. I've been to this spot a few times, so I'm chatting with one of the bartenders, just passing the time until Rick gets there. He finally comes in and I'm shocked to see that he still looks handsome to me."

"Uh, yeah, that's very weird."

"Shut up! Anyway, he comes over and gives me a hug, and then we get seated and just kind of sit there for a while, not saying anything. You have to remember this is the first time I'm seeing him in years, so we do a lot of small-talking and basic catching up. He told me he always had a feeling that I was into women, and even really into you."

"No way! How the hell did he say he knew that? Did you tell him that we messed around the night of the key party?" Nikki asked Lynda.

"Nooooo! I didn't tell him that; that's our secret, right?" Lynda reminded her, wanting reassurance from Nikki that she didn't blab to Kay or Chris or somebody.

"Yup! I haven't told anybody how much I turned you out that night!"

"Whatever. You wish, bitch. You know you dream about me every once in a while," Lynda cracked.

"Yeah, maybe once in a while," Nikki conceded.

"That's right! Anyway . . . can I finish my story, please?"

"Okay, okay. Sorry. So what did Rick say when you asked him how he knew about this supposed chemistry you and I had?"

"He just said it was a feeling he had."

"And what about his own issue? How long did he know that he was bisexual?"

"He told me that he had never confided in anyone about the story he was about to tell me; I guess that was supposed to make me feel special or something. But, anyway, I agreed not to tell anyone, so we could move on. And he began to tell me about this thing that happened when he was in high school. He said that when he was seventeen, he and his best friend since elementary school, Travis, were hanging out at Travis's house after a football game. Travis's parents weren't home, so they snuck beers into the house and got wasted while they listened to music and chilled. He said that Travis was always with a different girl, and they talked about how big of a ho everyone thought he was around school. Rick said that Travis at one point walked over to where he sat on the couch in the living room, sat down next to him, and handed him a cold beer.

"Hey, man, how come you're not as big a ho as me? I mean you do like girls, right?" Travis asked Rick. Rick told him that he had always just been kind of shy and that girls made him nervous. Travis said he understood and that the really pretty ones made him feel the same way sometimes. Then Travis told Rick that he was most comfortable when he and Rick were together. He said he could always be himself around Rick and not have to worry about being judged or picked on the way the rest of their crew would likely do. He told Rick that he was just different and that he was glad they were friends. After they moved on from that subject, Rick said that Travis asked him if he wanted to watch a porno flick. Rick said, "Sure," and Travis proceeded to pop one of

his dad's tapes in the VCR. The movie came on almost immediately, showing a graphic scene of two black guys getting a mean head job by these white chicks.

"I love that," Travis told Rick.

"Love what?" Rick asked.

"I love it when Shelly or one of the other girls I fool around with sucks my dick; it just feels so good, man. Makes me want to explode. Sometimes I do it right in her face."

Travis asked Rick if he liked blow jobs. Rick confided in Travis and told him that he'd never really had one. Then Travis asked Rick the question that probably changed Rick's life forever: "Would you think I was gay if I got on my knees and started sucking your dick?"

"Rick said he was shocked and disgusted. He told Travis that that was the craziest thing he'd ever heard and told him to stop talking stupid. Travis assured Rick that he had done it before and that he didn't think it made him gay, that mostly he let guys do it to him sometimes, but that he would be willing to do it to Rick because he knew Rick had never had one. Rick said that he was in such shock that he dared Travis to do it. The next thing he knew, Travis was on his knees in his parents' living room sucking Rick's dick—'and good, too,' Rick said. We both laughed when he said that."

"Dammmmmmn!" Nikki exclaimed. "What the hell was up with Travis?"

"I don't know. I guess somebody turned his ass out and had him really confused. Rick said there had always been talk that Travis's uncle was gay."

"So Rick got turned out by a guy, huh?"

"Yeah, basically. I guess it must have hit a nerve or something because Rick told me that he would think back to that time in his life even when I would be down there doing my duty at times."

"Girl, don't tell me that a seventeen-year-old boy gave better head than you!" Nikki laughed out loud.

"Fuck you, Nikki!"

"So is Rick gay, or is he bi? I'm confused."

"How the hell am I supposed to know? I don't think he knows himself. He said that he had only been with one woman other than me during our marriage—and that was the night of the key party. Other than that he had only been with men. Mainly T.J." Lynda noticed the silence on the other end. "Nikki? Did you hear me?"

"Yeah, I'm still listening." Nikki was dying to tell Lynda that Rick pulled Kay's key the night of the party, but she couldn't betray Kay that way—even though Lynda was her best friend. "Oh, man, T.J. Good ol' T.J. Waffle House T.J, right?" Nikki confirmed, remembering the day Rick told Lynda that he was in love with another man.

"Yeah, Waffle House T.J.!"

"So whatever happened with that?" Nikki asked. "Does he still see him?"

"Well, you remember he met T.J. at that escort service he started going to while we were married."

"That is so fucked up," Nikki said.

"I know, but anyway, he said that the T.J. thing was kind of a mistake or maybe fate or something. He contacted an escort service that one of his colleagues had used before, and they sent a guy out instead of a girl for some reason that night. Talk about making a fucking mistake. Rick said when he heard the guy's voice at the door he opened it and was totally confused, but let him in so they could figure out what had happened. He told me that the actual idea of a man coming to his room turned him on. After that he said he would see T.J. every now and then and just do shit like jack off on him or let him suck his dick. He claims he never actually had sex with him until after he and I were divorced."

"Ewwww!" Nikki squealed. "Girl, Chris is here." Nikki heard a car in the driveway. "Let me go."

"Oh, damn! We never got back to you and your drama, did we?" Lynda asked. "Are things any better in the bedroom?"

"Whatever. Good-bye!"

"Okay, okay, I'll let you go. Call me this weekend, Nikki. And, remember, if you don't fuck him today, Mina will gladly do it for you tomorrow." Lynda hung up before Nikki could tell her to go to hell.

Chapter 31

Good Advice

Penny passed by Chris's office and noticed that he was in deep thought. It was late Monday evening, and she was wondering why he hadn't signed off and gone home. "Hey, boss, what are you doing here so late? It's seven o'clock. Go home," she said, feeling like she was his mother at times. She just loved Chris to death. He was truly the most wonderful person she had ever worked for. She had a secret crush on him. For him being such a good-looking guy, she was always so amazed by his kindness and generosity. He never came across cocky or conceited, like so many men she had worked for in the past. Chris was truly a genuine guy. Ever since she lost her husband she had been quite lonely, and she envied Nikki for having such a wonderful man to come home to every night.

"What's up, Penny? Yeah, I'm headed home right now; I was just finishing up some reports."

"You looked like you had something other than work on your mind. Wanna talk about it?"

"Nah, it's nothing. Nikki and I had a fight over the weekend, and I was thinking about it and wondering if I need to make a move to remedy the situation so that we can stop fighting over the same thing."

"Mina?"

"Penny, how do you know me so well?"

"Oh, I make it my duty to know all of my bosses—inside and out." Penny chuckled. "It makes it much easier to work with them."

"Yeah, it's Mina. You're not going to believe this one, Penny." Chris told Penny all about Mina being Angel and how Nikki freaked out and forbade him to see her again.

"Well, what's the problem, boss? You know what you have to do, then, right?"

"Well, I know that Nikki was really having a hard time with our friendship, but I'm in such a weird place because I really like Mina and our relationship is truly innocent. But at the same time I don't think that Nikki really believes me."

"She probably doesn't, boss; I mean, Mina is a really beautiful woman."

"And, so what? She doesn't have anything on Nikki, not in my eyes anyway."

"Yeah, I know that's probably true, but Nikki probably doesn't believe that you think that."

"I tell her all the time. Every time we fight about Mina, I assure her that Mina doesn't even compare."

"Yeah, but us women have a hard time believing you men when it comes to that kind of thing. I mean, what else would you tell Nikki? She is looking at the real picture: There is this beautiful, sexy, young, unattached woman spending a lot of time with her husband—while she is at work or at home with the baby. Nikki is used to being that sexy, young woman. She is probably struggling, thinking that she can't measure up to Mina and that the reason you are spending so much time with her is that you are attracted to this girl who reminds you of who she used to be."

Chris was shocked by how right Penny was. He didn't want to admit it—even to himself—but he did love Mina's energy and her spunk. She did remind him of Nikki and how she used to be before they were married and definitely before they had Corey.

"Well, Penny, you are definitely a wise woman. I don't know what to do. I mean, I guess what you are saying could make some sense, but I love Nikki. Mina and I are just friends; I don't have any romantic feelings for her."

"Are you sure, boss? I mean really sure?"

"I'm sure, Penny." Chris lied his ass off. He knew that he found Mina attractive and that he fought that attraction every time they were together.

"Well, I don't believe you, boss. And I think you're the best. I know your intentions are good, but I think that this is a game that you're playing with Mina." She turned to walk away.

"Wait. What game?"

"Seriously, it is a game. It may be in your subconscious, but it's a game just the same. It's exciting seeing Mina each day wondering if you can resist her again and again. It probably makes you feel strong and in control knowing that she wants you but can't have you."

"Penny, you sound like you're talking about a soap opera; this is real life, girl. Mina doesn't need me; she has men falling all over her everywhere she goes."

"And you're sounding naive, boss. She doesn't want all of those other men; she wants you. Why do you think she spends so much time around you?"

"Uh . . . because I'm a cool friend to hang out with. I mean, the only difference is that I happen to be a man. Why can't we be friends? Just friends?"

"You can, boss, but I'm just saying it's a dangerous game. Nikki knows it, I know it, and Mina probably knows it, too. But you're just being way too stubborn to admit that you may have feelings for Mina. And you can't tell me you don't have feelings for her now that Nikki has asked you to stop seeing her and you clearly have not."

"Penny, I do have feelings for Mina, but they are not physical."

"So you don't think she's just a little sexy?"

"Um. Sure. Of course she is, but I think Beyoncé is sexy too; that doesn't mean I'm going to sleep with her."

"Yeah, but you're not playing racquetball with Beyoncé, you're not going to lunch with Beyoncé every day."

"I don't go to lunch with Mina every day."

"Okay, boss, whatever. Anyway, you need to end this, I think. Those thoughts that I caught you having earlier when you were in a daze were telling you the same thing I'm telling you now, and you know it. You just don't want to give Mina up: That's what this is really about."

"Penny, that's ridiculous. Give what up? I mean, I can end things with Mina any time I want."

"Then why haven't you? Your wife has asked you not to see her anymore." She hated to see Chris go down this path. She'd been around long enough to know that nothing good would come from it.

"I will end it. The only reason I haven't yet is that I feel sorry for Mina. She is really innocent in all of this. How am I supposed to tell her after I befriended her that we can't be friends anymore?"

"Now, that's just plain silly. Do you hear yourself? You need to end this relationship!"

"Penny, you're trippin'. You are not playing around, huh?"

"Well, boss, you know I consider it my duty to watch out for you. I care about you and I don't want to see you or Nikki get hurt in any of this."

"Well, what about Mina? Doesn't anybody care about her?"

"Mina seems like a nice young lady, but I don't think her

intentions are good. I think she wants you and will do whatever she can to have you and she is willing to wait for as long as it takes for you to break."

"How do you know so much about all of this? And, trust me, I won't break."

"I'm very observant. And you *will* break soon if you don't get out of this situation."

"Okay, okay, I'll talk to Mina and see if I can get her to understand that I can't see her anymore."

"That's what I'm talking about. I love it when you take my advice," Penny said, helping Chris out of his chair. "Now get out of this office and go home to your wife."

"All right, Penny. I think I should be calling you boss."

"Hee-hee." Penny blushed. "See you later, boss."

"Night, Penny . . . oh, and thanks." As Chris took the elevator down and passed the fourth floor, he thought about Mina and all that Penny had said. He knew she was right—he was being unfair to Nikki. He decided not to wait and to go ahead and end it tonight.

Chapter 32

Wrong Turn

Chris checked in with Nikki at home and told her that he had something important he had to take care of, which meant he would be home a little later. She didn't sound too happy about it but told him she would put his dinner in the oven. He was a bit nervous, unsure of what he was going to say to Mina. He didn't want to come across like a punk by making it seem like his wife didn't trust him or that he couldn't handle being around her—which was exactly what Mina was going to think. It was odd how well he felt he knew her in the brief four months they had been friends. She was not going to be happy about it, and he didn't want to hurt her. He decided to give her a call to see if they could meet for a drink.

"Hey, Chris," Mina answered, recognizing his number on her caller ID.

"Hey, Mina. What's up, girl? What you up to?"

"Not much. I just got out of the shower and was planning to sit down and do a little reading. What's up with you? Where are you? Why aren't you at home? Late night at work?"

"Yeah, something like that. Hey . . . I know this is kind of last minute, but I need to talk to you. Can you meet me for a drink?"

"Right now?"

"Yeah, now."

"Aw, Chris, you're killing me. I'm so comfortable; I don't feel like getting dressed up."

"You don't have to get dressed up. We don't even have to go drink; we can just go to a park or something."

"What's going on? Are you okay?"

"I'm cool, but I just really need to talk to you."

"Well . . . talk."

"No, not on the phone."

"Okay, well, why don't you drop by my place, then?" There was silence. "Chris? Did you hear me? Hello?"

"Yeah . . . um . . . I don't think that's a good idea. Come on, Mina, stop acting like you don't have any spontaneity in you; you know you can just drop everything when you feel like it and come on out."

"True, but I don't feel like it. So if you want to talk to me face-to-face, then your only option is to come by."

"You're tripping."

"Chris, give me a break. You really need to get over this fear you have of being alone with me at my place."

"I'm not scared of you, Mina, trust me."

"Well, you've never been here in all of the time we've known each other."

"Didn't you say you were ready for bed?"

"Yes, but I'm not lying over here butt-ass naked . . . if that's what you think. Give me a break."

"Whatever, Mina."

"You're the one that has to speak with me this minute, so if you want to speak to me that's what you're going to have to do."

"All right, that's cool; how do I get there?"

Mina gave Chris directions to her studio and promised that she would be fully clothed when he got there. She thought it was cute how he always told her that he didn't see her as anything other than a friend, yet he couldn't stand to be alone with her; they had made it a point to never see each other in private. Chris reasoned that it was inappropriate, but Mina knew better. She knew he was attracted to her. She could tell by the way he looked at her when he thought she wasn't watching him, but she respected Chris's wishes and always met him on his terms—until tonight. She was tired of playing by his rules; if he wanted to see her, he was going to have to come to her. She was shocked that he agreed.

Chris arrived at Mina's front door about forty minutes later. Her studio was pretty strange-looking from the outside. He had to go through an underground parking garage and up a flight of shabby stairs just to get to it. As he reached Mina's door he suddenly felt saddened by the thought that he was there for one reason and one reason only: to say goodbye to her. He did really care for her as a friend and did have some really good times with her; walking away was not going to be easy.

Mina opened the door wearing the tightest, tiniest white T-shirt he'd ever seen—it fell just above her belly button—and a pair of short gray fleece shorts that accented her legs perfectly. He knew that she knew what she was doing. But he was going to be strong; he wasn't going to let her get to him. "Come in," Mina said, leading Chris inside, with a big smile on her face.

"Let me take your coat." She helped Chris take off his jacket. "Don't you look nice?"

"Thanks. You too. Is this what you sleep in?" He looked her up and down.

"Yep, just a T-shirt and shorts; I don't like nightgowns.

Never have. They get too bunched up when I'm tossing and turning. You don't mind, do you?"

"Mind what?"

"That I'm in my PJ's."

"Nope! Do your thing. Listen, this won't take too long." When Chris stepped into Mina's place, he immediately loved her taste. He was surrounded by deep, rich red walls, hardwood floors, ethnic paintings, off-white leather furniture, candles, and crystal vases filled with fresh flowers. He was very impressed. "Hey, this is really nice, Mina. Really nice."

"Thanks, Chris. As you can see, I'm trying to get it all together." She nudged him. "Hey, do you want a drink?"

"Hmmm. Nah, let's talk first, okay?"

"Chris, what is up with you? Are you okay? Come on into the kitchen; let me make you a drink."

Chris agreed. He felt like he was going to need a drink to get out what he had to say to Mina. He took a seat at the breakfast bar on one of her cast-iron stools facing the kitchen. "Is vodka and cranberry okay?" Mina asked, holding a bottle of Grey Goose.

"Yeah, that would be great, thanks."

"Okay, so what's going on, Mr. Reynolds? It sounds serious."

"Well, I don't know really how to say this, but—"

"Uh-oh, before you get into all of that, let me show you something; you're going to crack up." Mina ran off down the hallway.

He assumed she was heading for her bedroom. Chris's curiosity was piqued, so he stood up and followed her. He didn't dare go into the bedroom, so he stopped and took a seat at her solid wood, glass-top desk neatly tucked away in her guest bedroom. "Hey, this chair is comfortable as hell. I need one of these at my desk at work," he yelled, letting her know that he had changed locations. Chris was stunned when Mina walked out of her bedroom. She had all types of gadgets with her: a black leather whip, handcuffs, and thigh-high black leather stiletto boots. "What the hell is all of that?"

"This is my dominatrix getup. I decided to spare you my leather catsuit, but I figured I could at least show you the boots. This is what I use when I'm at Suede," Mina bragged.

"Girl, you are all the way off the chain. Why are you showing me this stuff?"

"I just wanted to show you what I do. You sounded so interested when I was telling you about it; I figured it would be cool for me to show you."

Chris was starting to get aroused. He tried to hide his discomfort but couldn't. He was sitting in the chair with his long legs spread open. She was looking hot as hell in those boots. What had he gotten himself into? He knew he had made a bad choice coming to her house. Mina was feeling way too free. Chris strategically placed his hands on his crotch, in an attempt to hide the bulge that was starting to protrude from his pants.

"This stuff really turns these men on; they love women in control."

Chris wanted to get up so bad but he couldn't let Mina see his hard-on. So he was stuck for the time being. "Hey, Mina, put that stuff away. Can we talk now?"

"Dang! All right, all right, my bad. I guess I did get a little carried away. Hold on, let me put this stuff up." Then Mina walked behind Chris and before he knew it, he felt her yank his wrists together and then heard the distinct sound of handcuffs locking. Chris couldn't believe it. He felt so vulnerable as he sat there clearly with a hard-on and no way to hide it now as Mina ran off to her bedroom.

"Mina! Come on now, take these off. This isn't funny!"

Mina could tell Chris was mad, but at the same time she noticed that he was turned on. "Well, well, well . . . what do we have here?"

Chris couldn't say a word. He looked up at Mina in desperation. She looked so damn good. He could tell she didn't have a bra on. He could see her dark nipples poking right through her shirt. It was too much for him to take. He was frozen. Then Mina did the unthinkable—she straddled him, taking a seat right on top of his hard dick, and kissed him gently all over his face.

"You have such beautiful eyes," she whispered, kissing them.

Chris continued to gaze at her. He felt hypnotized. Her dark, soulful eyes staring into his were enough to make him come right there. He thought so many times of what it would be like to have her. *If only I wasn't married,* he would say to himself every time he saw her.

"And I just love your mouth, that smile, those lips. How many times have I fantasized about kissing these lips of yours?" She was so close to him, he could feel her breath against his face.

"Mina, you have got to stop this; this is not what I came here to do. I—"

"Shhhhh. It's okay." She placed her index finger gently on his lips. "Don't worry, I'm not going to make you do anything you don't want to do, I promise," she whispered.

Fuck, he thought to himself. She had him and they both knew it. He had tried so hard all of these months to fight his attraction for her, and now here he was, sitting in the most compromising position he could possibly find himself in. "Mina, seriously, this isn't funny. Take these handcuffs off, please. I mean it."

Mina wasn't paying attention to what Chris was saying. The only thing she could focus on was his hard dick and how good it felt against her wet, throbbing pussy. She started to stroke Chris's freshly shaved head as she pressed her breasts up against him. Chris was completely lost at this point. He was worked up, yet angry that he had gotten himself into this, and Mina was taking full advantage of the situation. Then he felt Mina reaching down to unbuckle his pants.

"Stop! This is crazy, Mina; I can't do this. You know I can't."

"Say *please,*" she said softly.

"Mina, this is for real. You're killing me here. This is not Suede, and I am not one of your customers." Chris made a weak attempt to get Mina off him. He was having a hard time since his hands were cuffed behind his back and the chair, and Mina, though tiny, was sitting on top of him. No one was going to believe that this was the way it had gone down—no one.

"Come on, Chris, you know you want me; stop fighting it. That's why you're here; admit it." Before Chris could respond, Mina had managed to take his dick out of his pants. "Mmmmm . . . it's so big—just like I dreamed it would be. I know you want me, Chris; I can feel it oozing out of you. I want you inside me; I want you inside me right now." Mina threw her head back and moaned in ecstasy, stroking Chris and rubbing it against her stomach.

Chris wanted to taste her; she smelled so sweet. He resisted, though; he couldn't encourage her. He just sat still . . . in shock at what was happening. He was so confused. His head wanted her to stop, but his body wanted her to continue. He wanted *her* to do it; he didn't want to be responsible. Then she did. She slowly slid her shorts to the side and carefully placed him inside her. She was so wet, his dick slid right in. She started to ride him slow at first, so she could feel all of him. Then she quickened her pace. Chris's body was trembling all over. He literally ached with desire for her. Mina grabbed his head and kissed him, slipping her tongue in his mouth and wrapping it around his. He could no longer resist her; he responded to her kiss. He was lost in the moment.

"You're so damn wet." Chris finally spoke up. "Is all that for me?" he whispered softly in her ear.

That only made Mina want him more. "Yes, it's all for you. You make me wanna come right now . . . mmmm." Her legs were burning now, but she kept sliding her pussy up and down on top of Chris. She wanted to take the handcuffs off to feel his bare hands on her. She wanted him to take her on the floor, on the kitchen table, in her bedroom, but she feared that, if she let him go, he would be gone forever. So she left his hands right where they were.

Chris didn't want to say it, but he had to let her know that he was about to explode. "Mina," he whispered.

"I know. It's okay; do it. Do it now; I want you to come inside me. I want all of you." And then, panting heavily, they both came in unison. Chris's juices flowed out of her like a river, as Mina's limp body lay trembling, hunched over him. They were both trying to catch their breath. He was in awe of what had just happened. After all of the warnings Kevin and Penny had given him, he still hadn't listened . . . and now look at him.

Mina didn't want to move. A small part of her regretted what she had done. She knew Chris pretty well. She didn't even want to look at him; he was going to be so upset with her. Their friendship was over, and she knew it.

Chris didn't say a word when Mina rose up and stepped off him. He sat there with his eyes closed and his clothes wet with sweat and sex. Mina took the cuffs off his hands. He rubbed his red, aching wrists, as he slowly stood up and managed to gather himself somewhat, adjusting his clothes, but he still looked a mess. How could he go home to Nikki looking like this—smelling like this? He looked at her with sheer devastation in his eyes as he walked away to find her bathroom.

Mina heard the water running in the bathroom and felt a little sad at the thought of him washing away what they had just shared. She went into her bedroom and changed into her bathrobe. When she came out, Chris was standing in the living room drying off his hands with a towel. He still did not say a word to her.

"Chris, are you okay?" Mina asked, concerned.

"Nope." Chris stared at Mina with contempt. "I'm not okay at all. What just happened here, Mina? What the fuck was that?"

"You know what it was, Chris. Don't try and pretend that you didn't want this; don't you dare say that to me."

"Mina, are you kidding me? Do you really think I came over here to fuck you tonight? After all of this time, I just decided to forget about my wife and kid; I just have to have Mina tonight? Do you really think that?"

"I'm not saying that was your intention in coming here, but you know good and damn well that you wanted me. You could have stopped me if you wanted to, but you didn't."

"Mina, let me tell you something. I came over here to tell you that I had to stop seeing you, that we had to end our friendship because it was starting to upset my wife and taking a toll on my marriage: That's what I came here to tell you—before you damn near raped me."

"You lying bastard! You wanted this and you know it!" Mina screamed. "You had plenty of opportunities to tell me that it was over, that you didn't want to see me anymore, but you were too busy getting off to get the words out, I guess. Too busy grunting and moaning. I mean, look at you. You're, what, six-four, two hundred and something pounds? Are you trying to tell me that you couldn't find a way to get out of that chair if you wanted to? Give me a fucking break, Chris! How dare you mention the word *rape*! You're a fucking bastard. Get out!"

"All right, all right, just calm down. This is the deal—I'm not going to have this fight with you. I'm going to tell you now since it's done . . . over . . . finished: I'm done with you,

Mina; don't call me; don't look at me at work. None of that shit. You were obviously planning this since we met. Calculated—that's what you are. Just fucking crazy. I can't believe I had the nerve to compare you to my wife. Ha! What a fucking joke!"

"Oh, don't flatter yourself, Chris. Planning what since we met? To seduce you? Are you for real? Do you think I couldn't have had you long before now if I wanted to? You were hot for me from the first moment you laid eyes on me. I knew it; you knew it. But I respected that you had a family; I loved that about you."

"Well, there wasn't much respect in the atmosphere tonight."

"Go to hell, Chris! If you want to pretend that you had no part in this, you go right ahead. I don't need this shit. And as for comparing me to your wife—your sweet Nikki, right? That's laughable—give me a break, she's more calculated than I could ever be."

"What the hell is that supposed to mean? You don't know shit about my wife."

"Is that what you think? I know your wife is a fucking liar; I knew that from the first moment I saw her."

"Please . . . you wish. You don't know Nikki; she is one of the most honest people I've ever met. Don't even try to compare yourself; there is no comparison."

"Reaaaally? Okay, well then, I guess you know all about her membership at Suede?" Mina blurted out.

"What? You're crazy. What membership?"

"Hmmm. Why don't you ask your honest, perfect, little wife?"

"No, I'm asking you: What the hell are you talking about?"

Mina started to feel a little guilty. She had no intention of going back on her word to Nikki about keeping quiet about seeing her at Suede even after Nikki had betrayed her. But she got sick of listening to Chris go on and on about how perfect Nikki was. She wanted to hurt him; she wanted to hurt him bad. "Whatever, Chris. It's not my story to tell; ask your wife."

Chris marched up to Mina and grabbed her by the arm forcefully. "Tell me what the hell you're talking about—now!"

"Or what? Do you think I'm afraid of you? You couldn't hurt me if you tried. You couldn't hurt me any more than you already have. Get out!"

"I'm not leaving until you tell me what the hell it is you think you know about my wife."

"I already told you; use your imagination to figure out the rest. Now get out!" Mina screamed, pushing Chris as hard as she could. She began to sob, and Chris realized that he had really upset her. He wasn't going to get anything else out of her tonight, so he shook his head and walked out of her studio—out of her life.

Chapter 33

Rain

The rain was coming down like nothing Nikki had ever seen before. She seldom worried about Chris, but this weather had her a little nervous, especially since she hadn't heard from him. She was hoping the thunder and lightning wouldn't wake Corey up. He had only been asleep for an hour or so, and she was sure she would hear him crying at any moment. She peeked in on him expecting to see her little one stirring around in his crib, but he was sound asleep. She walked over to him, kissed her hand, and rubbed it over his forehead. Just then the phone was ringing in her bedroom. She closed Corey's door and hurried to catch it. *It has to be Chris,* she thought.

"Hello," Nikki said, expecting to hear Chris on the other end; instead she heard what she thought was a woman crying. "Hello?" Nikki asked again, a bit of annoyance in her voice; she didn't have time for games and was about to hang up.

"Hey, Nikki," a female voice on the other end finally said.

"Hello. Kay, is that you?"

"Yeah," she sniffed, "it's me."

"What's wrong, Kay? Are you all right? What happened?" Nikki hardly gave Kay a chance to respond.

"It's me and Kevin; I don't think we're going to make it. I'm so sick of this marriage shit I don't know what to do."

"Okay, wait. Slow down," Nikki interrupted. "Back up. What in the hell happened to make you so upset?"

"It's the same shit; nothing new at all. I guess I'm just this insecure loser that cannot let go of the fact that I'll always feel like I'm in second place when it comes to Renee."

"Did something new go down?"

"Not really. I mean, earlier tonight I had gone out to pick up a movie and some food for us and when I came back Kevin was on the phone. I assumed he was talking to Chris because he was laughing and smiling so much; I just figured they were talking shit, you know. So I'm getting the food all ready on plates and shit, popping the DVD in, and this motherfucker is still on the phone. So, of course, I start giving him the signal to cut the conversation short, but he's still talking. So, finally, I grab the phone and get on the line and I'm like, 'Chris, your boy has to go; we're about to watch this movie, man.' Silence. Nothing but silence on the other end of the line. So I'm like, 'Chris? Hello? Chris?' And then I hear my sister's voice and I want to just die. 'Renee?' 'Yeah. Hey, Kay, I called to talk to you, but Kevin said you ran out to get a movie and something to eat. I guess you guys are about to chill now, so I'll just call you tomorrow. It wasn't important, just wanted to talk to you about what we're getting Dad for his birthday or whatever.' Somehow I kept my cool because I didn't want Renee to know how fucked up this whole thing had me at that moment. I told her it was cool and that we'd talk soon. She even said she loved me, and somehow I was able to tell her I loved her, too. But what I was feeling right at that moment was so far from love I didn't know what to do. Kevin didn't say a word; he knew better. He just waited for me to say something because he had no idea how hard I was about to go off."

"Uh-oh! What the hell did you do?"

"Nikki, it was so bad. I mean I couldn't help it. All that stuff from the past just came rushing back in, and I threw all that shit in his face and then some. I told him that if he wanted Renee he could fucking have her because I was tired of feeling like I was constantly fighting to win his heart. The whole time he was pleading with me that I was wrong and that he really loved me and that somehow he wished he could make me understand that it was me he wanted and not Renee. I threw my wedding ring at him and told him that I didn't trust either of them and that I hated the situation we were in. I told him I wanted a divorce and—"

"Whoa, whoa, whoa! A divorce? Kay, come on now. You were trippin'."

"I know, Nikki, but I was too far gone to stop myself; I just kept talking."

"So what did he say after that?"

"He was pretty quiet the whole time and then finally he got up and looked me dead in my face and told me that I should be careful what I ask for and that I was walking a really thin line with him."

"Damn!"

"I know. I was like, 'Oh, shit, this nigga is pissed!' I fucked up this time, and I knew it. But you just don't understand the position I'm in and how crazy it makes me to know that they even talk. I try, Nikki. I have tried hard as hell to get past it, but I think I realize I won't ever be able to. And I know that's not one hundred percent fair to Kevin."

"Maybe you guys need to try counseling."

"We need to do something because this isn't going to work."

"By the way, you're not PMSing, are you?"

"Why do you ask? Could it be because the story I told

you is completely irrational and I sound like a freakin' lunatic for going off on Kevin just because he was talking to Renee on the phone? Hell yeah, I'm PMSing!" Kay said. Then they both started laughing.

"You're crazy, girl."

Kay let out a big sigh. "You're my girl, Nikki. Thank you for listening to my bullshit."

"Whatever, girl. You know I'm always here for you. You guys can get through this, but you both have to want to."

"You're right. I'm working on it. I love him. I really do so I just have to start trusting him. That's my biggest hurdle right now. I will go crazy if I keep this up."

"Just know that he loves you and that Renee loves you and that what happened between them, whatever happened between them is over and there is nothing you can do about them having a relationship now. He's your husband and she's your sister. They *will* always be connected."

"I know. You're right. I'm going to let you go, though. I didn't even ask if you and Chris were busy."

"That's cool, girl. I'm straight. I'll holler at you tomorrow. Call me if you need me." Nikki didn't feel like talking to Kay about Chris and how worried she was that he wasn't home. After hanging up, she tried calling his cell phone again but got voice mail and didn't leave a message.

Chapter 34

Spite

Mina couldn't stop the tears from streaming down her face as she pictured over and over again Chris walking out her door. Then it hit her—Nikki. She went back into her bedroom and picked up the phone. She had to calm herself down first. She wanted to set it straight, to try and make things right, if at all possible. She decided she had to call Nikki and warn her that Chris knew and that it was her fault. Even though she and Nikki weren't friends, she felt bad about betraying her in that way. *That was a low blow,* she thought. Even lower than what Nikki had done to her. The phone rang several times before Nikki picked up.

Mina felt sick when she heard Nikki answer. "Hello?"

"Hi, Nikki; this is Mina."

"What's up? What's going on?"

Mina could hear the tension in Nikki's voice—the suspicion that Chris was, or had been, with her. "Listen, Nikki, I'm calling because I want to tell you straight up that I made a mistake." There was silence at the other end of the line. "I told Chris about seeing you at Suede."

"You did what?" Nikki asked in a tone that made Mina feel nervous. "Why? What did I ever do to you to make you want to throw me under the train like that?"

Mina knew Nikki had a point. "Well, you told him all of my shit for starters, but that's not what this is about."

Mina just couldn't live with the fact that Chris thought Nikki was better than her, and she had chosen to do something to tip the scale in her favor.

"So now you expect me to thank you for something? For looking out for me? Fuck you, Mina! Fuck you and your home-wrecking, scheming ass!"

"Wait, Nikki. Don't do this. I'm trying to be—"

"You're trying to be what? You told Chris about Suede to make me look bad, so don't even try to clean it up now; it's a little late for that. I gave you the benefit of the doubt, and you ended up screwing me over . . . like all my girls said you would. But let's be clear on something right now, you've done enough to try and ruin my family, so just leave us alone; stay away from my husband."

"Me stay away from Chris?" Mina fired back. "That's funny. Tell your husband to stay away from me. You know what, Nikki . . . I was trying to be nice, to do the right thing, but you're making this really difficult. So I'll leave you with this to consider, since you want to act a fool and call me names and shit—Chris just left my house." Mina waited for a reaction from Nikki.

"I already knew that, Mina," Nikki lied, "so don't think you're telling me something that Chris didn't already tell me."

Mina was caught off guard—she didn't know Chris had told Nikki he would be stopping by her place. "Oh, that's right. I forgot I'm dealing with the black version of Romeo and Juliet. He tells you everything," Mina said sarcastically. "Well, make sure you ask him to tell you how wet my pussy was when he had his dick all up in it. He said it was the wettest he'd ever felt," Mina said spitefully, hanging up and leaving Nikki with a hard pill to swallow.

Nikki held the phone in her hand in total shock, shaking. Chris wouldn't. He couldn't have, could he? Her first instinct was to call Mina back, but what was there to say, really? Nothing. She felt a tidal wave rush through the pit of her stomach and ran to the bathroom, getting there just in time to let it all out. She stayed on her knees for a minute to make sure nothing else was going to come up. Then she stood up and washed her face and her mouth out. Mina had to be lying, she thought or her marriage was over.

Chapter 35

Vodka on the Rocks

The rain was coming down harder than ever when Chris decided to stop at Frankie's before heading home. He had no desire to see Nikki right now. Not only did he feel guilty as hell for what had just transpired, but he couldn't get Mina's last words out of his mind; "*I guess you know all about her little membership at Club Suede."What did Mina mean by that?* Nikki would have told him if she were a member. *And when did all of this happen, anyway? Recently? In the past?* It was killing him; he needed a drink bad.

Frankie reached under the bar, grabbed a shot glass, and slammed it down in front of Chris. "What'll you have, my friend?"

"Hey, Frankie, man, give me one of those *lethal weapons* you let me try a few weeks back, the one with five or six different kinds of liquors in it."

"Whoa! That kind of night, huh?" Frankie said, mixing up the shot. "Here you go; drink up."

Chris threw the colorful shot to the back of his throat and asked for a vodka on the rocks next.

"What's going on, Chris? What's got you in this mood? I don't think I've ever quite seen you like this—you look a little rough."

"You wouldn't believe me if I told you, man. You wouldn't believe me if I told you."

"Try me."

"Nah. I just want to drink." Chris didn't want to talk about it. He wanted to pretend it hadn't happened. He was grateful for the rain. He imagined that it could somehow wash away every sign of what he had done. He finally stopped smelling Mina. He looked around Frankie's spot and thought about the fact that it had all started right here—in this very spot where he was sitting. And this is where it would end; he would never see her again. He couldn't now, even if he wanted to. She hated him for the things he said. He could still see the pain in those engaging eyes of hers.

Chris must have had about four shots and five or more drinks when he heard his cell phone ringing. It was Nikki for the third time now. He didn't want to talk to her, even though he knew she had to be worried and needed some reassurance that he was okay. It was going on midnight and he was drunk, his head starting to spin. He watched customers walk in and out as the hours went by. Frankie had served him his last drink about an hour ago. He decided to leave the bar and headed to the empty black chaise longue across from the television. *Sports Center* was on, and he figured he would take a peek at the highlights and sober up a bit before attempting to drive home. It felt like hours had gone by when he looked up and saw Nikki walking right past him toward the bar. He was a bit confused because she was dressed pretty provocatively, something he hadn't seen since Corey was born. She had on a black halter dress that tied around her neck. Her breasts were protruding out of her plunging neckline, and she was wearing the highest pair of black heels he had ever seen her wear. She looked like she was waiting for someone. She kept checking her watch, looking around the room. He called out to her, but she didn't answer him. *What the hell is she doing here?* he thought. *Where is Corey?*

Then the front door opened. A tall, dark man walked in with a pretty white woman with short red hair. She, too, was dressed to kill in a red slip dress. The dark stranger was decked out in what looked like an Armani suit and tie. When Nikki saw them she waved and motioned them to come over to her, her cherry-colored lips spreading from ear to ear. Chris had never seen her with so much makeup on her face. He wasn't prepared for what came next. When the mysterious stranger approached Nikki, he immediately slid his hand up her thigh underneath her dress. She then uncrossed her legs and invited him to probe farther. Which he did. Nikki, appearing to be experiencing things she had never felt before, threw her head back.

Chris was stuck. He tried to get up, but his legs gave out on him. He was paralyzed. He called out again to Nikki, and this time she looked his way. Instead of looking stunned to see him, she smiled deviously and then reached over and kissed the redheaded woman, while still focusing on Chris. Chris watched as his wife slid her tongue down this stranger's mouth—a woman no less. Nikki then reached around the back of her neck and untied her halter dress. Her breasts were now completely exposed as the dark man caressed them. He then started to suck on them, biting her nipples. Nikki continued to look at Chris, smiling at him. The redhead then knelt down and made her way between Nikki's legs as she sat on the bar stool. Nikki didn't appear to be wearing any panties, so the redhead slid her tongue inside Nikki. Then the man got on top of the bar, unbuckled his pants, grabbed Nikki's head, and shoved all of it inside her mouth—it was the biggest dick Chris had ever seen. He couldn't believe what he was witnessing. His stomach was sick, he felt faint, and he couldn't breathe. He tried to call out to Nikki but couldn't; he lost his voice. He looked around the bar and noticed that it was completely empty. Where was everyone? Where was Frankie? Why wasn't he stopping this from happening? "Nikki," he called out. "Nikki! Nikki!"

"Chris! Chris! Wake up, man. Wake up."

"Wha? What's happening? Nikki?" Chris muttered in a drunken stupor.

"Chris! It's me, Kevin. You okay, man?"

"Kevin? Where's Nikki? What's going on? Where's my wife? Where is she?"

"Nikki's not here, man. She's at home . . . where you need to be. What happened to you?" Kevin asked.

"Damn! I must have been dreaming," Chris said, finally starting to come around.

"That must have been some dream. You were screaming out for Nikki, all sweating and shit. What the hell is going on with you, man?" Kevin helped Chris up from the chaise longue where he had passed out.

"Shit! What time is it? How'd you know I was here?" Chris asked Kevin.

"Wow, man, you don't even remember calling me telling me to come and get you?" Kevin said.

He knew then that Chris was in the worst shape he'd probably ever seen him in. "You don't want to know what time it is, trust me. But don't worry; I already took care of Nikki. She called me, and I told her that you were with me and that you had too many drinks and had fallen asleep."

"Damn! Good looking out, bruh," Chris said, still thanking God that he was only dreaming. "This has been one hell of a night, Kev, man. You wouldn't believe the shit I went through tonight. Hey, what about Kay? Does she know what's really up or what?"

"Nah, she was asleep when I left; it's three a.m., man."

"Shit! Three? I've gotta get home."

"You sure that's what you wanna do? You sure you don't want to talk about it first? I mean, clearly, you're in a bit of trouble."

"Kevin, I had sex with Mina, man."

"What? When? Today? How? Why? Well, I know why," Kevin mumbled. "When? Come on, man, let me take you home; you're in no condition to drive right now. Yo, Frankie, we're out. Thanks for keeping an eye on my boy."

"Yeah, thanks, man; I owe you one," Chris slurred, throwing his hand up.

Kevin left Chris's truck in the parking lot and drove him home. On the way there, Chris told him all about what had happened with Mina.

"So what are you going to do now?" Kevin asked. "I mean, you know you were wrong for going off on Mina like that, right?"

"I don't know, Kevin. I'm still pissed at her, though. That was shady how she did me; she knew that I wasn't trying to go out like that. She took advantage of me, man."

"Listen to you! You sound like a punk, Chris. Don't even try it! I told you she was trouble, but you didn't want to hear it; you always think you're so in control of shit. Tonight she just proved that you're a damn man, that's all."

"Come on, Kevin. So you don't think that what she did was wrong?"

"Nope! You asked for that shit. You knew you wanted that chick all along. I knew it; she knew it. Hell! Nikki probably knew it. You can't fuck around with a woman like that and expect not to suffer some consequences."

"Oh, you got a lot of damn nerve judging me after the shit you pulled with Renee."

"Don't go there, Chris! And I'm not judging you. It's not about me. And I never fronted like I wasn't into Renee—not once."

"True. You're right, man. I could have stopped her if I wanted to. Damn! I didn't say shit, man. Nothing. I just let her do her thing. She had me so turned out, I didn't know what the fuck to do. I tried telling her to stop, but it was so weak, the way I said it. I wouldn't have been convinced either. I was just tripping on how bad she wanted me, man. She was all over me, dog, all over me; I couldn't resist it. Damn! I shouldn't have gone over there. I knew I shouldn't have."

"What are you going to do about what she said about Nikki? Do you believe her? Do you think she's been to Suede?"

"I don't know. She was pretty upset with me, so she could have been saying it just to get back at me. I'm damn sure gonna ask Nikki about it, though."

"You gonna tell her about Mina . . . and what happened?"

"Hell no! I can't, man. That would be the end of my marriage. Nikki would leave me, period."

"All right. This is you right here. Good luck, man. Keep your head up and be strong; don't let Nikki rattle you. You can do this," Kevin said, giving Chris a pound as he pulled off.

Chris was still struggling to get to the front door. His head wasn't right. That dream was so real to him, it made him wonder if Nikki really had been going to Suede. *And if she had, what was she doing while she was there?* He couldn't even think about it. He just wanted to sleep. He prayed as he turned the key in the front door that Nikki would be asleep and that he could just pass out somewhere in the living room downstairs.

Chapter 36

Confrontation

Chris slowly opened the front door. The darkness in the living room was a good sign. If she was up waiting, she would most likely have been in there watching television. He crept slowly up the stairs and was disturbed to see a dim light shining from their bedroom. *Damn!* he thought, bracing himself for Nikki's wrath as he approached their bedroom. He was surprised to see Nikki still up, dressed in the sexy red nightgown he bought her for Valentine's Day. When Nikki saw Chris, she greeted him with an unexpected hug. Chris was taken aback. *Why is she being so nice to me?*

"Hey, babe, what's going on with you? Why aren't you asleep?"

"I was worried about you. I missed you tonight," Nikki said, unbuttoning Chris's shirt.

"Whoa! Whoa! What are you doing?" Chris asked, placing his hands on Nikki's.

"I'm taking your clothes off; you're all wet. Let's get you dried off."

"No. I mean don't. I'll take my clothes off. I'm gonna head to the shower," Chris stammered.

"Mmmmm . . . now you're talking," Nikki whispered, unbuckling his belt.

"Nikki! What are you doing? Let me get in the shower. What's gotten into you?"

"I want you, babe; I've been horny all day. I've been waiting for you ever since you called and told me you'd be late," Nikki said, kissing Chris aggressively. "Mmmmm, you taste so sweet, baby."

Chris was utterly confused. *What should I do?* he thought. This was not the reaction he expected coming home drunk at four in the morning; he expected her to be pissed, angry. Not horny. He didn't know what to do, but he knew he couldn't make love to Nikki—not when he had just been with Mina. He didn't even have a chance to clean himself up properly; he just washed his hands and face at Mina's. He couldn't let Nikki take his clothes off; she would know instantly. Surely, she would smell Mina all over him. He had never lied to Nikki before now. Suddenly, he felt his entire world was about to come crashing down.

"Nikki! Stop!" Chris snapped. He pushed Nikki so hard that she fell back on the bed.

Nikki looked up at her husband as if he were a stranger. "Chris, my God! What the hell is going on? What's the deal?"

"Man, Nikki, I'm so beat. Can we please talk about this in the morning?"

"It is morning!" Nikki reminded him, not giving in.

"You know what I mean. It's been a really long night; I just wanna take a shower and head to bed for a few hours. I'll go into work late, so we can talk tomorrow morning. Is that cool?"

"Hell no! That's not cool! Start talking! Where the hell

have you been, Chris? Kevin told me that you were with him all night, but I know that's not true. So tell me where you've been," Nikki demanded, pulling Chris into the living room.

Chris was devastated. He wasn't prepared to lie to Nikki, but he had no choice. He couldn't hurt her like that. She would never understand. "Well, I was at work late until about seven o'clock. You know that. I called you on my way out."

"Right. And you said you had something important to take care of and that you would be home a little later. You never told me what it was, though. And here you are—nine hours later—looking a mess. You can't even look at me, you won't even let me touch you. What's up? You're scaring me."

Chris had no words. He had no clue how he would explain this to her. "Well, I did some soul-searching and thought about how many fights we have had regarding my friendship with Mina, so I decided that I was going to end it. I was prepared to tell her that I couldn't hang out with her anymore."

"What? I'm not liking this, Chris. Why didn't you tell me that's where you were going then?"

"I didn't want you trying to talk me out of it. I know how you are. You would have continued to try and convince me that I didn't have to do it because of you. I just wanted to handle it myself."

"Okay. Please tell me you're not just leaving her house, Chris."

"Just let me get this out. You asked me what happened; give me a chance to explain."

"Okay, continue," Nikki said, sitting Indian style on the couch.

"All right. So I called Mina up and wanted to meet her somewhere to talk."

"Why couldn't you do it over the phone?"

"Nikki, please let me finish. I didn't want to do it on the phone. I mean, it's not like we weren't friends. I, at least, owed her that much—to tell her this in person."

"Oh, please . . ."

"Nikki!"

"Sorry. Go ahead."

"Anyway, Mina didn't want to meet me out. She was in for the night and said that if it was so important I should come to her place."

"How convenient!" Nikki interrupted again.

Chris just gave her a frustrated stare and she shut up. "Okay, so I went to her place, for the first time I might add, to tell her that it was done, that our friendship had to end, and that was pretty much it."

"What do you mean that was pretty much it? What did she say?"

"She wasn't happy, obviously, but what could she say? She had to accept it."

"So you left then? How long were you there?"

"Ummm . . . just about an hour. Maybe an hour and a half, that's all."

"And then you just left? That's it? So why the hell are you so drunk? And why did Kevin feel the need to lie for you?"

"Kevin didn't lie. I went to Frankie's and then headed over to Kevin's, where I had a few more drinks and fell asleep. That's it, Nikki."

"So why did Kay tell me that she hadn't seen you all night?"

"Kay didn't know I was there; she was asleep."

"Chris, you're a lousy liar. What the hell are you not telling me? You better say it, Chris. I swear to God, you better tell me now while I still give a shit."

"Say what?"

"Say that you fucked her—that's what!"

"What? Why would you think that? Nikki, I didn't, I swear."

"She called here, Chris. She told me that you know about Suede. She told me that your dick was in her wet pussy, so I decided to put you to the test. I figured that, if you had sex with her, you would never let me touch you, much less make love to you, and I was right; you reacted just as I expected—guilty! Guilty as hell!"

Chris wanted to die right where he stood. He couldn't believe that Mina called Nikki. He hadn't counted on that.

"Oh, what's wrong, Chris? Are you surprised? Surprised that your little adorable Mina could say such a thing? Well, she said it, so I'm going to ask you again: Did you fuck her? Did you have your dick in her wet pussy?" Nikki wanted desperately to hear the truth, but when Chris opened his mouth he said just what she expected him to say.

"Nikki, that's crazy. She was upset, that's all. I did *not* have sex with her, and the reason I don't want to have sex with you right now is that I'm tired as hell. Damn! It's four o'clock in the morning; I've been drinking all night. I probably couldn't get it up if I tried. Give me a break!"

"You give *me* a fucking break, Chris; I don't believe you. You would never turn me down unless you had a reason . . . like guilt. Sex, sex, and more sex! That's all you've been crying about since Corey was born. How I never seduce you anymore. How I never wear sexy nightgowns anymore. How I never initiate anymore. You've been begging for this. The fact that you're too tired and drunk is complete bullshit as far as I'm concerned. *You fucked that bitch!* How could you, Chris!"

Chris knew he was stuck. He tried to turn the tables on Nikki.

"Forget about me; what about you? What's up with Suede? Is that shit true? Are you a member there . . . at that sex club? Jesus, Nikki! What about Corey? What about me?" he pleaded with an Oscar award–winning look of despair on his face.

"What *about* Corey? What does he have to do with this? Listen, I'm not a member now, but I was for a short while. It was before Corey was born."

"You're lying, Nikki. I can't believe you lied to me about this."

"I am not lying, Chris! I just didn't tell you *one* thing. There was just one thing in my life that you didn't know about me. You know what? You have a lot of nerve asking me about this now!" Nikki yelled in Chris's face. "So fine, you want to know what I did at Suede? I did what Nikki does, Chris! I went there to see how that side of the world was living; I was curious. And there was a time when I could talk to you about my desires and you would listen, even understand and support me. You used to love that side of me—that wild side—it excited you. Then you just decided one day that you wanted me to stop being who I was and to start a family. But what was I supposed to say? I mean, you were looking at me with those beautiful, trusting eyes of yours. You were practically begging me to change, be someone that I'm not, and I did . . . because I love you and I wanted to please you, make you happy. But it was hard, Chris. Really hard."

"Damn! I didn't realize starting a family with your husband was too much to ask. So, basically, you're saying that you had Corey for me; you didn't want to be a mother?"

"Chris, don't do this; don't fucking do this to me."

"What do you want me to say, Nikki? I mean, according to what you just said, I was the one that made you change to become someone you're not—a mother!"

"No, that's not what I said; don't put words in my mouth. You know Corey is the best thing that's ever happened in my life. I said that I am who I am. I always have been. I always will be. I didn't say that a baby couldn't have been a part of that. I said that we didn't have to change our life to become parents. And that's what you asked me to do."

"No, I asked you to change *your* life, not mine; you were the one that was out of control. I wasn't the one going out there, taking risks with our friends, playing all those silly-ass games; that was you. I just allowed it to happen, and that was my mistake. I mean, look what happened after the key party. Look how many lives you affected."

"What? Are you blaming me for what happened to our friends? Are you serious? Look, Chris, you need to take that back. I had nothing to do with what happened to Lynda and Rick. Their marriage was in trouble long before I came up with any party. And I know you're not going to try and blame me for Kevin and Renee's situation. And Jason was messed up when we found him. All I did was put the idea out there; they could easily have turned me down. It wouldn't have been the first time, but they didn't; that was *their* choice, not mine. And as for the outcome of all this, it is what it is. I had nothing to do with that," Nikki fired back in anger. She couldn't believe what she was hearing. She never knew how Chris really felt about her until now. It hurt her to the core. She felt as if she were standing in the room with a stranger.

"I'm just saying that you put all of it in motion, and that wasn't your place."

"Chris, I'm just glad that now I know how you really feel about me. That's a fucking eye-opener."

"Nikki, what do you expect me to say after what Mina told me? Mina, not you. Do you have any idea how that made me feel? I felt like a punk, an idiot. There I was ranting and raving about how great you were, how honest you were, and it all blew up in my face. Tell me this: How did you find out about this place? Who did you go with?"

"Oh, so I'm not great anymore? That's funny. Mina can kiss my ass thinking she told you some big, dark secret . . . because we both know the real reason she told you: She wanted to make me look bad so she could have a chance with you. You said so yourself. She's a jealous, conniving bitch! So did you give her what she wanted, Chris? Did you?"

"Nikki, just answer the question . . . since it's not such a big deal: Who the hell did you go with? One of *your* male friends? It damn sure wasn't me!"

Nikki paused, looking at Chris, her eyes welling up with tears. She knew she owed him an explanation but she was pissed because she felt like she was answering to Mina. "A friend of mine told me about the club, and it sounded intriguing. *She* told me that I wouldn't have to do anything, that I could just watch. I figured there would be no harm in just watching, and that's what I did. That's *all* I did. I just wanted to get out there and see something I'd never seen before. I didn't even touch another person while I was there. So, to answer your question, no—I didn't sleep with anyone there, nor have I ever cheated on you and our marriage!"

"So you expect me to believe that you didn't fuck anybody?"

"No! Absolutely not! I did a lot of watching, like I said, and I masturbated a few times. That's it!"

"That's it? So, basically, you're telling me that you were parading around this sex club naked, masturbating in front of fucking strangers? What the hell is wrong with you, Nikki?"

"Chris, don't you dare try to turn this around on me. Don't you dare. This isn't about me; it's about you and the fact that you've been out drinking with Mina until all hours of the morning!"

"Nikki, I was not drinking with Mina. I told you what happened. You either believe me, or you don't. If you choose to believe Mina over me, then go right ahead, but I did not fuck her."

"Have you ever been intimate with her?"

"No, I haven't," Chris lied.

"So you've never kissed her? Never? Not once?"

He lied again. "Nope. Not once."

"So why was she upset? Why did she take it so hard? I mean, she sounds whipped to me, or worse . . . in love. What did you do to make her get so angry at you that she felt the need to call me and tell me you were there fucking her tonight?"

"I didn't do anything; it was just her ego. She didn't understand why our friendship had to end, and then I talked about you and told her how great you were. That's why she told me about you being a member at Suede. She wanted to show you up, to tell me that you weren't this great, trusting wife I always told her you were." Chris had never lied to Nikki like this before, but he was in too deep now; he had to keep it up.

Nikki stood up and started to cry as she paced the room. She didn't know who or what to believe. She wanted to believe Chris, but he had become a completely different person ever since Mina had entered his life, becoming more and more like the typical guy. But how could she trust Mina over Chris? It made sense that Mina would lie to get back at her. After all, she was acting like a bitch when Mina called to warn her that Chris knew about Suede. Maybe she did tell her that just to hurt her.

"Nikki, do you believe me?"

"Take off your pants!" Nikki stepped to Chris.

"What?"

"You heard me. Take off your pants."

"Nikki, what the hell is going on here? I mean, what has gotten into you?"

"Chris, take off your pants, or I swear I will rip them off you right now. I wanna see it. I want to smell your dick."

"You've gone crazy, Nikki."

"No, I haven't; it's called 'getting to the bottom of

things.' I'll know if you've been with her or not, once you take them off. If you refuse to do it, Chris, I'll have no choice but to believe Mina."

Chris just stood still. He was in such a quandary. He knew if he took off his clothes, she would instantly know Mina was all over him, her smell, her sweat, her come. All of her. How devastated she would be to smell another woman on him. He couldn't do that to her, so he refused.

"Okay, well, I have my answer, then: You fucked her; you fucked another woman." Nikki began to sob again.

"Nikki, please don't cry. It's not what you think."

"You're a liar . . . and a cheat. I can't believe this is happening to me. I was warned, but I didn't listen; I had too much pride. I wanted to trust you so badly. I'm such an idiot."

"Nikki, please . . ." Chris pleaded, attempting to wipe the tears off her face.

"Go to hell!" Nikki snapped, slapping his hand away from her face. "How could you do this . . . and then lie to me about it?"

"Nikki, I didn't have sex with her; it wasn't like that. I mean, I—"

"Chris, we will never be okay again if you don't admit this to me right now. If you care about me at all, you'll tell me the truth. If you respect me, you'll tell me what you did with her. I want to know all of it. You owe me that much."

Chris looked at his wife, his soul mate, his lover, the mother of his son, and realized what he had done finally, what his relationship with Mina had cost him. His eyes were filled with tears. One more blink and they would come pouring down. "Nikki, I wasn't with her; I wouldn't betray you like that."

"Prove it, then. Let me see. Why won't you take off your pants?"

"Nikki, I'm not going to do this anymore; this is ridiculous. I'm tired and I'm going to bed. We'll have to talk about this tomorrow." Chris walked away, leaving Nikki alone. He almost reached the top of the stairs when he looked down at his wife and saw the unbearable pain he was putting her through. He wanted to reach out to her and tell her everything, but he couldn't bring himself to admit what he had done. The words just wouldn't come. He knew that his not complying with Nikki's demands probably meant losing her trust forever, but he had to take the chance that in time she would let it go and forgive him. He knew that there was nothing more that could be said tonight, so he continued up the stairs.

Nikki lay on the sofa crying uncontrollably. She knew now that Mina was telling the truth. Somehow, it confirmed what she knew all along. She pondered on why she let their friendship happen, why she didn't stop it before it got out of hand. She told herself over and over again that something bad was going to happen, but she let her pride get in the way. *How will we ever get through this?* she thought.

Chapter 37

Closure

By the time Chris woke up and got himself together, Nikki and Corey had already left to start their day. Nikki left him a cold note that didn't give much hope for their future. She'd said that she was leaving him to go stay with her parents until she decided what she wanted to do. He tried to call her several times, but she wouldn't take any of his calls. He knew he'd fucked up in a major way. His head was pounding from an awful headache from all the drinking from the night before, not to mention the pain he was experiencing in his stomach for all of the lies he'd told Nikki. As he got in his truck and headed to work he thought about all that had transpired with Mina. He wondered how she was doing . . . if she cried herself to sleep like Nikki did. Did she hate him? He thought about the person he'd become since he met her and tried to make some sense of where he went wrong in his friendship with her and his marriage. The only conclusion he could come up with was that he didn't listen. He didn't listen to his hormones when they were raging and out of control the night he met Mina. He didn't listen to his heart when it was telling him how much he loved his wife and didn't want to hurt her. He didn't listen to his friends when they warned him to stay away from Mina. And, most of all, he didn't pay attention to the signs that Nikki gave him every time she looked away when he mentioned Mina's name, every time she cursed him out for the simplest thing, and every time she pleaded with him to stop seeing Mina without really saying a word . . . until she finally broke and did. But by then he was too far gone . . . too caught up with his feelings for Mina. He put Mina's feelings above Nikki's and that was his biggest mistake. He wanted so badly to make it right, but he knew he had a long journey ahead of him.

When he got to work, he closed his office door and tried to keep busy so that he wouldn't bring any attention to himself. He was sure the pain he was experiencing was all over his face. He hadn't seen Penny yet that morning and he was grateful. He knew she would be able to tell right away that things had come to a head and he didn't want to have to hear the dreaded words *I told you so.* Just then, there was a knock at his office door.

"Come in."

"Hey, boss. Sorry to be late, but I had an appointment with my eye doctor. You did remember, didn't you?" She knew that Chris could barely keep up with his own appointments and hoped he hadn't noticed her being late. Then she noticed the sadness in Chris's eyes; he knew what was coming next. "Are you okay, boss?"

Chris wanted desperately to pour his heart out to her. He just needed someone he trusted to tell him that he hadn't screwed his marriage up for good. "I'm all right, Penny; just a rough morning, that's all."

"Oh no! Things are a mess, aren't they?" Penny said, knowing the answer to her question.

Chris thought about lying and pretending to not know what she was talking about; instead, the truth came pouring out. "It's over, Penny—my marriage, my friendship with Mina, everything. It's all over."

"Boss. Listen to me. Whatever has happened, I promise it will be okay."

"No, Penny, I don't think so, not this time."

"Listen to me. Take it from someone who's been around the block once or twice."

"I told Mina we couldn't be friends anymore."

"You did the right thing, no matter how bad it feels right now; it will all work out, you'll see," Penny tried to assure him.

Chris shook his head from side to side mainly because he knew Penny had no idea of how bad things really and truly were. "I don't know, Penny. Nikki is really pissed at me."

"I know she is, and she probably has every right to be."

Chris looked at Penny with a defensive scowl on his face. "Nikki left me, Penny. She took Corey and she's gone to stay with her parents."

"And I suppose you think you're the only man who's been left by his wife before. I left my husband on several occasions, but I always went back . . . eventually." Penny paused a moment. "Don't look at me like that. You men just don't listen, so hardheaded, thinking you can have it all; you can't. You need to be grateful for your family and leave the rest to those single men out there. Remember these words, Chris: Men and women cannot be friends; it doesn't work out. Not when one is married. Everyone has to learn that the hard way, though, at least once, just like you're doing now."

Chris had been convinced that he was stronger than the rest and that his love for Nikki would be able to withstand the attraction he had for Mina. He didn't want to think that he was just like all the other men out there . . . a statistic . . . and he definitely didn't want Nikki to feel that way.

"I know you're right, Penny, but for now I just can't see how this will ever be okay again. I know Nikki very well.

She's not going to forget this for a long while and—I'm not gonna lie–I'm afraid of what she'll do."

"We'll see," Penny said. "It will be okay, I promise."

"If you say so. Listen, I'm going to grab a bite to eat; do you want anything while I'm out?"

"I'm okay. I'll check back in on you later this afternoon. By then your wife will probably be taking your calls." Penny walked out of Chris's office, closing the door behind her.

Chris tried Nikki's office once more before leaving but got her voice mail just as he'd expected. He hung up and left for lunch. On the way to the parking deck Chris tried hard to think about something other than his current situation. He had no idea what he was going to have to do to get her trust back but was willing to do whatever it took and more.

Chris heard a familiar voice on his way to his SUV. "Hi." It was Mina. He turned around and saw her standing a few parking spots over from his. He had been so deep in thought that he hadn't even heard anyone walking in the parking deck along with him. Chris had no idea what to say; his emotions were all over the place. He was happy as hell to see Mina but pissed at the same time.

"Hey, Mina."

"So that's how it's going to be, huh?" Mina asked.

Mina was walking toward him now. She walked right up to him and looked directly up into his face and told him she had two questions for him. Chris didn't know what she was going to say, nor how she expected him to respond. Mina had tears welling up in her eyes. She was trying her hardest to keep them from rolling, but that was impossible. Chris held back the urge to wipe her tears away. The anger he had inside him wouldn't allow it. They stood in silence for a few seconds experiencing the moment for what it was.

"Do you really believe that I had bad intentions for you and your family?" Mina asked, barely able to talk.

"I don't know what to believe Mina, I don't. I think we're

both at fault for how things ended up, but I won't ever forgive you for what you did to me at your place."

Mina looked down in an attempt to gather herself and then looked back at Chris into his eyes as if she was searching for something she wanted so badly to find. Her next question was coming. He could feel it.

"Chris, did you love me?" Mina asked, lowering the boom.

He paused for a minute trying to figure out what to say. "Mina, I—"

"Chris, tell me the truth; you don't have anything to lose by being honest with me. At least send me on my way with the truth."

"I liked you a lot but any possibilities of me coming to love you were ruined the other night. I thought I knew who you were to a degree, but now I realize I had no idea. I only have myself to blame, though. I never should have allowed myself to get this close to you. To let you get this close to the one thing in life that matters to me most, my family. Now we have no choice and it's the best thing for both of us and for me most of all. It's best if we don't talk anymore. Let's just let this be it."

Chris could tell that Mina was hurt by his response. She wanted him to say that he loved her and wished he could be with her. It was clear that she was disappointed beyond words. Mina started to walk away, and Chris realized this was his chance to let her go. He knew that he and Mina would never be able to have a friendship again, and so he decided to honor her request and leave her with the truth. It was all he could do for her at that point.

"Mina, I, umm." She turned and looked at him, anticipating what his final words would be. He was too mad to let her walk away with the satisfaction of knowing he had fallen in love with her.

"Never mind," Chris said. "Good-bye, Mina." He didn't

wait to hear her response or see the look on her face. Walking away toward his car Chris had never considered that it was possible for him to love another woman—until Mina had come along.

He got in his truck and saw that he had missed a call from Nikki on his cell phone. *The timing couldn't have been worse,* he thought, as he dialed Nikki's work number and watched Mina drive out of the parking deck. His heart sank when Nikki answered the phone.

"Nikki?"

"Yes."

"Hey, babe. Hey . . . um . . . can we please talk?"

"Not right now, we can't."

"Are you and Corey all right?"

"We're fine, Chris."

"Nikki, I love you, and I'm sorry, babe. I'm so damn sorry that I've made you doubt me."

"Unbelievable. You're still denying it. Even now. Are you ever going to admit that you had sex with her?"

There was silence on the other end. Chris wasn't getting anywhere, and he knew it.

"Nikki. Don't do this now. Please. Can't we just move past this? I mean, I could have tripped on you a lot harder about your membership at Suede but I didn't."

"Yeah. You didn't because I was too busy tripping on you about fucking Mina."

"Awwww, come on, Nikki. We're better than this. We can get through this. Just give us a chance. Please."

"I can't talk to you now, Chris. I just can't. I'm too hurt. Seriously broke down. I never would have expected this from you. I think that's why I was so cool with you being friends with her in the first place. I trusted you."

"Nikki, that's bull and you know it. You didn't trust me. You never trusted me with her."

"Yeah, and I guess I shouldn't have, right?"

"Let's not do this. Seriously. I'm never going to see or talk to her again. Can't that be a start?"

"Nope! Because first I would have to believe you. And I don't! I can't!"

"Are you leaving me, Nikki? Are we over?"

Nikki paused before saying . . . "No. But I can't promise you when we will be together again."

"What can I do?" Chris begged. "Is there anything I can do to make this better? I love you and Corey so much. I would die without you."

Nikki wanted so badly to tell him she loved him too. That her life felt over without him. She wanted so desperately to feel his arms around her. But all she could think about was Mina. She could never imagine being with him again without thinking of her and the fact that he held her, kissed her, had sex with her. The thought of it made her sick as she dropped her cell phone and pulled over and threw up on the side of the road.

"Nikki? Are you there? Are you all right?"

"I have to go, Chris. I can't talk to you anymore. Not for a while. Not for a long while. I'll let you know when I'm ready to talk to you. Until then, just give me my space."

Chris, not having much of a choice, agreed. He was dying inside. He felt so helpless.

"I love you, Nikki."

"Good-bye," Nikki said. She couldn't bear to talk to him anymore. She loved him, too, but at the moment she wasn't feeling anything but contempt. She wasn't sure what made her angrier—the fact that he'd had sex with another woman or the fact that he didn't have the guts to admit it to her. She couldn't imagine her life without him, and she had no desire to raise her son alone, but she knew without a doubt that her marriage was broken, possibly beyond repair, and she had some really hard choices ahead of her.

Chris let out a long defeated sigh and started his truck. He had to believe that they would be okay again one day down the road. For now, he figured all he could do was give her what she asked for. Space. He knew it wouldn't be easy, but he felt confident that he made the right choice by not admitting to what happened with Mina. Mina . . . he thought as he sighed again. He couldn't believe how much she turned his life upside down in such a short while. If someone would have told him this was how his life was going to turn out, he wouldn't have believed it. Just then his cell phone rang. It was her. Mina. He let the phone ring three times before he hit END. He had no desire to speak to her. He doubted that he ever would again. He finally decided to delete Mina's number out of his phone.

As he sat there listening to the radio he caught the tail end of an interview with author Michael Baisden. It was "relationship week" on V-103 and Michael was being asked if men and women could be friends without sex getting in the way. Chris quickly turned the radio off.